PRAISE FOR
THE SOUL CHARMER SERIES

"Rogue Souls is fantastic! ... I was really reminded of the early Kate Daniels books by Ilona Andrews."

— *Red Hot Books*

"Snappy, snarky, and oh-so-sexy."

— Darynda Jones, *New York Times* bestselling author

"I'll be once again counting down the days to the release of book three to see what comes next."

— *Fiction Vixen*

"Do not miss, fantastic urban fantasy"

— Lauren Dane, *New York Times & USA Today* Bestselling Author

"Mueller is definitely an author to watch."

— *Scandalicious Book Reviews*

"Mueller explores an intriguing concept in a seedy, visceral setting that pops to life on the page."

— *Publishers Weekly*

ROGUE SOULS

CHELSEA MUELLER

Chelsea Mueller

©2018 Chelsea Mueller

Formatting by Uplifting Designs

All rights reserved. No part of this publication may be reproduced, distributed, or transmitted in any form or by any means, including photocopying, recording, or other electronic or mechanical methods, without the prior written permission of the publisher, except in the case of brief quotations embodied in critical reviews and certain other noncommercial uses permitted by copyright law.

Printed in the United States of America.

First printing, 2018

BOOKS BY CHELSEA MUELLER

Borrowed Souls

Rogue Souls

Lost Souls

In memory of Loki,

who was at my side for every word on the page.

ROGUE SOULS

CHAPTER ONE

Callie Delgado was familiar with poor choices. She'd made plenty.

She'd eaten only Hostess products for a solid month when she was twelve. She'd cold-cocked one of her mom's boyfriends when she'd caught him raiding the pantry. She hadn't turned her brother in when he'd stolen drugs from a hospital where she'd worked. She lost her job and career path because she chose family first. Always. She didn't regret those decisions. Not really. Not in the keep-you-up-at-night way. Not in the wonder-who-you've-become way.

But this?

Tiny beetles burrowed beneath her skin. Instead of grinding a palm down her arm to still the sensation, she had to "embrace the magic." Whatever the hell that meant. The black stone flask was buzzing hard enough to make her question if her fingers had gone numb.

She squeezed the flask, and the heated thrum of the container now pulsed beneath her palm. The flask was ready, even if Callie wasn't.

The woman standing before Callie stomped her foot. "Can we get this over with? My husband will be home soon, and we are attending the seven o'clock services."

Services. Callie was about to pull a soul out of this woman's body, and she wanted to pretend that faith was a priority. Fucking Gem City. "You could have come to the shop if you wanted an appointment."

The woman reeled back like Callie had swiped at her gaudy pearls. "The children…need me."

Three kiddos ran around in the next room oblivious to the fact mommy was doubled up on souls so she could sin without feeling *dirty*. "What'd you need the soul for anyway?" Callie asked. She popped the cap of the flask, and then keened her head to the right until her neck cracked. Like she needed to be limber for this shit.

"With this?" She gestured to the three kids, all too young for school. "I need a little thrill. So I pick up a thing or two I don't pay for, and thanks to your boss the Church doesn't need to worry about it."

This lady had no shame. Maybe that's what renting souls did for you. It took away your shame. Your guilt. Your honor. Callie wasn't certain. She'd only had an extra soul in her once and it didn't make her feel protected or powerful or prideful. It'd squicked her out, and mostly she just appreciated that it'd concealed her fingerprints, because she'd also done some illegal shit while using a borrowed soul. Unlike this woman, though, Callie had zero desire for a repeat.

This conversation was pointless. Callie extended her arm until the metal mouth of the flask pressed against the woman's sternum, beneath the trio of druzy pendants that cost more than Callie's rent. Heat blossomed and wilted beneath her palm. She capped the flask, and tucked in her back jean pocket. Her hoodie was already zipped, but Callie tugged the tab upward until it was fully sealed.

Her shoulder grazed the other woman's as she strode to the door.

"Am I square with him?" the renter asked.

In the last several weeks of repossessing rented souls for the Soul Charmer of Gem City, Callie had heard this question a dozen different ways. Most were variants of fear. They didn't want to have a man who could steal your soul mad at them. They didn't want him to send the muscle out to beat them black and blue. They weren't all too scared of Callie, but then they didn't know what she could do. Neither did she. That was the problem. This woman, though, that lilt and pleading tone in her voice? She wanted to make sure he'd be ready to rent to her again. Callie ran the pad of her thumb across her fingernails and the thin layer of ice coating them. Yes, this woman was square with the Charmer, but did she understand what she'd given up? The ice on Callie's nails proved this woman was broken, missing pieces now, and she was ready for more.

Callie could almost relate. "Yeah. Your account is

settled." It was the most comfort Callie could give her. If only the Soul Charmer would settle with Callie. His magic snapped and roiled within her body, demanding release. Callie wished she could oblige, but despite yanking souls out of delinquent renters, she didn't know enough to control it. Not owning her own body, not controlling the power within it, was more painful than she cared to admit. At least she wasn't innocent. None of them were.

Callie ignored the chill beginning to lock her fingers in place. She was getting good at it, and that worried her. She tucked her hands into her pockets, and hurried out the front door. Gravel from the yard peppered the sidewalk. She sidestepped the small rocks, and kept her eyes on the motorcycle idling at the curb.

Derek held out a helmet to her. The bike was massive, but he looked natural atop it. Broad shoulders wrapped in a well-worn leather jacket and the right amount of scruff on his chin presented every bit the image of badass. He'd cultivated the look, but Callie softened as his gaze met hers. She took the helmet from him, but didn't immediately put it on.

"Remind me why I had to do that," Callie said, voice low.

Stretching her fingers didn't erase the echo of ice. The chill lingered in her mind, even if her hands were no longer supernaturally cold. Streaks of ruby and gold slithered behind the snowcapped Taos Mountains in the distance. The roads weren't icy in Gem City yet, but winter in the high desert might be enough to make her perpetually cold. At least then she wouldn't have to acknowledge every soul renter she passed at the 7-Eleven.

"Because he pays you to."

"He doesn't pay me, actually." Callie's grumble punched past the wind whipping against her back.

Derek's response was a deep rumble of a sigh. He climbed off the motorcycle. Callie took a half step backward so she wouldn't have to incline her head to meet his gaze. He brushed a few loose strands of her dark hair behind her ear. The wind must fear the powers of the Soul Charmer's muscle, because her locks didn't budge. "I don't want to argue over your *apprenticeship*."

Spitting the term suggested otherwise, but Callie didn't correct him. "I meant why you didn't come inside with me to collect the soul."

They were a team. Since the beginning, which didn't feel like the mere weeks it'd been. She was just the one with the magic in her bones to get the flask to pull the souls out of people. She needed someone to scare them into compliance. She was short, did not know how to wrestle, and the heaviest thing she lifted on a regular basis was a 25 lb. bag of flour. She needed Derek's muscle and menace. The bonus of having someone she trusted at her back? Also very important.

"You got it done without me." He grazed his scarred knuckles along her jaw. Callie leaned in to the touch.

"It would have been easier…"

When they were alone he laughed with his whole body. People were peeking through blinds at them now, and Derek's chuckle barely passed his lips. "Not every job requires me."

Callie took his hand in hers, and squeezed. "Disagree."

"The boss thinks otherwise. He wants you to try doing the easy retrievals solo."

"He hasn't taught me shit. He can't go shoving me out of the nest like a demented mama bird."

"Please never call him a mama ever again."

Callie laughed loudly imagining her de facto boss covered in feathers. She let her voice carry around the cul-de-sac. Let them listen. They were the ones pretending to be better than who they truly were. At least she was upfront about her shit.

The woman Callie had retrieved the soul from opened her front door to shush them. Callie flipped her the bird, and then tugged on her helmet.

Quality time with deadbeat soul renters in upscale housing who set her teeth on edge and forced ice into her palms was not exactly making her feel like a magician. If she was going to be able to pull souls from people's bodies she should at least feel like a goddamn magician.

"Fine, let's go talk to the old man."

CHAPTER TWO

November carried that ominous threat of real winter. It was too cold to be riding a motorcycle. Callie hadn't said anything, because a piece of her enjoyed the cold wind crushing against her. Derek dodged the potholes and puddles littering the road as they eased into downtown. It was still early enough that the shops throughout the Plaza were open. When the streetlights popped on, everyone would be gone though.

Not the Soul Charmer, though. His business boomed when the others fled for the suburbs. Restaurants and bars stayed open nearby. Socialization with access to booze led to bad ideas in Callie's experience. Based on the number of stumbling men and giggling couples falling in the door of the soul renter's emporium, she was right.

The sun stretched toward them between the squat,

adobe buildings. Derek parked the bike down the alley from the back entrance of the Soul Charmer's shop. The store's front didn't offer much more appeal, but at least you knew what you were getting into. If you had to enter a store by walking past broken beer bottles and Dumpsters, either it was selling some shady shit or it didn't want your money. The Charmer was willing to barter—as Callie knew all too well—but he generally liked taking people's money and fucking with them at the same time.

No wonder Callie hesitated after Derek had stowed their helmets.

Derek extended a hand to her. "C'mon, doll."

She took his hand. It was warm and calloused and *familiar*. No matter how many times she'd walked in the unmarked employee entrance, it set her teeth on edge like it was the first time. She squeezed Derek's hand, and focused on the warm pulse of the full flask in her back pocket.

"Right. Let's go refocus the old guy."

Turns out the Charmer was plenty focused already.

They pushed their way into the back office, and the Soul Charmer already had his hand out for the flask.

"Did she give you any trouble?" he asked. Somehow the white stubble on his chin only sharpened the grizzled old man.

Callie shrugged. "She whined about it."

He took the flask from her, and whirled to face his desk. The oak behemoth was odd in the tile-and-glass laboratory chic of the room. The Charmer popped the cap with gnarled, knobby fingers. Callie's stomach hollowed out. The soul was so close, and she didn't want to feel it. His gold rings clinked against the container, but Callie's heartbeat rang far louder in her ears. The soul leaped from the flask and into the opaque black jar her blackmailer-turned-boss held. He had yet to explain how he controlled the transfer of the souls from one object to another.

Rented souls weren't obedient. The Charmer would tell his customers his soul magic was safe, and it was easy to extract them. He told Callie the magic he'd infused in her wouldn't harm her. He'd lied to her and he was certainly lying to them.

Sure, Callie's body was still intact despite the magic pumping through her veins, but in the quest to crush his rivals the Soul Charmer had turned her into the human equivalent of a metal detector dialed to a "soul" setting. Her body reacted to soul magic levels in others. The ice layer on her fingertips earlier was, unfortunately, not new enough to shock her. It was still far better than what happened when extra souls were present around her. Callie suppressed a shudder at the memory or the last time she'd stood near a person with multiple souls in their body. The sensory skills were good when you were tracking down those reneging on their soul rental agreements, but a shitty one when you were trying to buy groceries and your hands froze to the cart. What was worse, though, was the power bound her to the jerk.

She'd agreed to work for the Soul Charmer a month ago to save her brother from a mobster. Nothing like having a murdering drug dealer shunt you off to the guy who dealt in souls, right? It was supposed to be a quick job. In and out. Her brother was safe at her apartment now. So why was Callie still in this back-alley shop, still toting a flask for the guy? Because the Charmer had refused to remove the magic, which meant Callie had to push back. Keep your enemy close or some shit. She demanded the Charmer teach her how to wield soul magic.

She already regretted that decision.

Standing near the Charmer as he poured the freshly collected soul into a jar crafted of the same onyx as the flask she carried? Definitely a regret. Heat began to pool in her palms. The sensation didn't bring pain, but it overwhelmed her. The florescent lights overhead focused to a spotlight on the jar, the sharp tang of astringent clogged her nostrils, and the fire filled her. The dozens of times she'd watched the Charmer complete this transfer, he'd close the lid on the jar quickly. He didn't this time, but the soul stayed inside.

Callie hadn't ever put much thought into what a soul would look like. It was supposed to be intangible… at least until the Charmer brought the ability to rent a soul to Gem City a decade ago. Even as she slapped the opened flask to people's chests to collect the borrowed souls, the pass from body to container was invisible. Now, though, she could see an opaline white swirl in the jar. Gossamer threads moved like a jellyfish in the container smaller than a jam jar.

She would have been mesmerized if sparks weren't igniting along her fingers. "Enough," she muttered, not sure if she was making the request of the Charmer, her fingers, or the soul.

"Rein your magic in, and it won't be an issue." The Soul Charmer gestured widely with his right arm, and the billowing sleeve of his purple pajama top flapped and snapped. She would have been impressed at the seventy something's dexterity, but she was busy trying to stop the magic from roasting her.

Callie curled her fingers toward her palms. Steam hissed out from the edges of her squeezed fists as though she were crafting a custom lava rock within them. The temptation to try to knock out one of the old man's gold teeth burned almost as hot as the fire in her fists. He'd been offering her the same advice for the last three days.

"Care to tell me how to do that exactly?" she asked.

He did not. He shoved the open jar closer to her. The skin on either side of her hand began to blacken. Callie had been through this before. It would heal quickly. Her brain did not care for facts now; it cared that her skin was visibly charring. She began edging backward. The Charmer followed her. Mint mingled with musk in the air between them.

The last time Callie's hands had charred, she'd seared the flesh off another woman, but had felt no pain herself. As the Charmer edged toward her now, though, the flames contained in her clenched fists grew hotter and the sharp snap of million rubber bands cut into her mind. She sucked in a breath, but it only urged the pain to build like bumblebee stingers wedging themselves beneath her skin. She opened her right hand. Angry red welts began to rise, and then they burst open. Blood trickled down the edge of her pinkie finger and dripped onto the polished tile floor.

The Charmer moved closer again.

Callie's right shoulder hit the wall.

Nowhere to run.

Her employer simply moved the jar closer to her oozing, flaming flesh. Fear lanced her, and she doubled over. Her instinct was to make herself small enough to hide from the roiling waves of pain crashing against her mind and thrusting fists upward into her stomach. She screamed loud enough to rattle her ears and raze her throat. She called for him to stop, but her cry was an unintelligible keen.

The ground shook or maybe Callie was simply hyperventilating.

"What the fuck are you doing to her?" Even over her cries she'd recognize that tone of gravel spit into a bonfire. Derek.

A flash of gold glinted before Callie's gaze, and the pain disappeared. Not dulled. Not faded. *Disappeared.* Immediately. She sucked in short, panicked breaths, and reminded herself she would be fine. Magic was scary, but it hadn't ever damaged her physically.

It also hadn't been painful before. She'd never needed to scream and go full-on fetal position as a result.

Callie ignored the jar the Charmer still held. Her entire right hand and much of the left looked like spent charcoal briquettes and she wasn't about to look away until she saw them healed completely. Derek huffed and grunted at her side, but otherwise the tiled workroom in the back of the Soul Charmer's seedy downtown storefront remained quiet. Her pulse pounded in her ears, and with each *bu-bump* the ashy flakes softened and lightened. Eventually her flesh was unmarred again other than the jagged scar near her elbow from an unfortunate incident with a summertime slide when she was eight.

"What was the point of that?" she asked when she was finally healed. Her voice was pure hangover rasp.

"You wanted to learn." The Soul Charmer rotated the opaque jar left and right as though he could still see the white wisps beneath the shiny lid.

"I wanted you to teach me," she corrected.

"Apprenticeships are about hands-on learning. Either you have the ability or you don't." The Charmer shot a derisive glance Derek's way, but Callie's partner—with his lack of magical ability—just ground his teeth harder.

He continued under his breath, "I'm starting to think I was wrong about you."

Callie wanted him to be wrong about her. She didn't want to spend her nights next to his slimy ass. She didn't want to frequent drug dens. She didn't want to help criminals cover their crimes through the use of rented souls. She knew from personal experience the way the borrowed soul affected the body. The way it blurred fingerprints and muddied DNA. Mob boss Ford had seen to that. Now she regularly saw his goons and men like them. She pulled the rented souls out of their bodies after they'd tainted and stained them with sin and corruption. She'd spent years getting out of her mom's con-artist shadow and scraping her addict brother off various floors. She was only here because of them. She was here because she'd saved Josh with a rented soul. She was here because the Soul Charmer had changed her.

Well, she told herself those were her only reasons. It was easier to blame loyalty or family to make bad decisions look inevitable. A tiny part of her had liked being able to protect herself with the magic. The thought was a pinprick of light in the dark recesses of her mind, the kind she could only see when her thoughts cleared moments before falling asleep. She'd demanded this apprenticeship if the Charmer wouldn't take his magic back. If he was going to use her, she'd use him right back.

She'd regretted the decision before she'd screamed in agony. Now she was in full-on, fuck-this-place-and-this-job-and-that-asshole-with-his-jars-and-his-shiny-fucking-teeth.

"Shoving souls at me and changing whatever magic surrounds us in here—" he still refused to tell her what he'd done to the backroom, but the energy was obvious "—so that it hurts and then not telling me what I'm supposed to do isn't teaching. Fuck, Charmer, I could learn that same way on my own."

His crazy old man cackle sputtered into a hacking cough.

"She tell a joke?" Derek's tone was even. He'd been aligned with the Soul Charmer for a lot longer than Callie. The edges of Derek's ears were red, but otherwise his emotional shield was solid.

The Charmer wiped his mouth on his sleeve. "She's learning the way I did. Sink or swim."

"I thought you taught yourself."

"Exactly."

Callie rubbed her hands together, pleased to confirm sensation was normal. Her irritation spilled forward, but she didn't meet the Charmer's gaze. "Either teach me how to use the magic or I'm done."

"We both know you wouldn't run, Calliope. My magic is in you. I'd find you."

She believed him. That was the problem. No leverage. She said nothing, because he was right. She was stuck with his magic. She was stuck without the skills to contain it. She was about to be stuck working for him solo.

Fucking.

Stuck.

The Soul Charmer turned and shuffled across the tile floor, and around to a back wall lined with honeyed wooden shelving. He replaced the jar in its spot and turned it so the label faced outward. Without looking at either his employee or his apprentice, he said, "We can try something else next time, but you need to practice control. Figure it out."

Figure it out? Callie bit back the urge to roll her eyes. Story of her fucking life.

"Until I—" she swallowed her irritation and her

worry "—figure it out, I need Derek with me on retrievals. Not everyone is going to give it up without a threat of muscle."

The Charmer didn't even bother turning around. "You'll get used to it."

"That's not good enough."

He whirled on her. "You know my business is more than this." He gestured between the two of them. The simple action twisted violent from the power in the room and the sharpness of his words.

"I get it." She held her own hand up in supplication. It didn't gather the energy in the room, so she continued, "I'm not sure I'm ready for solo stuff yet."

Understatement.

The Charmer harrumphed, but didn't disagree.

"I'm going to help her when I can either way, boss," Derek said. He was already edging Callie toward the door.

He was reading this room better than she was, which was exactly why she needed him at her side if she was going to keep repossessing souls and doing this magic shit. Derek led the way to the back exit, as though he knew she didn't want to risk running into a customer. She pushed herself through the first doorway. It had heavy magical wards that always left her feeling slicked with grease and gasping for breath. Like being birthed from the Charmer's workspace. The ick factor was worth it to be done with the Charmer for the night.

"Want me to make you dinner tonight?" Derek asked her as they edged down the hallway.

"All I have is bread, I think."

"Nah, you've got cheese, too."

"Are you making me a sandwich?"

"You don't know how impressive my grilled cheese sandwiches are."

Callie slammed her palm into the push bar on the door. "I guess you're going to have to—" her words were lost, swallowed by the scene in the alley.

A dead body blocked her path.

CHAPTER THREE

The kid was sixteen or seventeen, but lying there disjointed and lifeless on the craggy concrete he looked younger. His dark hair was smooshed to one side, slicked with something even darker like he'd slapped a spot with motor oil. His eyes were open, but unseeing. The milky white haze around his irises indicated he'd been a soul renter from a distance, but Callie was wedged in the doorway and close enough to the body for the lingering magic to press against her.

Ice crystals formed a lattice across her fingernails; the dark blue she'd painted them shifted into the smoky grey of the clouds before the first snowfall. Her hands only went icy when she was near someone who had used a rented soul before. The Cortean Church and the Soul Charmer might say the rented soul was the only one bearing consequences, but that wasn't the truth. Tiny fragments of the host's soul were snipped away with each interaction, and Callie could feel it even in this teenager at her feet.

"Tell me the Charmer wouldn't rent to a kid," Callie asked Derek over her shoulder, her voice barely a whisper.

"Cash is cash." His words were casual, but his voice shook. They were looking at the same horror. They were seeing the same teenager staring at them through glassy eyes. They were both faced with the reality of *dealing* with it.

Callie's hands began to ache from the cold, but she couldn't back away from the boy. His cheeks still held color. His throat held more as a trio of vivid, red gashes were open on the right side. Callie's gut bottomed out and shifted like it might flip. She'd worked in a hospital, and bore the iron stomach that went along with a medical gig. It wasn't the blood or the torn flesh offering the mule-kick to the belly. No, she had a damn good idea what she was looking at, and that was the problem.

"But Tess is gone," she said.

Derek's hands were light on Callie's shoulders as he edged around her. He leaned over the corpse, and then agreed, "Doesn't make sense."

Tess had the ability to take people's souls. She'd been after only those that belonged to the Soul Charmer, but Callie had seen the three-strike mark before. Those who had refused to give Tess their rented soul wore those same hatch marks as a scar of the forced extraction. It was the sign of a stolen soul. Callie didn't need the Soul Charmer and his shitty mentorship to make that clear to her. The problem was Callie and Derek had delivered Tess to the Charmer. Tess was gone. The Soul Charmer had believed he had more enemies, more people wanting to steal his magic and steamroll his business. It's why Callie was infused with magic. The thing was, this didn't look quite the same as what Tess had done. Callie squeezed her hands into fists, and would swear they crackled like ice cubes dropped into a glass of tap water. She ignored the freezing sensation and studied the clean edges of each wound. Clean. She shook her head. Such a poor way to describe the pink fileted skin. That was it, though.

"These are from a knife," she told Derek.

He grunted one of his non-committal huffs, and she knew him well enough now not to take it personally.

"Tess used her fingernails or something else more dull. She raked the skin. This… this is precise. Someone meant to damage this kid," she continued like his response had propelled the conversation.

"If they're dropping a dead kid at our doorstep, this was planned." Derek was right, but Callie really wished he wasn't.

She glanced toward one entrance of the alley and then the other, but they were alone. "Why would someone want to murder a kid, though?" She wished she were still young enough to wonder why anyone contemplated murder.

"Got your attention, didn't it?"

The freezing cold encapsulating Callie's hands began to dissipate. She hadn't moved. The soft pink of the boy's cheeks began to dull, too. Whatever was left of him was gone, and now only the oozing knife wounds could maintain their vibrancy. The proof of his murder, of what had been done, couldn't flee as quickly as this teenager could rise to Heaven. Callie liked to mock the phrase and the Church's reliance on it. It's what sent people to guys like the Soul Charmer who would take all their money and promise them a sin-filled loophole. However, in that moment, she prayed it was real. She prayed this kid found peace.

Derek knelt next to the body. "Ford's the knife guy."

Fuck wasn't that the truth? "Why would he…"

He shot her a look that said both that she should know better (and she did) and that it could be dangerous to have this discussion here.

"Right," she said.

"We need to move him and tell the boss."

Callie squeezed her eyes shut. She did not want to go talk to the Soul Charmer again. It wasn't only the trial by literal fire; it was also that he was goddamn scary when you gave him bad news.

"Why do we need to move him? Shouldn't we call the cops?" As soon as the words left her mouth she recognized how dumb they were. Weeks ago she'd broken into a police substation and stolen files. She was certain there was a bigger charge than burglary when it was stealing from the cops. She did *not* need to be talking to them, and none of the Charmer's crew needed Gem City PD anywhere near the soul rental shop.

Before Derek could explain, she added, "Do you need help moving him?"

He gave her the most genuine smile; the kind that made his eyes warm and her chest fill with light. "You're not going to touch him. I'll take care of this. Go back inside."

Callie wasn't a coward, but it was purely her pride and ego that kept her from asking Derek to be the one to tell the Soul Charmer about the dead kid door drop. "Okay. I'll go break the news."

She thought she'd infused the words with confidence. She'd been faking it for years. But Derek focused on her like he could see the little secrets and tiny fears she lined her ribcage with. He rose, walked to her, and wrapped his arms around her. She buried her face in his jacket and pulled in a deep breath of the leather, clean soap, and Derek. She was quickly associating the scent with comfort, which should have scared her more than saying a few words to her soul magic boss.

She squeezed him back for a brief moment, and then pulled away. "I'll go tell him," she repeated.

He nodded, and then turned back to his task with the teenager.

The Soul Charmer had told her someone was after him. He'd said they were after his souls. He'd said he'd need her.

Now she had to tell him he was right about the first one, and probably the second. The pompous asshole was going to revel in it, but Callie was clinging to hope he wasn't correct about her.

Finding one corpse was one too many, and if someone was ballsy enough to start dropping dead people at the shop's door, this could only be the beginning.

CHAPTER FOUR

Disposing of a body took a damn long time.

This was Callie's first foray into the world of illegal removal of corpses, but she had—incorrectly—thought it would be faster than calling the cops. When the police came for a body there was crime scene tape and chalk outlines, people to question, photos snapped, and hours upon hours of note taking and waiting around for a coroner to take the person away.

Callie had waited inside the Soul Charmer's shop while he and Derek had decided where to dump the kid with the shitty luck to be used as a threat to the main man in Gem City who wielded soul magic. Derek wanted her inside for her safety. The Charmer only cared about managing information she had access to. Either way, it was better than looking at a dead teenager.

The Soul Charmer returned inside alone. It was

hours until Derek returned. Hours spent answering her boss's questions. The same questions. Repeatedly.

Did you recognize him?

No. Each time he asked, Callie bit the urge to ask him if he did. That tang of magic came from somewhere, and she sure wasn't slipping sixteen-year-olds second souls.

Was there anyone in the alley?

No, again. Or if there had been, she had been too focused on the horror closest to her feet. She assumed Derek would have run after anyone nearby, though. He had a knack for keeping his eyes on the edges of any space he entered. He had practice. Callie was new to the clandestine craziness. It was probably for the best that she wasn't adapting quickly. People shouldn't be comfortable with criminal shit.

What did the slices look like again?

Heartbreakingly bloody and raw. The urge to sob beat steady against her sternum, but letting it free would only complicate matters. Where was Derek? He could divert the Charmer and spare her a few private moments to freak the fuck out. Oh, right, he was busy relocating a corpse to a place where the police could find him in a couple days, and not link him back here, to the Charmer, to her.

By the fifth or sixth go-round of these questions— she'd lost count—the Charmer's tone had become harsher, but his focus then turned to his wares. He carefully selected jars from his soul shelves. The black jars took on an even darker tone behind his pale, bony fingers.

She sucked in a deep breath, drawing side-eyed disdain from her vicious companion as he carefully set three jars onto his massive Oak desk.

Did you feel the magic coming off "the boy?"

The tone of this question changed each time the Charmer asked it, to the point Callie was now certain he thought she could make the ice crystals on her hands form at will.

"I didn't just feel the cold, Charmer. Ice formed on my nails." She held her hands aloft as though he could see the echoes of the magic there. His derisive snort suggested he could not.

"But you said it went away." He nudged a jar closer to her end of the room with a gnarled knuckle.

Callie tracked the jar's movement with her eyes, but resisted the urge to step backward. It was capped and a good four feet away. Now was not the moment to panic. She could do that at home. In the privacy of her shower. Possibly with a beer.

"Yeah, when his body went cold, my hands went back to normal." The longer she was around this onerous old man, the more her irritation found its voice.

He puttered around the storage room so often Callie had begun to think of it as his office. There weren't bills lying atop his desk though, and the only writing instruments found were the basic, black markers he used to label the jars storing souls. Still, it was his workspace, and in the weeks she'd been visiting the shop—working there, if she had to be honest—it was the only place she'd witnessed him at work. She'd shill souls in the lobby, and he'd hustle with the game of her mom working a three-card Monte scam on tourists. But it was back here, in this room, that he worked the real tricks. It was here he tried to make her control her magic. It was here that he was the most dickish and scary.

"Perhaps you finally succeeded?"

He meant blocking the magic from the souls, and they both knew she hadn't. "Is it not normal for the effects of soul renting to disappear after death?" she asked.

Lord, if someone had told her months ago she'd be having existential conversations with the Soul Charmer, she would have told them to cut back on the booze.

He'd dropped the subject suddenly when the crisp call of the bell beckoned him to the store's front. She appreciated the reprieve, or would have if the asshole hadn't gotten into her head.

Could she have saved that kid? Her brain screamed the question louder and louder each second she was alone in the sterile room stacked with shelf upon shelf of souls. Today hadn't been the first time the Charmer shoved a soul at her to see what she could do. The Charmer had been nudging jars closer and closer the last several days, and Callie hadn't been able to control her reaction in the least. The Soul Charmer wanted her to "take it," which had been about as useful instruction as her mother Zara's "just go" when she'd first put Callie behind the wheel at twelve.

Her brain was not wired for this magic shit, and

now that her sketchy boss had quit spitting questions at her, she had time to think. To marinate in her worries. Even despite the pain and discomfort of being in the Soul Charmer's den, there weren't any major consequences. She'd try, fail, and the Charmer would take his magic back. Only that hadn't happened yet. She hadn't learned enough to leave on her own, and she hadn't failed enough for him to punt her out the front door, and now she'd damn near stumbled over a dead body.

A dead kid, she mentally corrected.

She'd stood there, feeling the soul magic fade. Probably feeling his soul fade. Fuck if that wasn't going to be the thought screaming at her every night she couldn't sleep for the next decade.

It was with that fresh hell caught in her mind that the Charmer returned. The door from the customer-facing portion of the building was covered in rich velvet, which muffled sound between the spaces but also offered a gentle *whoosh* when moved quickly. And the Charmer always moved quickly. Callie sucked in a breath and sent a speedy, silent prayer that he wasn't toting a fresh soul with which to test her. She was burnt out for the day. Pun completely not intended.

The heavy fall of a boot covered the clapping of the Soul Charmer's bare feet. A tiny piece of Callie relaxed at the familiar sound of Derek walking into the room. Not a piece she'd show anyone. Not a piece even the Charmer could glimpse. She'd spent decades reinforcing the wall to keep out strangers. Even a magic man couldn't excavate an opening in mere weeks.

She turned, and the sight wasn't what she expected. It was Derek, yes. That part was good. The Charmer was at his side, which was also expected. It was his store after all and they were in this mess because he was a jackass. (Or because of magic. Whatever.) It was that Derek was supposed to be her reprieve. He was going to tell her it was all going to be okay. He'd been acting as a buffer as best he could between her and the Charmer, which was saying something because he refused to hide how awful he thought the whole arrangement was.

This wasn't her "let me fix that" guy. That guy held his chin high and his shoulders square and didn't care if you saw the deep scars on his knuckles. Hell, he wanted you to see them. He didn't back down. He didn't get scared. The man before her, though? He ground the knuckles of his right hand into the leather of his jacket sleeve. The light was bright enough for her to see the dark smudge there, but Callie couldn't tell if it were dirt or blood. Maybe that was enough to explain the hunch of his shoulders and the way he stared at the knobby feet of the bookcases against the far wall. The metal and brass and the stone tiles beneath them wouldn't look back. They wouldn't judge.

He'd "taken care" of the boy. He'd disposed of a body that didn't deserve to be dead. He fixed yet another problem he hadn't caused, and yet the look on his face wasn't "fuck it, I'm out" frustration. Callie long ago learned when her bullshit tank hit max others needed to clear a path. Derek was better than her. More controlled. He didn't stick by people simply because he always had. He didn't come from a family that placed loyalty above all else. So why was he standing in this room with lowlifes like she and the Soul Charmer and wearing a sheet of shame so saturated in self-loathing and disgust that it had to weigh two tons and carry more sins than Callie could amass in a lifetime?

The urge to go to him hooked a meaty paw under her ribs, gripped her heart, and yanked. She took a staggered step forward. Derek cast a look in her direction—she couldn't be sure if he was telling her to stop or begging her for help—but the hollow shadows beneath his eyes didn't ease. It didn't matter either way. This situation wasn't under her control. It never was.

The Soul Charmer's voice cracked against the stark surfaces surrounding the three of them. "Well?"

"It's done." Derek's rumbled reply squeezed that paw around her heart.

The Charmer rolled his beady eyes and began pulling jars from the nearby shelf. He cradled another three in his right arm before he spoke again. "I've known you long enough to know you would take care of that taunt."

Callie audibly sucked in a breath. The Charmer was slimy, but the teenager they'd found outside was more than a teasing jab. At least he had been to someone. He could have just as easily been her brother Josh a handful of years ago. She could have been the one weeping. The pit of disdain she had for her evening employer welled a little more each day, but today it had damn near doubled.

"What else?" When in work-mode Derek shifted to single-syllable communication as often as possible, but she'd never seen him do so with the Charmer.

Maybe their boss heard the weariness underneath the words. "Who left him out there? We can't simply expect this was pure luck. Dead bodies don't drop on our doorstep unless someone is making a statement."

Callie stood five or six feet away from the men, but took another shaky step toward them. Derek squared his shoulders toward the Charmer, but Callie saw the quick, soft glance he directed her way. He licked his lips, and then spoke. "I don't disagree. Kid wasn't a fluke. Someone cut him. Ripped a soul right out of him. Signs were obvious. But they didn't leave a note or their blood or anything on the kid. I don't know anything more than you do at this point."

The Charmer released a fresh armload of jars onto the tabletop with a *thu-thu-thu-thump*. "We need answers. That vile Tess started ideas. Ideas are not good for our business."

Callie got him. Ideas led to ambition, which might be great in school, but when it came to cutthroat business anyone getting ideas, thinking they knew how the magic worked, how to win the market when the kingpin could steal Heaven from you? Those ideas wouldn't bring anything but a bucket of trouble and a bag of regret. Callie damn sure planned to stay on his good, non-lethal side and wasn't about to try to scheme to steal from him. Hell, she couldn't even keep a contained soul from fucking up her hands.

"It isn't Tess—" Derek started to say, but the Charmer cut him off.

"I know it isn't her, but you know we have other

enemies." The Charmer cast a dark look at Derek, but continued to them both, "We need to find the source of the problem and shut them down now. Yesterday. Hellfire would be too kind a resolution. I want blood and ash."

His rage wasn't for the teenager who never got a chance. Not for that kid who he'd almost certainly rented souls to, and was dead for it. The Charmer cared about what was his simply for the fact it belonged to him. He didn't notice that his loyal collector was broken after burying or buying a cover story for a kid who'd lost his life on the other side of the far wall. He ignored the grief etching along Derek's jaw, and the defeat caked to his skin.

Callie saw it all, and fuck if she didn't want to fix it.

"We'll find them," she said with the confidence of a woman who wielded a badge and a gun, though she had neither.

The Charmer arced a brow like some B-movie villain, but it didn't faze her. "Oh you will?"

"Callie—" Derek shook his head, but it wouldn't change her mind.

She rushed the final steps forward to stand solid at his side. Her emotions were making her reckless, and it wasn't for family this time. What. The. Hell? The paw at her heart gave another yank, and she quit thinking about why she was offering to get further enmeshed in the Soul Charmer's bullshit and just did it. "We found Tess for you. We can figure this one out. Give us time."

"Time? I'm being robbed and dead children left at my door and you wish for time?"

Yes. She needed time to bring her emotions in check. Time to think. Time to let Derek *not* think. Time for him to process. Time to pretend they weren't part of this seedy, vicious underbelly of Gem City. She didn't tell him that, though. The Charmer would have no pity for her feelings. She pulled a card from Derek's play-book, instead: "We need to plan. Smart moves."

The Charmer's huff would have been a gentle agreement from anyone else bearing his grandfather looks. Callie had gotten plenty of sighing and grum-bling acquiescence at her day job at Cedar Retirement Home. The Charmer's age was a moving target—some days he looked to be in his seventies and other nights he aged a couple decades more—but he wasn't like the elderly men at the Home. He was magic and violence, and his response only made her gut tighten as though readying for a heavy blow.

"At least you've been listening to him, if not me," the Charmer finally said.

Callie had never missed a word out of the Soul Charmer's mouth, but now was not a good time to point it out. "We'll find out who's behind this."

"You'll do more than that, but—" the Charmer shooed them with his hands "—that's a start for to-night. You can go."

Callie opened her mouth to make sure he knew she wasn't doing jackall tonight, but Derek's hand cupped her upper arm and the warmth and warning it carried kept her from speaking her mind any further.

"Thanks, boss," Derek said, the words finite and conversation ending.

He escorted Callie to the back of the room, and toward the side exit. She used the time to think about how much of an idiot she was. Who volunteered for more work with the Soul Charmer? She already hated her time with him—and not only because it invariably ended with her screams—but she hadn't ever wanted to be part of this world. She wanted to believe she was better than the drug addicts and criminals who were at home among the soul renters. She needed to believe she deserved a life without threats and pain. Only that nasty black pit buried in her belly reminded her none of that was true.

That truth tingled through her skull as Derek popped open the back door again. Callie held her breath until she was certain the alley didn't conceal any more trouble. No bodies, no weapons, no magic. Just a flickering yellow street lamp, crumbling adobe on the wall of the adjacent building, and a hulking Dumpster that had been emptied earlier in the day. Derek's fingers found hers and he held her hand as they walked through the alley. Callie sidestepped a beer can, and Derek stretched his arm toward her so he wouldn't have to break the connection.

For once, Callie didn't know if he held on to soothe her or himself.

Since when had she become the comforting one outside the Soul Charmer's shop?

Oh, fuck, Derek was one of her people now. Like family. An honorary Delgado.

CHAPTER FIVE

Callie and Derek had stood next to his motorcycle for a solid five minutes before deciding to head to Dott's. It was their favorite greasy spoon. They weren't alone in loving it. The popular diner was busy for late on a Thursday. But they had pie and beer ready to serve, and the combo would make a perfect midnight snack for Callie. Provided she had money, which she did now. At least until she paid the electric bill next week. Then she'd be redlining it again.

They sat in their usual back-corner booth. When was the last time she had a "usual" anything with anyone? Until a month ago, Callie's "usual" was making a PB&J, reading half a paperback, calling family to touch base, and then crashing out. The only parts of her routine that remained intact were sleeping and checking in on Josh and Zara. She had four days to finish the latest mystery book she'd checked out from Gem

City Library, but she doubted she'd have time to get through the last hundred pages. Not with a recovering addict on her couch and a murderer leaving gifts at the Charmer's back door.

"Bette's coming back," Derek warned her. They'd come here often enough to have a regular waitress, too.

Callie had cradled the chilly beer bottle in her hands, but now pulled them away. Just in time. Bette approached and Callie's fingers began to stiffen and shift to a subtle blue hue. She shoved her hands beneath the table and onto her lap. Their waitress was in her mid-40s, always got their orders right, and was a soul user. She wasn't renting now, but each time she returned a rented soul a snippet of her own disappeared. Callie hated that she could feel the change in Bette, but hated more that the woman had no idea how her dabbling with the Charmer had changed her. At least Bette didn't have a bonus soul right now, but Callie still wasn't particularly comfortable around her.

The library book she'd been reading had a main character who could touch an object and know its history. Callie's hands could burn people, they could get coated in ice, but they could not answer questions about whodunit. Naturally. That would have been useful.

"You two want your usuals?" Bette asked with the sweet tone she probably used around her four-year-old.

That motherly tone helped Callie ignore the way her fingers had locked beneath the table. She nodded, and Derek answered for them both, "Yep."

Once the waitress left to put in their orders for a cheeseburger and a patty melt, color began to return to

Callie's fingers and they thawed. Derek was watching her closely. Deep grooves had set up shop between his eyebrows.

"Do I want to know?" she asked, still rubbing her hands together to shake the echo of a chill.

"You just got in deeper with him." He meant the Soul Charmer.

"Not any deeper than I already was." She shrugged. "Apprentice, remember?"

"Don't remind me about *that* deal. It was bad enough, but you didn't need to offer to get involved with whatever shit fell at his door."

"Did you also not need to spend your night disposing…" she looked around the diner and then opted to incline her head in his direction instead of announcing their crimes in public. They didn't kill that kid, but Callie was pretty sure moving a dead body and disturbing a crime scene were pretty damn illegal.

"That's part of my job."

"Are you going to tell me what the whole 'we have enemies' business was about?"

Derek remained silent. That non-verbal 'no' stung.

"What else is he trying to make you do?"

"Normal shit, Callie. I'm keeping tabs on the competition for him. Nothing to worry about." Exhaustion lanced his words, and Callie's unease doubled.

"What competition is left? Tess is gone—"

It might have been mentioning the woman who'd tried to take over the Charmer's business or reminding him of how the Charmer had turned Callie into his own weapon or the memory of singed skin, but Derek cut her off with a ferocity she'd not seen. "Don't change the subject. Tonight was pure shit. You need less awful in your life, and now you volunteered to help find out who did *that*."

That. A murdered teenager.

"He was going to make us do it anyway." Wasn't he? He'd made them find Tess, he'd blackmailed Callie into interrogating Tess, he'd used her connection to Derek against her, he'd refused to take his magic back before. She'd had to demand to be his apprentice to shift the power dynamics.

"At least this way we control the terms with him," she added.

"He's always in control," Derek said under his breath. For not the first time, Callie wanted to know how the Soul Charmer had earned the loyalty of a man like Derek. The dark slashes cutting beneath his eyes and the hunch of his shoulders held the questions at bay for now.

"Are you okay?"

Derek let out a derisive laugh—brief and cutting. So that was a no.

Maybe her worry was showing, because after a moment he said, "I'll be okay."

The song of the martyr.

"It's okay if you aren't," she said quietly. Her mother had often lashed out when Callie offered emotional help. *Feelings* weren't what Zara had wanted help with. Picking pocketbooks from purses, distracting the utility guy, funneling cash to Josh—those were real ways to help.

Derek wasn't like her family. He pulled a long swig from his beer, and then nodded slowly. Booze and empathy steadied him. "I know. Tonight was fucked. It'll be a couple days until I get over it."

A couple days to forget what he'd done? Doubtful. They'd aborted the plans to go back to her house and make sandwiches because Callie couldn't be around Josh yet. Her brother was still crashing on her couch. He would want to cheer her up, but he still needed so much work from her. He was a recovering addict, who was leaning a lot closer to addict than recovered. He'd been kidnapped by drug lord and mafia boss Ford, and Callie had earned his return. She wasn't about to let him double back into a pattern that resulted in her big brother dead. It was that thought that brought them to Dott's. Callie was unnerved by what she'd seen tonight. The flames dancing on her arms? Nothing compared to the cold, fading stare of that teenage boy.

Trying to deal with her worry for Josh and his care while her brain was still battered from the stark visual from the alley was too much. "Do you have any idea who would have done that?"

It was plain what "that" she was talking about. Derek stilled his features as if what was happening behind the scenes was so volatile he needed to pre-emptively cover it. "No. Whoever did *that* knew those marks would mean something to us, but the precision worries me. We haven't seen it before, but it sure as shit looked like they were aces at stealing souls."

"I haven't even heard the Charmer whine about small-timers trying to offer soul rental services recently."

The dark noise rumbling from Derek's chest wasn't his normal grumble. Callie didn't recognize the sound, but it sharpened her attention.

"No one has dared a storefront or a newspaper ad since what happened to Tess," he said.

"Is that common knowledge?"

"Those who need to know are aware she crossed him and now she's gone."

Neither the Soul Charmer nor Derek had told Callie what happened to Tess after they'd captured and questioned her. Callie would have liked to pretend that Derek didn't know, but he probably did. Just another act of his protection. For her. Maybe stepping up for him at the shop earlier hadn't been a completely terrible idea. Provided getting more involved in this mess didn't get her killed. Her life was fairly shitty, but it was hers and she'd prefer to keep it.

"Who would have the balls to do something like this, then?" She hadn't meant to say the words aloud, but now that they were out, she was curious what Derek's answer would be. He'd been a part of the Charmer's soul magic world far longer than she. She needed him to have enough extra insight to calm her worry.

Instead he said, "Bette."

She was saying "what?" as her fingertips went icy. Her right index finger and thumb froze to the waxy paper label wrapped around the brown bottle. Callie hissed, but managed to school her features while Bette set their plates on the table and asked if she could get them anything else. Derek quickly replied no on their behalf, and the waitress left. Callie's fingers returned to normal, but when she pulled them away from the bottle, the paper clung to her.

"Damn it," she muttered and began rubbing her fingers together to pill the paper. It fell to the table in a small pile. At least it looked like there was a fidgety kid at the table instead of an adult woman who froze her beer label to her fingers.

She hadn't forgotten the question she'd accidentally asked, and she doubted Derek had either. "Any ideas who?"

Derek groaned, and Callie's stomach dropped. She hadn't even had a bite of her sandwich yet.

"That bad?"

"Anyone who heard about the burns Tess had, the ones Bianca had, and didn't flinch is not going to be someone you want to meet."

She winced, not because of the fear of who was to come, but at the way he danced around her history. She was the cause of the others' fear. She was the one who had burned Bianca and Tess when they'd hoarded souls within themselves and turned her palms into incendiary devices. Her brain finally processed the last part of what he'd said though. "Someone *I* want to meet?"

"We need to distance you from this."

"Because you don't want me using these?" She

held her hands up like exhibits A and B.

"That, too. You don't need more guilt weighing on you. Or the Charmer forcing you to do darker, nastier shit you can't forget." He spoke with that eerie blend of pain and knowledge. If they'd sat on the same side of the booth, she would have hugged him. Instead she extended her arm across the table and opened her palm to him. He took her hand in his.

"I don't want him forcing you either."

Derek looked over her shoulder, but she waited to continue until he met her gaze again. "We're in this together," she said.

"I know, doll. I just wish the thing we were working together on could be some mundane shit like assembling furniture."

"I don't think you would need help putting together a bookshelf."

He smiled and meant it. "No, not really."

She laughed.

"Do you need a bookshelf?"

Not now, but someday. If they got out of this. If she got Josh back on his feet. If she could keep working a steady job and save up, then she could start buying books. She could need a bookcase. She'd put her mysteries on one shelf and the romances on another and use vases as bookends.

But first she had to sober up her brother (for real this time), figure out how to cover the increased expenses of an extended houseguest, and find out who had it out for the Soul Charmer.

CHAPTER SIX

Home. The simple concept had eluded Callie for too long. Her mom's house had been a place to sleep when she was a kid, but not a safe space. Her first few apartments came with roommates, which hadn't made them any safer. She'd never had much in the way of possessions, but even the small amount she'd left in the ten by ten allocated to her in each of her previous communal digs never looked right against the stark walls.

She'd lived in Crest Winds Apartments for more than a year and a half. Alone. It was hers. The space was Spartan—partially because all her cash was continually sucked into family shit and partially because she wanted what was hers to be clean and sharp. She couldn't scrub the stains off her insides. She couldn't box the blocks of guilt wedged low in her gut and drop them at the curb. She could, however, make a sanctuary without cracked dishes, without dust dotting tables. Her clothes could be neatly put away. She'd spent money on them; they deserved to be treated with care. It was in this tidy, one-bedroom apartment on the second floor, she'd found home. Her past lingered, but she'd found the first place where she could close her eyes and not want to cry or run. A place where she could let the tension in her muscles ease. She knew the locks were shit, but in the twenty-two months she'd lived in Crest Winds, no one had ever tried to bust it. Not even Ford or his goons when they were in peak shakedown mode.

Apartment 231 was home.

Or it had been. Before the brother who knew her deepest betrayals—the times she didn't put family first, the times she'd tried to distance herself from their mother—had taken that from her.

The door wasn't ajar or even unlocked when she got home from dinner with Derek, but tension lashed Callie's back. Her brother Josh was crashed out on the couch. His black hair was growing out and it was squashed against and swirled over the top of a pillow he'd jacked from her bed. She'd given him one for the couch, but it must not have done the trick. The orange pillowcases were only for her bed, but here was one in the living room. His shoes were on the coffee table. His shirt had been flung across the back of the couch. The laundry basket near the coat closet at the front of the living room was empty.

She latched the door behind her, and then closed her eyes. And waited. Seven seconds later she opened them, but the sight hadn't changed. Her older brother was still passed out on her sofa. An empty bowl and a fork glared at her from the small counter separating her perfunctory kitchen from the aging living room. At least he'd eaten. Callie picked up the dish and utensil, and placed them into the sink. She'd wash them tomorrow. Or maybe Josh would. He'd been sleeping so much since she'd gotten him back from Ford. He claimed he went through the worst of the detox from his meth addiction while the mafia leader's captive. Callie remembered how high he'd been when she'd spoken to him on the phone all those days ago. He shouldn't be at the sleep-nonstop part of recovery. She ignored the medical training she'd received in her hospital days. Maybe things had changed. Maybe she didn't remember correctly.

She pulled her phone from her back pocket ready to get an answer on the timeline of withdrawal side effects. Ugh. The internet icon was off. She tried reconnecting, but her next-door neighbor must have changed her password. The neighbor's sister had visited last week. The jerk probably let her know the "123456" password was not entirely secure and anyone could hijack her connection. Which was exactly what Callie had done. Digging into why Josh was sleeping—at almost midnight—was not worth using any of her data. She'd be at work in a few hours, and could look it up on her break. Cedar Retirement Home had legit Wi-Fi and their IT guy gave no fucks what anyone looked at.

It didn't matter right now anyway. She had Josh back. He was alive. Ford and his thugs hadn't done so much as a drive-by of her place—Derek had been checking—since they'd completed their exchange. She'd stolen soul magic research files from the police for Ford in exchange for Josh. She wasn't about to let a little bit of extra sleep stop her from enjoying having her brother home.

Family first, right?

Lucky bastard was getting more sleep in a day than she'd had in a week. She ran the sleep math, and she was going to get a solid four hours before she'd have to get up for work. The real work. The reputable, non-magical work that kept the heat on and the water running. If she wanted to renew the lease on this apartment—her home—she'd need to make sure regular checks—even small ones—continued hitting her bank account.

She needed to stop letting Derek grab the tab at dinner, too. He liked to pay and didn't act like it was a hardship, but she wasn't a mooch. She'd seen women—okay, mostly her mom—who went on dates because they were hungry or wore minimal clothing to the bar so they wouldn't need to pay for drinks. Derek needed to know she wasn't like that. She wouldn't take advantage of trust or kindness simply because she could. She wasn't Zara. She shook herself. Derek kept looking past the dark clouds roiling inside her to see this tiny golden shaft of good, and that's all he cared about. He'd recognize the rest eventually, but if she could hold her own to keep them equals it might delay the inevitable discarding and heartbreak.

She just needed to come up with a way to cover Josh's bills. The food and heat budget went up with a second person staying in the apartment, especially when he was there alone so much.

Worrying over money never made dollars manifest. Callie washed her face and tried to let the financial stress slide down the drain. It mostly worked. She climbed into bed and tucked the comforter around her bunting style. *The cash flow will correct itself*, she thought as she closed her eyes.

Color fading.

Blood dripping.

Eyes pleading.

Callie's eyes opened in a flash. She slammed her head back against the pillow. Who was she to worry about covering rent when a teenager had lost his life? What were the odds of ever getting a night's sleep again with that scene burrowed in her brain?

Leaving for work when the sun was asleep wasn't something new for Callie. She'd worked the early shift at Cedar Retirement Home for a couple years, and the routine didn't suck. Since beginning a second, unpaid, and exhausting gig as the apprentice to the Soul Charmer, though, that pre-dawn walk to the car was different. As soon as she stepped into the breezeway outside her apartment, her muscles snapped in bands across her stomach—natural armor tightening and locking in place. She locked up, tucked her elbow tight against her purse, and hotfooted it down the stairs. Ice dug a groove alongside the curb. Her landlord hadn't salted. Callie stepped over it. *At least it isn't on my hands. Too fucking early for that,* she said to herself.

Her beat-to-shit ride was bathed in a halo of yellow light in the back of the lot. A six-foot cinder-block wall rose solidly from the hard-packed earth in the front of the car with a tall-for-Gem-City streetlight towering above it. One of only three such lights in her complex's lot. Callie reminded herself safety made the extra distance worth the walk, but this morning she was simply too exhausted to accept the illusion of safety as anything other than that.

Her right calf muscle twitched when she pressed on the gas pedal. Not enough sleep or water or fruit was making her shaky. At least she could *be* shaky. That poor kid left on the cold ground outside the Soul Charmer's shop wouldn't be on edge or sleep deprived again. That memory of his body fading wasn't going to leave Callie. Derek would assure her that time would help, but Callie wasn't so new to tragedy as to believe that waiting long enough would make her forget. Scars didn't have to be on the outside to remain forever.

CHAPTER SEVEN

It didn't matter how shitty your life had been, there were always standout shit moments. The worst of the worst. Those memories that curled in the corners of your brain waiting for their chance to light up, vivid and real, in quiet moments years later. Callie was counting frozen beef patties to be thawed for the lunch shift. Maybe it was the chill of the walk-in freezer or the menial task, but one of the handful of egregious memories flashed bright and bitter.

She fingered the crimped seal on the next pack of patties. The pattern puckered beneath her fingertip, and Callie remembered the stitches. Her first stitches. Some people went their whole life never having been sewn back together. Callie was a patchwork of mended wounds inside and out. Not all her scars were visible. Not even the first five stitches she'd received beneath her left eye.

Callie's mother hadn't been home in eight days. She had a line on a married business guy who wanted to escape, and Zara wasn't about to miss her chance to cash in. It hadn't been the first time her mom had disappeared chasing a "sure thing" or losing track of time at the casino. However, the teachers at school were making note of Callie arriving for a free breakfast. It wasn't that she wasn't already on the list, but the more people watched you, the more they saw. That fact hadn't changed in Callie's twenty-four years. Nothing good had ever come of being watched. Not for Callie. So she'd skipped her last class—seventh grade geography—that day and walked the alleyways behind the shops on the Plaza. She'd seen Saint Catalina's statue as she crossed streets, and pretended not to feel the holy glare burning into her back. Callie had spied an open door and ducked in. The retail shops consistently had their employee spaces at the back, and the shoddy electrical work in historic buildings forced their refrigerators and microwaves against the back wall. The space Callie snuck into was empty aside from the humming appliances. She snatched a twenty-ounce soda and a baggie of carrots, and shoved them in her backpack. Josh had taught her the trick last summer. Flexing it solo made her bolder, braver. She ducked back out of the building, and continued down the alley looking for another opportunity. Hopefully one with an entrée or two.

She'd continued the process until her bag had three sandwiches, the carrots, three sodas, and a sealed bag of chocolate covered pretzels. She should have quit while she was ahead, but her twelve-year-old mind really wanted some chicken and thought she'd snag some soon. Her luck had run out, though. Her last stop was the back of a rowdy bar. She'd made the mistake of assuming everyone would be busy in the front at a place like that. It was the kind of shithole that served minors and never cleaned its floors or bathrooms. It was also, Callie learned, the kind of place where stealing was really fucking off limits.

When the two guys—barely adults—caught her pilfering from their stash, they weren't above kicking some tween ass. They'd broken her orbital socket, and she'd passed out from the beating. They'd left her in the alley like one of the bums who spent the evening scouring the dumpsters for leftovers.

Josh had found her. Rescued her.

He cleaned her face as best he could with his shirt, and took her to St. Mary's hospital. The assholes who clobbered her hadn't taken her bag. So she and Josh still had food, and even then Callie's gut had twisted with how happy that made her. She wanted something real in her stomach. The nurse in the emergency room had given her a sports drink and a bag of chips, but that wouldn't sustain her into the weekend. Her stealing had gotten her another day. The cost hurt more than her hunger pangs had.

The difference between that day and all the other ones when she'd needed stitches or went hungry or feared she wouldn't rise to Heaven or felt alone and like a degenerate? The reason that memory took hold of her in the quiet moments? She learned two important things that day. One, that she was poor. Good and truly. Broke-ass poor. The kind of poor that made your insides hurt and your mouth dry. And, two, that no matter your reasons crime was crime and once you crossed that line it was hard to get anyone to see you as anything other than a criminal.

"Callie! Can you grab me an extra box of eggs while you're in there?" Louisa called from the other room. Her voice yanked Callie back into the present.

Callie hollered back an affirmative, and tried not to let the memories of aching for food rumble too hard against her sternum as she hefted a third box of beef patties on to her stack. She was surrounded by food every morning at work. She touched it, helped cook it, and often ate the leftovers. Day-job leftovers were a whole lot better than the back-alley scraps she'd scrounged all those years ago. It was part of the reason she liked this place. Working in a kitchen was a guarantee of one solid meal a day. Sometimes two. She made enough to keep a loaf of bread, some processed cheese, and cereal in her cupboards, generally, but one doesn't forget what it was like to be without food. She doubted there'd be a time when she believed food would always be on the table.

She brought the stack of pre-packaged beef out of the freezer, and set each box on the stainless steel prep counter in the corner near the far door. Louisa was stirring a batter and humming. The tune was off-key, which was the norm for her boss. Callie pulled a fresh box of eggs from the refrigerator and brought them to the short woman.

Lou's hips twisted and rocked to her own lyric-less

version of "Lord of Love." Callie had heard the song at least three times a week growing up. The Cortean Catholic Church nearest her mom's place still had it in regular rotation.

"Eggs, as requested." Callie strived to keep amusement from tainting her words. It wasn't that the song was particularly amusing, but the sight of her fifty-something supervisor rocking out to a church hymn was likely to be the best sight she'd see all day. She wanted the kind of joy that burst from you in dance and song in her life, too. Maybe once she was done with the Charmer. When she was back to being Callie, and Josh was sober, and she and Derek could hang out without having the Soul Charmer and their respective connections to him dangling above them.

"Callie?" Louisa said her name like she'd already said it more than once.

"Sorry. Didn't get enough sleep last night."

Lou must have been able to tell she meant the apology. She smiled. "Can you go ahead and beat the eggs for me?"

"Sure, how many do we need today?" Callie asked, already turning to the smaller of the home's two industrial mixers.

"Twelve dozen should do it. Don't know why you use that thing."

Callie's laugh was real, and it made the weight on her chest much more manageable. "Yes, you do. My arms would ache and it would take infinitely longer if I did it your way."

'Her way' was to do everything by hand. Louisa continued to work a wooden spoon through a thickening pancake batter. Her seventh batch of batter this morning. "Hard work builds character. Plus you could have guns like these."

Lou flashed an arm muscle in a classic body builder pose. Callie had to admit, the muscle was legit. "Well, then you'd expect me to carry even more boxes."

"You have to carry boxes anyway."

Callie shrugged, and started cracking eggs into the mixing bowl.

The radio played the oldies station at a level-two volume in the background, and Callie and Louisa worked quietly.

"Your brother keeping you up?" Lou spoke so softly that Callie almost didn't hear her.

Callie's chest tightened as though the threat against her brother was imminent again. As though someone would show up at her doorstop with a knife or a gun and demand her big brother.

Josh's kidnapping by mobster Ford was an entirely secret affair. Callie's family had plenty of those—those dark truths that wouldn't be understood by those who weren't blood. Ford must have felt the same way, because no one had mentioned Josh's time with the goons to anyone. The only non-family member in the loop was Derek, and each day he was moving a little closer to being considered family. At the very least, Callie found herself sharing more with him. Her fears and secrets had started seeping out in the soft moments with him. Maybe her brain lacked filter during the wee hours in bed, or maybe it was simply nice to have someone to trust. Either way, as much as Callie loved Lou, she wouldn't share Josh's secret.

Lou knew Josh was a junkie, though. It was more common in these parts than any governmental official would admit. If they acknowledged the issue, they'd have to allocate funds for mental health care. Un-fuck-ing-likely. Her boss's kid was in the same boat, and Callie had been able to share the frustrations of trying to keep a loved one from rock bottom and failing—repeatedly—with Louisa.

The immediate truth was fair to share, though. "He's sleeping all the time."

"He clean?" Lou asked. She dropped a pat of butter into the bowl, and kept her gaze locked on the mix.

Callie turned back to her own work. It was easier to watch the mundane act before her, than catch any pity in Louisa's eyes. "I think so. Hope so. It's just I don't think he should be sleeping so much…"

"When Michael detoxed last time, he slept a lot."

"Really?"

"He had to get past the shakes and the sweating and the hours of heaving in my favorite mixing bowl, but then he was asleep for a day or two. I think their bodies have to rest and recover after the trauma that stuff put them through."

Neither woman ever said methamphetamines. They didn't need to. The bathtub drug lingered over the conversation, unspoken and abrasive.

Callie opened her mouth to say Josh hadn't done the puking thing and wasn't crusting up his pillowcases with sweat every night, but she didn't want to break the spell. It was too much like admitting her brother hadn't hit rock bottom. That he hadn't gone cold turkey. That he was still using.

"I'm sure you're right, Lou."

He probably went through the gross battery of detox at Ford's place. He'd only been high at the beginning of the two weeks the mobster had kept him. A drug kingpin known for chopping his enemies into tiny pieces wouldn't have funneled free drugs to a guy so in debt his baby sister was working for a thug. Right? A heavy stone settled in her stomach, but she swore she wasn't lying to herself. It didn't matter, because she she was done with Ford.

She'd stolen the documents he'd needed. He'd wanted to know how close the police were to linking fingerprints and DNA from criminals using rented souls back to the original ones. So far renting souls from her *other* boss The Soul Charmer wasn't illegal, but the fact that sticking a bonus soul in your body altered your DNA and fingerprints—the best options for forensics to catch a criminal—meant The Powers That Be needed to figure out how to fix that. They needed to prove it was a problem, they needed to undo the changes, and they needed to make it illegal. Which would seriously suck for Ford.

She'd gotten him the information. She chose not to think about what he had done with it—or what he might still be doing with it. As much as she wanted to protect everyone, she had to prioritize. Josh, her mom, all the Delgados, and Derek came before worrying over who else Ford might target. As long as the jerk wasn't banging on her door right now, she could move forward. She could get back to distancing herself from the shit side of town. She could get her raise—just another four weeks—and renew her lease, and be on track to getting her life back together.

Other than the magic coursing through her veins. *Thanks, Soul Charmer.*

She'd almost been able to forget, because Louisa—bless her—refused to ever partake in soul magic. The kitchen at Cedar Retirement was a safe space, and Callie was going to take it.

CHAPTER EIGHT

The safety of Cedar Retirement Home did not extend to the parking lot. At least not today.

Ford's favorite goon was leaned back against an aging SUV in the parking lot. The vehicle didn't belong to Nate. He had parked a douche-y sports car outside her apartment on more than one occasion that was *all* Nate. He was a spindly man with smears of black beneath the too-thin skin atop is cheekbones and a mouth perpetually set in a sneer.

Callie kept her eyes trained on her beat-up sedan. Nate and his causally crossed ankles were next to her car. She supposed she could be happy he wasn't up against her vehicle, but she didn't think the two feet between the man and her car were going to stop him from hassling her.

"Hey, sugar, how's about—"

"Not in the mood, jackass." She kept walking, her

hand held up to block her view of him.

"Now is that anyway to greet a friend?"

She dropped her hand. He'd pushed off the car, and now stood next to her driver's side door. She stopped with a few feet between them—enough to keep out of his arm's reach.

"We aren't friends." Her voice sliced sharp. She didn't sound scared, but her stomach tried to roll beneath her ribcage anyway.

"We could be." He waggled his brows, and she wished she could punch his smug face. Derek would. Derek would pop that fucker so fast.

"Well, we're not. I'm full up on friends."

"That's a shame. Are you saying Ford isn't your friend?"

Callie opened her mouth to launch a snappy comeback about how people who blackmailed you were never categorized as friends, but then remembered the time she'd seen severed fingers at Ford's home and decided to fold her arms across her chest and glare instead. Silent malevolence was the way to go here. Probably.

Nate's grin sent the same snap of tightness across Callie's nape that a haunted house clown would. "Well Ford considers you a friend, and was hoping you might be interested in doing him a favor."

She'd thought she was done with these people.

"I don't have time. Tell him I'm sorry, but I can't."

"What's got you so busy that you don't have time

for Gem City's favorite son?"

Ford was more than a mobster. He was also the son of one of the most successful and wealthy men in Gem City…who was probably also a mobster. The family owned slaughterhouses, and Ford let word spread he was familiar with blades and a bone saw. Callie doubted that common thread was a coincidence.

"I'm helping my brother sober up, for one, but also working two jobs."

"Yeah, we heard you're now working for the Soul Charmer. Ford wouldn't have sent you his way if he'd known you were going to align with him."

"I didn't see it coming either," she said more to herself.

Nate took a step toward Callie, and she mirrored his movement in the opposite direction. She wasn't about to let him get close enough to lay hands on her. That wouldn't end well for anyone.

"Ford would like to know more about the soul rental business. He thinks you could be a real asset to our team."

Callie's stomach sank to the soles of her feet. She shuffled to the right a smidge to be sure she could still move. "I already have too many jobs. Sorry."

"You'd keep doing whatever it is you're doing for the Soul Charmer, but just fill us in. No big." The light behind Nate's eyes said it sure as shit was *big*, and while a little part of her wanted to know why, a bigger part blasted that bad news warning to her brain like a powerful thunderstorm moving into her cerebellum.

Maybe it was the mental jolt or maybe she was simply over being everybody's pawn, but Callie balled her fingers into fists and took three hurried steps toward her car. She shoulder-checked Nate to get past and to her car door. An icy bolt shot down her arm so sharp and fast she'd almost believe it was God striking her for her repeated bad decisions—if she thought the Big Man really would smite people, which she didn't.

She'd reached the car and her escape, but her balled hands couldn't open to grip the handle. She struggled to unclench her fists, but Nate crept closer behind her. In another circumstance she would have felt him hovering over her shoulder. She would have thought about jabbing her elbow back hard into his gut and running. Touching him wasn't going to solve his situation. Running wouldn't either. If there was anything she'd learned from her family it was running from your problems didn't solve shit. It merely delayed the inevitable.

She turned to face Nate. He didn't acknowledge her struggle to open her hands. Even if the tendons and muscles in her forearms were screaming, at least she wasn't visibly straining. She angled one arm closer to him though it ached from the prolonged freeze. She edged the tips of her fingers on the other hand outward a smidge.

He leered down at her. Why did this guy have such a hang up with her? Maybe he was a douche nozzle with every woman in his presence, but there was something that reared that red-light warning in her belly when he stood mere inches from her, and it didn't have fuckall to do with the magic locking her in ice or the fact he was missing tiny pieces of his soul. But maybe it could buy her time? Get her space? Get her out of there without more pain?

Callie lifted her chin in far more of a "don't even try it, asshole" act than in order to meet his gaze. Though, the move achieved both. "If your boss wants to know about renting souls, why don't you just answer his questions?"

The lurid glaze over Nate's dark eyes evaporated. His black eyebrows knitted together tight enough to edge into uni-brow territory. "I ain't working for the Soul Charmer, cupcake," he said, but the illicit tone he'd leveraged before had fallen limp. Like a teenager bragging about having sex when he hadn't even kissed a girl.

"You rent them, don't you? You can tell him about the process." Callie kept her voice even. She slipped her left hand behind her, and while her fingers remained cold she was able to extend them completely. It hurt, but she moved them enough to be confident she could grip the door when the moment struck.

This time Nate took a full step back from her. "Charmer tell you that?"

A tiny tendril of glee tickled Callie's throat. Nate was unnerved and it was fucking fantastic. About time someone else was put on edge. She was pretty goddamn done with being the only one teetering on the cliff. "Does it matter how I know?"

She took a half step backward, too, so her body grazed the side of her car and she now had breathing room between she and the mob henchman.

"It matters," he said under his breath. He turned to look away, but continued to speak, "Thought your man kept people's secrets."

"He's not my man, and I can't speak to his secrets. Why would your boss care?" She'd adapted to avoiding Ford's name. It helped her pretend she wasn't talking to mobsters who had no compunction about disposing of bodies.

Nate shrugged. Callie fingered the door handle. It wasn't locked. The one time running late and not having anything worth stealing paid off. She could move enough to lift the handle now.

"Doesn't most of your team, crew, whatever, use rented souls? That's kind of the point of them, right? No fingerprints, no DNA, no problems with the boys in blue." The parking lot was empty of people and light on cars, but Callie pitched her voice low. It would make Nate feel like she cared about his privacy, and would keep any of her coworkers from checking up on her if they heard her voice out here. Empty parking lots were like caverns at the right time of the day. Sound carried.

Nate grumbled unintelligibly for a moment. His shoulders were pulled tight, like he ached to fold his arms and pout. Instead he rocked back onto his heels. "Yeah. Well, he has questions about how it works."

Callie took his moment of distraction to pivot. She quickly lifted the door handle, opened it, and slipped inside the safety of her car.

Nate rushed to the door, too, but didn't move to open it. Small favors. He rapped a single knuckle against the glass.

She lowered the window an inch.

"I have to get home. I have obligations," Callie said with the full punch of the truth.

"I'll give you a couple days to think over Ford's offer."

Callie was tempted to notify him saying "give me information" was not exactly an offer, but wasn't about to find herself negotiating with a guy who scared the shit out of her. She did that once before, and how her hands went into an icy death grip when she was standing by a heavy soul magic user. So, hard pass.

Nate must be taking his vitamins, because it was like he read her mind. He gave her car a dramatic sidelong look. "Ford pays better than the Charmer. Keep that in mind."

He tapped twice on the top of her car with an open palm, and walked away. He hadn't really threatened her, but it still took her three tries to start the car. It had nothing to do with the POS engine.

Callie rolled out of the parking lot without a destination. She should be going home. She should be checking in on Josh or at least finishing the paperback mystery she'd checked out from the library. Feeding both her and Josh left zero room for library fines, and she would not be okay until the book's crime was solved and she knew who had done it.

They needed groceries, too. The store wouldn't be too crazy now, but she wasn't in the mood for the mental math required to mete out the proper goods to feed them both and not kill her bank account. There was still cereal and milk in house, and she and Josh had existed on less for longer than a day when they were kids.

Callie headed north. She could almost call it the long way home, if you considered looping out near the airport so you could take dirt roads and avoid other cars and streetlights a way home. She needed to quit kidding herself. She had a few hours until she was due at the Charmer's again, and she wanted to avoid people. All people. Those she liked, those she didn't, those who would turn her hands icy and those who would threaten to chop them off if they didn't get their ways. Not that Nate had even insinuated there would be slicing or dicing if she didn't get Ford the information about the Charmer. She'd been to Ford's house, though. He hadn't been coy or ashamed by the severed fingers resting in the inbox pile on his desk. He'd wanted her to see them, and this was why. His henchman asked for a favor and she immediately assumed if she didn't comply he'd take a digit or two.

Nonverbal threats were the most effective for her anyway. Callie's brain would sputter and whirl and spin the most terrifying scenarios. Whatever her mind could conjure would be the most detailed horror. More than whatever Nate could cobble together with a tenth-grade education.

The sky was a pure, soft blue above her, but smudges of grey hovered above the Sangre de Cristo Mountains. Callie dialed the car's heat up a notch, as though she could already feel the ice and snow storming near Taos. Like she knew it would come down the mountain for her. Her hands already carried the weekend blizzard, but the storm that darkened the horizon chilled her core in an inescapable way. Whatever was coming was going to hurt.

So Callie splurged on some hot chocolate from the McDonald's drive-thru, and drove twenty-five miles per hour along the gravel roads at the edges of Gem City while she drank it. Thirty minutes later she gave up, and returned home and to her real life.

Josh was still sleeping—or maybe sleeping again—when Callie got home. She flipped the deadbolt behind her, and let out a long sigh of relief. She was home where zero gangsters were going to pop up and block her path to the refrigerator.

That was a solid plus. Her home had taken on a musky scent that wasn't that "man" scent every romance novel she read referenced, but more the funk found after many days of not showering and keeping the windows latched. Her brother was ripe and it was funking up the place.

The television blinked brightly across the living room. The news was on, but she doubted Josh had been catching up on Gem City goings on. The anchor's voice was soft with the low volume, but Callie followed. "The dismembered body was found in the Railyard District. The police are investigating the identity of man, but as yet have no leads. Potential suspects were not shared with us at time of broadcast."

Ford was everywhere. The news anchor and her perfectly coifed hair knew as well as Callie did that crime lords coiled beneath their city. What Callie didn't know was how Ford kept avoiding the cops. Maybe the goods she'd stolen for him were icing on the bribery cake.

Callie grabbed the tufted red throw pillow from the closest chair at her dinette set and threw it across the room at Josh's sleeping form.

He grunted, but didn't fully wake or acknowledge the light weight of the pillow on his shoulder. A full bowl of cereal sat on the carpet next to the couch. Josh's hand dangled a couple inches from it. At least he'd gotten up at some point and wanted food. Even if he hadn't eaten it. It wasn't for show if he did it when she wasn't here. Her stomach did that keening move it reserved for real worry. Josh had a way of bringing that sensation forward. She wanted his sobriety to stick this time. Since he was zonked, she opened the front closet door. She rolled the vacuum cleaner out. Though the place needed a good cleaning, that wasn't her goal now. She had stacked her hopes in a pile in the back of the closet. She was used to keeping secrets, but this was more about hiding from her failure.

The books she'd bought when she was training to be a medical assistant had bent corners, faded covers, and in-your-face ocher stickers proclaiming their USED status. She knelt on the carpet. It was the standard "accessible beige" of every apartment, but hers hadn't been replaced in several years and was more of a "beat-down brown" these days. She sat aside her anatomy and physiology books, and tugged out the fat book in the middle. The DSM-V had to have a guide for what Josh's comedown would be like. You'd think she'd remember this from ER stints, but she only saw those patients in fleeting moments in the first forty-eight hours. She'd known nurses and other PAs that picked their specialty for personal reasons. Their grandma had cancer, so they went into oncology. Their dad had a valve in his heart, so they found themselves working in the cardiology department.

Callie was the exact opposite. She should probably want to help people like Josh. She should have been driven to save the lives of addicts, but at the time it'd been this insurmountable task. Josh had bounced out of the second rehab center at that point. The professionals were trying and failing with him. She knew what addiction looked like. She had seen it in the pockmarks on Josh's arms, in the twitch of his left eye, in every sudden glance at the blank spaces in the corners of the room. She didn't need to see that shit at work. So, she'd found herself in the ER clinic. She'd still seen the junkies hustling for opioids, but she also had helped with broken bones from less-than-successful first bike rides and asthma attacks and the flu (as well as every virus that people wanted to think was the flu and that she could not actually dispense the flu vaccine for). Callie smiled at the memory. She'd loved her work then. Until it was gone. Until Josh ruined that for her, too.

No. She shook herself. She couldn't pin her problems on her brother, and she shouldn't dwell on the past. It didn't fix a damn thing in the future. She skimmed the sections of the DSM-V on addiction, but most of the details were focused on how to know if someone was on drugs. The small comedown part focused on increased sleeping and eating in the first couple days to a week. It'd been a couple weeks since

Josh went clean, but maybe he'd been doing meth so long his body needed more recovery time? The fact he had food at the ready was a good sign. Maybe that was bowl number three for the day. Callie relaxed onto her heels. She was getting herself worked up over nothing. It was kind of nice to have a moment to realize she might not have to be as worried.

She had plenty of trouble on the table. She'd vowed to find out who had set their sights on the Soul Charmer. Her ballsy move would bite her in the ass most likely, but at least Callie wanted to find the answer to who killed that kid. She might not care who wanted to dick around with the Charmer; the bastard probably deserved it. She did, however, care a lot about who would leverage a teenager like that. Who would value life so little as to cut a kid? To take away whatever potential he still had. Soul user or not, that boy could have gone somewhere. She'd fucked up her life, but at least she could get retribution for the kid. He could have helped feed his brothers and sisters. Where would Callie and Josh have been without each other? Josh didn't keep Callie upright and fed anymore, but there was a time when he was the one smuggling sandwiches to her at lunchtime. One didn't forget shit like that.

Callie was determined to make sure the dead teenager found outside the Charmer's shop got peace, even if that was only in the afterlife knowing that whoever slashed him for the rented soul would meet the full wrath of a vengeful Soul Charmer and his apprentice who would burn her way to the truth if she had to.

And, let's be real, she had to.

CHAPTER NINE

Callie met Derek at the base of the stairs outside her apartment. Snow had started to fall. She shrugged a little deeper into her coat, letting the edges of the collar skim her earlobes for a brief moment.

"No scarf?" Derek said as way of greeting.

She shrugged. "It's okay. We're taking the car right?" Her breath steamed in the air.

His sharp nod would have riled her when they first met, before she discerned it was plain agreement. No hidden meaning. "You left your scarf in the saddle bag on the bike." He held the soft, grey knitted affair out to her.

His eyes tracked her movements as she wrapped the scarf around her neck and knotted the front in a quick, practiced motion. He didn't smile, not really, but she could see the tension in his cheeks that suggested he wanted to. He offered her a stiff nod of approval, and opened his right arm for her to cozy in.

The break from the wind coupled with the warmth of his jacket against hers was welcome, the sense of calm that came with his strength and the smell of leather that brought comfort were better.

They started toward her car. Derek's motorcycle was parked beside it. The chrome glistened even in the concrete-colored light through the snow clouds. Usually she was fine with riding on the back. Callie didn't have hang-ups about being behind Derek. It was safe there. Though when it was edging into the single digits temperature-wise, wind whipping your face was not a good thing. Scarf or no scarf.

"How's he doing?" He meant Josh. Derek had avoided her brother. She'd say the feeling was mutual, but Josh wasn't really awake enough to have vocalized a real stance on the dude she was dating. Still, Derek liked meeting outside the apartment. Callie assumed it was his conflict avoidance skills kicking in. For a guy who tracked down deadbeats who didn't return rented property, he really wasn't much for letting things get ugly. Which was nice, since she had plenty of ugly sneaking into her life as it was.

Callie didn't miss a step, though her heart stuttered with a flash of worry.

"He's sleeping," she said with the same weary tone she'd used the last three times she'd answered this way. She quickly amended, "Which is expected. The meth wrecked his system and now he needs to rest and recover. Sleep lets your body repair itself."

Derek made a rough sound in the back of his throat,

which Callie took as agreement. He gave her a quick squeeze, like he knew she'd been convincing herself and not him. He'd only asked the question because he cared about her. She knew it, but she also liked that they hadn't talked about it. He hadn't made it *a thing*.

Callie always put family first, but Derek put her first. It was weird, but nice.

She tossed Derek her keys, and walked around to the passenger side.

After she'd buckled in, she asked, "Do we have to go by the shop tonight?" Her usual disdain for the Soul Charmer's emporium was increased tenfold today. Memories of dead bodies will do that to you.

He tossed the flask into her lap. It had an onyx inlay, and in her hands became more than a way to sneak booze into a movie theater. It was the tool she used to extract rented souls from their hosts. The stone warmed to her touch, and she didn't hate the sensation.

"I'll take that as a no?" The question was playful, because the times when she could poke a little fun were dwindling of late and Derek was her one respite. Most of the time.

Derek started the car. "Boss is still..." When he paused Callie had the sense it wasn't because he didn't know the word he was looking for, but because he spent so much of his day communicating with as few words as possible that shifting into conversation mode with her was awkward at first. Even after weeks and weeks together. She'd pity him if she didn't second-guess why he stuck around her when she'd already broken his trust. He'd wanted to help with the Ford blackmail. He'd tried. She'd taken advantage of an injury he'd gotten on the job, ditched him, and broke into the police station alone. She did it to protect him, but it was still the wrong move and Derek was still fucking sore about it. Justifiably. He'd forgiven her, but building back that bond took time. They don't put that kind of shit in a Hallmark card, but it was the closest she had to romantic sentiments for now.

Callie waited for Derek to continue, because she knew he would. "He's still wrecked. Broke some jars against the wall. Probably good you weren't there. Shattered glass and my girl on fire would be too much shit to handle." He said it like a joke, but blocks of stress were building up around him, too. Locking his shoulders tight and forcing him to stretch his scarred hands every few minutes. His face when he'd come back from "taking care" of the corpse left outside the Charmer's shop had gutted her. He had worn the grim pain of a man who had disposed of a body. It had been horrific, but honest.

"If he'd give me a hint as to what he wanted me to do, it'd help," she muttered, trying to steady her thoughts. "Did the Charmer have any suggestions as to where to start at least?"

Derek shot her a look that said it was a dumb question and she should know that. The Soul Charmer wasn't big on specifics. It made her whole plan to be his apprentice one of her most idiotic of recent memory. "We need to do a quick collection, but then we'll start with what we know," he said.

"We know that a kid was murdered to get the

Charmer riled." She'd only employed that kind of under-the-breath vehemence when fighting with Josh in the back pews during Saturday night service until she started working for the Soul Charmer.

Derek reached over and gave her thigh a quick squeeze. "Right, and our next step will be to figure out why."

"Why that kid or why do they want to screw with the Charmer?"

"Both."

Luxe, modern homes shared city blocks with adobe shanties throughout Gem City. Most neighborhoods you could blend no matter your social standing. It was one of the reasons Callie had stayed here after high school. There was something to be said about never feeling like you lived in the bad part of town. There were shitholes everywhere. Only the commercial areas could truly be considered dangerous, and that was mostly after dark.

The Soul Charmer's shop was in a sketchy area, but he liked it that way. The Charmer was the kind of man who reveled in his customers feeling debased. It made little sense since the purity of their souls affected his gig, but she'd seen the glee in his eyes each time a well-dressed customer cast the floor an "oh, God" look when their heel sunk into whatever congealed beneath the thin carpet.

However, that hodgepodge neighborhood setup didn't apply everywhere. There were partitioned, planned communities on the edges of the city. Ones that constantly ran sprinklers to maintain green grass in the middle of the high desert. The residents were always transplants from the coasts. People who missed seasons and said everything was "too brown." The desert wasn't for everyone, but people who moved to the land of juniper bushes and hard-packed sand and thought they'd bring along Bermuda grass and oak trees should be kicked in the shins.

It didn't help that Callie's car was a yellow stain on the pristine street.

"Someone here needs his soul repossessed?" Callie didn't have to groan for Derek to know exactly what she meant.

"The prick pays triple list price for souls, if that makes you feel better," Derek said before getting out of the car.

The Soul Charmer loved his sliding scale for soul rental. It's how Callie ended up working for him in the first place. He'd bartered work for a brief rental. It soothed the memory's sting to know he was good about fucking people over across the board and not only people he could jam his magic into.

Callie slipped her hand into her coat pocket and palmed the flask. Her flask. The onyx almost hummed beneath her fingers. She wasn't certain if the flask was eager for the soul collection to be done, too, or if it simply fed off the magic buzzing through her veins. She squeezed it into her palm and let the energy heat her against the brittle wind whistling past her.

They hurried to the mark's front door. It wasn't just

the single-digit temperature or the white flakes falling from the sky. Derek and Callie had more important things to do tonight. Bigger problems to solve. Getting side-eyed by neighbors would only slow them down.

Derek thumped a fist against the door. The knock was hard and heavy and didn't require repeating.

"You can't be here!" The squat man who answered the door was already red in the face and they hadn't even spoken yet.

Derek shoved his way inside, and Callie followed. Their apoplectic host stood holding the handle of his front door, parting and closing his lips like he couldn't decide the best curse word to throw at them. Sage and citrus filled the air, but there was no sign of natural sources for the scents in the sterile entryway.

"Shut the door, Cameron," Derek's tone was drenched in disgust, too, and the implication that their host wouldn't want his neighbors knowing he associated with the scourges of Gem City.

Maybe he should have thought of that before he rented a soul. Callie stared at his puffy cheeks and his bird-like nose and tried to figure out what this guy did that needed a second soul. He slammed the door and clopped his way in fancy foreign loafers toward them. He certainly wasn't a jewel thief.

"What do you want?" He didn't meet either of their eyes. He damn well knew what they needed.

Callie took a step toward him. She didn't want to be here anymore than he wanted her here. The tendrils of warmth began to coil in her palms. Not the inferno she experienced around the raw, uninhibited soul in the Soul Charmer's shop or the full-on flames associated with a person stacking multiple rented souls in their bodies. No, Callie had come to recognize this burgeoning heat as the sign of someone storing a single bonus soul in their body. It was like holding her hand in the very edge of an open flame. Hot, but not enough to scorch if she didn't linger too long. She was not going to linger with Cameron. They had people to see, a murderer to find. Normal Tuesday night shit.

Cameron hurried backward on his heels.

Derek pointed to a nearby dining room chair. "Sit."

Cameron did. "Fine. Okay. What do you want?"

"When you borrow something from a friend, he's gonna want it back," Derek said.

Callie resisted the shudder slamming into her spine. Nate had played that *friend* card, too. She shook it off. Derek wasn't Nate. The Charmer wasn't Ford. She wasn't scared.

Cameron balked. "For what I pay him, he owes me an extra few days."

"It's been a week."

"Well, okay, but…" Cameron floundered.

Callie stepped toward him again. "So now you're giving it back, yeah?"

Cameron knocked his elbow against the grand table next to them. It was probably one, solid piece of mahogany that cost four-month's rent. He shifted his arm onto the table. His forearm covered a few pages of crisp white paper. Lots of blocky text with brackets and bullet points. If this guy thought she cared about his contracts, he really didn't understand how normal people functioned at work. She wanted to pretend they were forgeries and he was a crime boss, but the truth was probably something closer to securing retirement funds for other pencil pushers.

This house and this guy made her skin crawl. Every filigreed picture frame and every hand-woven rug looked like a lie to her. This guy wasn't wholesome or pristine or ready to be on the cover of Rich Asshole Monthly. He was as filthy as the rest of them, only he refused to admit it. Her breaths were coming shorter and faster. She didn't think it was the magic. It was this guy, and the way he made her feel. She didn't wait for an invitation or even encouragement from Derek; she plucked the cap off the flask and clapped the opening against Cameron's sternum.

He yelped, which was a first. The soul push/pull process wasn't painful. Maybe she'd smacked the container against him too hard?

"You can't just go around taking souls," Cameron muttered.

Callie tightened the lid on the flask, and small ice crystals began to form almost immediately along her fingertips. She shuffled backward until the chill subsided.

"We done?" she asked Derek, not bothering to hide her contempt for this place and its owner. She wasn't necessarily eager for a one-on-one with the kind of person who'd kill a kid outside the Charmer's store, but she was ready to get out of here. Plus, keeping the Soul Charmer happy was a good way to avoid an armload of agony.

"Just a sec," Derek said to her. Then he turned to Cameron and stalked forward until he towered over the man. He held a closed fist up against the mark's face. It covered a whole cheek, part of his nose and one eyebrow. If he punched the small man, it'd be more than a broken nose. He held the fist there until Cameron started to quake. "We don't do this again. We will not be nice again."

Derek turned to leave.

"Nice? You have the audacity to show up at my home—"

Derek cut him off, "Oh, and Cameron, your rates have just doubled."

He slipped his arm around Callie's shoulders and walked her out of the ostentatious home, and back to the comfort of her busted ride. Warmth wiggled its way around her waist, and the harsh squeeze of her chest eased. It was nice that a simple, protective gesture could make her breathe again. It hadn't always been that simple for her. Given the last few weeks, she was due for a simple joy or two.

CHAPTER TEN

Derek took the long way back into town. Instead of indulging on the perfectly paved roads leading out of Cameron's neighborhood, he went for the aged two-lane state highway road. While it, too, was paved, it'd already been graveled in the name of the weather. Tiny rocks plinked against the underside of the car. It reminded Callie of drizzle, only on the wrong side of the car.

They were back to regular duty for the Soul Charmer. Dusk was creeping in fast, and that meant their time belonged to the shady man who hawked souls. They could no longer ignore the memory of the dying kid outside the back door the other night. Callie wanted to know why he rented souls. This would lead them closer to answering why he was picked. It might also make her feel better. If he was into some really fucked up shit, it could let her pretend this wouldn't be the kind of trouble she got pulled into regularly apprentic-ing for the Charmer. It would maybe let her feel a little less gross about her night gig.

Derek agreed with the plan, but mostly because he thought they'd find leads for where to go next, who to talk to, and maybe discover who that kid would know that would understand anything about how soul magic worked. Other than the Charmer.

Callie cradled the still-warm flask in her lap, watched bushes and occasional street signs for civili-zation, and tried to count the soft pings against the car. It was easier than carrying a conversation right now.

She liked being in the car with Derek. When they'd first started working together for the Soul Charmer, riding on the back of his bike was her only respite from all the stressors in her life. Now, they tried to cultivate that same sanctuary in her car, but it wasn't working. Probably because the problems they had to solve now were rumbling in both their guts. Callie could taste the bitterness of the moment on the back of her tongue. She spoke anyway, and tried to control her tone. "We can't just talk to his friends. It'll make us look guilty."

"No it won't. He rented from the Soul Charmer be-fore. It'd be normal for us to come by to get back the goods."

This argument didn't assuage any of Callie's fears. Derek wanted to talk to the dead kid's friends, and that tightened a band of fear stretched around her belly.

"Right, but if they know he's dead—"

"They don't." Derek didn't look at her when he cut

her off. He stared at the road like he intended to refill the cracks and potholes with his stare alone simply so he could smash them back into place.

The tick in his jaw should have kept her from asking, but the boiling worry in her belly couldn't be contained. "How do they not know? I thought you…" Callie struggled to find the right word. One that wouldn't be a lash to her lover's back and one that wouldn't kick her upchuck reflex into gear. One that wouldn't make this real.

Derek's knuckles were white where he gripped the steering wheel. It made the crisscrossed scars on them pop in harsh pink relief. "He needed to be some place that bought us time, but he *will* be found."

The words weren't for Callie, but she absorbed the fervor behind them. "If he's found right away it comes back to us, doesn't it?"

Derek's jaw ticked again, but he nodded.

"It wasn't in the Railyard, though, right?" Fear seeped into her words. The newscast was too fresh in her mind.

"What? No." He opened his mouth to say more, but didn't find his voice. Callie didn't push. She shouldn't have even let the idea into her brain. She was so familiar with family fucking it up that she was putting her baggage on him, and it wasn't fair.

Whatever he'd had to do left a fresh scar, but this one wouldn't light his knuckles or track down his cheek. This was something deep and gutting on the inside. Callie understood. She kept all her scars walled inside her ribcage where their pangs could kick her, but she didn't have to share them with anyone else. Private wounds. It shouldn't have surprised her that Derek bore them, too. They shared this one, which made her wonder more about their relationship. They met because she was forced to work for the Soul Charmer. They bonded because he put her first, and no one outside of family does that. But their shared memories weren't pretty ones. Sharing scars wasn't the sign of a healthy relationship. Fuck it, she thought. She wasn't built for healthy at this time, and Derek had her back. It was probably selfish, but she was going to enjoy being with him. Besides, maybe now was her chance to pay him back for being there for her with Josh. She could be there for him as this new, torturous wound healed.

She sat up straighter in the worn passenger's seat. The seatbelt dug into her neck as it tightened with its hair trigger. When it released she pivoted in her seat enough to pull one leg up, and fully face Derek. The angles of his jaw were sharp enough to cut, but Callie didn't mind. She reached over and ran the back of her fingers down his cheek. "We are going to get justice for him," she said softly.

Derek jerked a nod. One quick, harsh motion. The speedometer ticked up another five miles per hour.

"How often has working for the Charmer allowed us to get justice for someone who deserved it?" She was speaking more to his past than hers. She was, after all, new to the whole soul magic shebang.

His responding grumble didn't carry the harshness of his earlier words. Almost an agreement.

"I think we'd find the person responsible even if the Charmer wasn't going to throw a tirade of exploding glass and souls."

"Don't tell him that," Derek rumbled.

"I have no intentions of telling him jackall, but he can see my soul. So he probably knows."

Derek huffed with enough humor to almost be a laugh. His grip on the steering wheel eased.

"Finding who did this will help me deal with it," Callie said.

"Punishing who did it will help, too," he replied.

He wasn't wrong. Callie wished the idea of vengeance didn't ease the tension in her torso. It did, though. Maybe they did belong with the Soul Charmer.

She nodded, but didn't voice her agreement. "You think this was just to fuck with the Soul Charmer?"

"No," Derek grated the word across the gravel beneath the car. Then, a moment later, added, "It's about the magic. It's always about the magic."

"If they have the skills, though, can't they access it?" There were always others trying to set up shop to compete with the Soul Charmer. Callie had helped him stop one of the few powerful ones from stealing the rented souls from the Charmer's clients. Tess had magic and she hadn't gotten it from him.

"He has access to more than any of the others."

Callie's lips parted, but words failed her.

"Don't ask me how. I'm not his fucking apprentice." The words should have sliced, but they came with a real underscore of teasing.

"I'll add that to my list of things to ask about. It'll be right below the 'How do I keep from bursting into flames whenever I'm near an unprotected soul?' and 'When do I get my secret decoder ring?'"

Now they both laughed and the sound filled the car. It covered the plinking against the undercarriage. It covered the rumble of the engine. It even almost covered the howl of a coyote in the distance.

The moment of levity focused Callie. They could do this together.

"Okay, so where are we going?"

"Kid his age had to hang at Deco's."

Callie knew the place. It was part arcade, part cheap pizza spot, and part skate park. Basically a teenager summer fever dream. Only it was November and that meant it became an after-school hot spot. Callie checked the clock. Only six. It'd still be packed.

"If there's time, I will own your ass at Skee-ball."

The corner of Derek's lips quirked up. "Thanks for the warning, doll."

***

Callie hadn't been to Deco's since she had been old enough to drive. Lights flashed—red, yellow, blue, pink—in rapid succession inside the trendy Railyard District hangout. The lights doubled against every hard, shiny surface, and blinked brighter through pint glasses and against the slick faces of the cell phones in nearly every kid's hand. When she'd last been in this arcade, no one shot video of high scores. Or maybe they had. Callie had rarely played the games unless a boyfriend was buying. She hadn't ever had cash for air hockey or Pac-Man or the car-racing game that she never won. That hadn't stopped her from coming to Deco's to socialize. It had been a good way to get gossip, and she hadn't hated watching friends play games. Interacting with people without the requirement of conversation was Callie's idea of perfect.

Men and women mingled on the far right of the room. The bar had happy hour pricing, and the button-downs looked at home amid the heavy beats and bright lights. Probably pre-gaming for a Saturday night at a club. Callie hated that shit, but the kind of people who ordered tapas at an arcade—like the plate of sopapillas she saw a waitress hurry to a nearby high-top—were totally the kind who wore painful shoes to dance in the dark and drop triple digits on booze. Two bucks for a PBR would have cut it for Callie right now, and she didn't even need a disco ball to refract the lights of children playing games.

Deco's used to be a rabbit warren of connected rooms, but in the last few years the management had knocked down most of the walls to connect the space. They'd built out a bar, added more pool tables, and made the place into a quirky destination for adults. She blamed them for the soul magic sifting in the air. The energy of the place pricked at her skin, pinching and pulling. No one nearby was pushing the temperature down on her, but her fingers twitched as though they knew she was going to be locked up and icy in moments. Callie hadn't quite experienced this before. She avoided busy places other than the grocery store, and there everyone was in such a hurry to get milk/bread/Pop-Tarts and get home to families that would devour the goods, the static second soul energy hadn't had time to coalesce like this. Arcades and bars might be breeding grounds for germs, but apparently they were great magic holding cells, too.

Derek elbowed her. "They look about his age, yeah?"

The group he'd spotted were old enough to have driver's licenses, but still clearly underage. The three boys and two girls huddled around a tall arcade game promising one fake shotgun to quell a zombie apocalypse. All five had hair coifed to look like they didn't care, but probably took an hour to do. Callie swiped a hand through her own. It was edging into rib-length territory. She needed to cut it soon.

"What are we supposed to say to them?" She would have whispered, but the whizzes and whistles whipping through the room from the array of electronics muted her voice regardless.

"Ask 'em if they know Cullen." A flash of pink strobe cut across Derek's jaw, slithering between the dark prickle of stubble. He didn't flinch, but he held his breath like he was readying to take a punch.

"How do you know his name?" She tried to keep the accusation from her tone, but her gut boiled with betrayal. *He said he didn't know the kid.*

"It was in his wallet. Cullen Stevens. Seventeen." His voice was even and easy to hear over the noise. At least one of them was solid.

Callie hissed in a breath. Now her stomach ached for a different reason. Several reasons. Why did she always expect the worst, and why didn't she *trust* him because he'd earned that from her? Oh, right. She grew up in fucking Gem City.

"I'm glad we know his name," she said and meant it. He had a family and a life, and while they had to find out answers for the Soul Charmer, they could also do right by Cullen. That made her feel like less of a shitty person. Some days, that really mattered. "So that means we know where he lives. We could go there and—"

"Lived," he corrected. His voice dropped low enough to scrape their ankles. He was reminding himself of their goal. It worked for her, too. That past tense should have shaken her again. Should have brought back the vision of the color fading from the kid's—Cullen's—cheeks. Instead it filtered her resolve until it was even and steady.

She opened her mouth intent to find out why they were taking the long route to answers, when it hit her, "His parents aren't going to know about soul renting."

Derek nodded.

"Unless they just want to make sure he'd rise to Heaven." That truth about Gem City always bubbled beneath the surface. Almost everyone in town was a practicing Cortean Catholic, which made them big on purity and guilt. Keeping one's soul light enough to make it to the celestial gates was paramount. It wasn't a shock soul renting was big business, but the fact the Church averted their eyes like they were trying to hit quarterly sales numbers continually kicked Callie's squick sensor into high gear. She thought of her own mother then—something she'd been avoiding lately. If soul magic had been an option when Callie had been busted shoplifting food when she was eleven, Callie didn't doubt Zara would have suggested she start using another's soul to get the job done. Anything to pretend they were good people. Then again, that would have meant Zara had to notice that her kids didn't have anything worthwhile to eat.

Derek curled his hand around hers and gave it a gentle squeeze. She offered him a half-hearted smile in return. Not every parent was Zara. Hell, most of them gave a serious damn about their kids.

They stepped in behind the kids, who didn't cast a single glance in their direction. At least one didn't have to be stealthy if they were doing business in an arcade. Callie waited for the icy sensation to coat her, for someone in this group to be using soul magic. Cullen had. He couldn't be the only teenager who dabbled in cheat codes for getting into Heaven.

"Don't forget the one shambling behind that box on the right," Derek warned as a way of greeting to the gamer and his friends. He pointed at the green and grey zombie near the corner of the screen, not that anyone was looking.

The guy manning the shotgun blasted the shambling one, but he must have realized that advice wasn't from one of his friends. He missed the next three zombies and earned a GAME OVER screen because he was craning his head back and up to see Derek.

It might have been Derek's size or the well-worn biker jacket doubling it or his glacial stare—maybe all three—but the gamer guy looked about to shit his pants.

One of the girls at his side shouldered closer. She put her back to her friends and kicked her shoulders back like she was not only ready for a fight, but also knew how to end one. "Aren't you a little old to be playing video games?" she brought the right amount of sass to make Callie like her.

Derek may have disagreed. "I'd annihilate that game, but I've got a day job." Each word was even and solid and disinterested.

Did he have to talk to teenagers often? How many rented from the Soul Charmer? She shook the ick of her current employer from her brain. Getting squeamish now wasn't going to change a damn thing.

"He looks like he beats people up for a living, Lizzie. Chill it," the tallest boy in the group said. He wore a faded black tee shirt for a band Callie had never heard of.

Callie got the impression these kids thought it was cool that Derek might know how to fight, but she didn't want to have to clean up any messes, explain blood and bruises to parents, or get anyone booted from Deco's.

"We just keep things moving for the Soul Charmer," Callie said making sure the creepy old man's name carried every bit of grit and gravity it warranted.

Five sets of eyes widened, and Player No. 1 dropped the plastic gun. They recognized the Charmer's name, but did they know Cullen *knew* him? Hell, did they even know Cullen, or were they traumatizing them for nothing?

The plastic shotgun clanked against the front of the machine. Just loud enough to be heard over the points tally from the nearby air hockey table.

"Wha-wha-what do you want with us?" the tall guy asked.

Derek's smile was a harsh slash of compressed lips that was more grimace than expression of joy. Definitely not friendly, but he was shit at fake smiles. "Information," he said. He didn't bother trying to soften his rasp or chip away the hard edges of the word.

One of the girls darted forward, checking her shoulder into Callie hard. It might have looked like she was scared, but Callie had been poor and desperate before. The lightness in her front pocket was immediate. She would have recognized the lift from that alone, but the immediate emptiness after losing contact with the warm thrum of her flask set her into action. Her arm shot forward and she looped it through the girl's upper arm, cupping her biceps and holding tight.

Callie preferred to keep her voice low and her body hidden. She did her damnedest to keep her head down, because attention lead to a whole kind of mess she didn't want. She didn't need to be scrutinized or questioned or have someone wonder and worry about her. All of that, though? Out the window when it came to someone stealing the Soul Charmer's property from her. Her arms had been burned from soul magic. She was not going to even contemplate what kind of hell would befall her if she lost that fucking flask.

Callie let every bit of kindness slip from her face. It pooled on the tile floor, ready to drop anyone who tried to run.

"We are the wrong people to steal from." The words grated from the back of Callie's throat like she had swallowed rocks and was ready to spit the buck-shot.

The girl tugged against Callie, but Derek had already shifted to flank her. He blocked the girl's path to the exit. He grumbled deep from his chest. The sound underscored Callie's message.

Heat coiled in Callie's torso. It wasn't a reaction to nearby soul users. This was her fear and anger igniting something fiery and black. Something she should not let out on anyone, much less a teenage girl. "Hand back the flask."

The girl opened her mouth to argue. Derek stopped her with one word, "Now."

She gave the flask to Callie. The onyx inlay snapped warm against her palm, and she almost smiled. Would have, but she didn't need strangers seeing her get giddy over a flask—magical or otherwise. She dropped the girl's arm and tucked the vessel for bonus souls back into her pocket. Sweet security washed over Callie, and she chose not to think too much about what that meant.

Derek nodded once at the girl. "Go."

She did. Her friends remained locked in place. Fear had glued them to the sticky floor. They were trans-fixed on their friend ditching them, a friend who didn't bother looking back. Callie eased her shoulders back, as though it would make her any less scary or any more casual. It did neither. Derek placed his hand on the small of her back, the touch doing more to relax her than anything else could. It was more than the warmth of his body. It was the subtle reminder they were in this together. It was still a rare feeling, but she liked it.

She and Derek turned their attentions back to the group silently watching them. It was eerie to have so many eyes so focused on her, but when Callie turned, two of the kids stumbled backward. Faking wasn't Derek's forte, which was good for her but kind of shitty in extracting info from a group who were increasingly staring at him like he was a giant ready to fe-fi-fo-fum their asses. Callie stifled a snicker at the mental visual of Derek sporting a burly beard and toting a hand-hewn club around.

She could soften her tone, though. She could be less scary. She reminded herself she wasn't *that* much older then them. Seven years was vast, though, in the difference between seventeen and twenty-four. "We aren't looking to hurt anyone. We're checking in about a friend of yours. Cullen?"

"We know Cullen," the gamer guy responded. He didn't meet Callie's gaze.

"You know anything about him renting souls?"

"Shouldn't you already know all about that if you work for the Soul—him?" The guy's bravado stuttered on the Charmer's name. Sketchy dudes could breed fear, which was good. These teens needed to stay away from renting souls. They were too young to start giving away pieces of themselves. Callie wished she could go back to before she started giving away her time, her heart, her energy, and snippets of her soul. Renting a soul to avoid tarnishing your own was one thing. Levering magic to polish your soul was another. It simply didn't work that way. Time travel wasn't real either. Fixing the past wasn't an option. Damn it.

"Lots of people work for the Charmer," Derek said.

"Can you just tell us what you know about his soul renting?" Callie added in a much kinder tone.

"I mean, yeah, he rented souls," Gamer Guy said. Callie was tempted to ask his name, but after the showdown with the potential flask stealer, they weren't likely to want to share personal information with them.

"Do you know how often he rented?" Callie nudged.

"On payday like everyone else," the tall guy said.

"No," Gamer Guy corrected, "He only rented whenever Jessica was in town. Just happened to be every two or three weeks."

"Who's Jessica?" Derek didn't bother hiding his impatience. The longer they stayed talking to teenagers in Deco's the higher the chance of being recognized. Of whoever killed Cullen and had it out for the Charmer seeing them.

"His step-sister," Gamer Guy said.

"Isn't she a drug addict or something?" Sassy Girl asked. Callie's gut plummeted. She knew all about drug-addled siblings.

The look Gamer Guy shot the girl suggested they weren't friends, but happened to hang out in the same circle. "She just likes to party," he said.

Derek got it. "He buy for her?"

"Not the souls. That's for him. He'll roll on molly with her and they'll go dance, but he doesn't want to miss his shot at Heaven because of it." Gamer Guy made a point of staring directly at their chins while he spoke. It was the kind of trick guidance counselors liked to give the "troubled" kids to help them "connect" better. Callie had been given a similar talk. Still, Gamer Guy shuffled his feet. His anxiety was starting to trip Callie's, which meant they couldn't push him too much farther.

"Do you know if he rented from anyone other than the Soul Charmer?"

Tall Guy responded first, "No one else in town can actually do it."

If only that were true, Callie thought.

"I'm not going to get him in trouble am I?" Gamer Guy asked with real concern built on the backbone of naivety. He'd already ratted on his friend regardless.

Callie and Derek shared a look. Cullen couldn't get into trouble anymore. They didn't say that, of course.

"No, we're making sure the scammers aren't screwing over our clients." The lie came more easily to Callie than it should have. She lifted her chin a little as pride surged. Getting better at this job was a heady, delicious feeling, even if it might be pulling her farther away from what was right.

"When he was low on cash, I think he tried those guys who hang out downtown by the art galleries."

He meant the men who tempted tourists into trying soul rental. They wore flowing shirts made of hemp and prayer beads as jewelry. Their "mystic looks" were far from reality, but Callie wouldn't have pegged them as more than hustlers. Not the kind of criminals who would murder anyone, much less to start a war with the Soul Charmer. It was a lead, though, even if it was a weak one.

They'd milked the group for all the information they were going to get. The fear coursing through their veins was going to overload them if Callie and Derek pushed them any more. They thanked the group, Derek passed them a handful of twenties, and she and he left the arcade.

They had more information, but Callie wasn't any less confused now. She squeezed the flask inside her pocket, and tried not to think about why the act comforted her.

CHAPTER ELEVEN

"You hungry?" Derek asked once they were back in the car.

The privacy the metal doors and dingy glass provided was enough to let Callie exhale. Her lungs ached from pretending she had some kind of skill for this shit.

"Did we just interrogate teenagers?" The absurdity of the possibility brought Callie's question forward on a laugh.

"We don't ever interrogate people." His words cut hard. Callie had interrogated someone before. She'd laid her flaming palms on the Soul Charmer's rival Tess to get answers for the man and keep Derek safe. He muttered a "sorry" and revved his vocal cords deep in his chest, a rumble of indecision. He didn't know how to make things right. Callie understood though. If there was anything she got it was screwing up hardcore when you didn't mean to and having to use a spoon to excavate your way out of the hole your idiot brain had just dug for you.

The minute shake of her head didn't miss his attention. His eyes locked on hers and darkened. Others might be terrified by that look, but she was safe here with him in the quiet of the idling vehicle.

"You're right. That wasn't an interrogation," she said. The hidden words, the truth of the realization of what a real interrogation would have been like and the fact Callie knew those details intimately were woven between the words of her agreement.

"So, food?"

"Are you just trying to avoid going downtown?" She didn't blame him if he was.

He shrugged. "A little, but I also skipped lunch."

Callie smiled. "It wouldn't be fair to let you loose on the grifters downtown if you're hangry."

"The grifters have nothing to worry about. It's the ones who actually can do basic soul magic that are going to be an issue. It's harder for me to tell them apart."

Callie slouched against the worn seat. "You need me to be a magic detector? Isn't that usually the Charmer's thing?"

Her shitty joke fell flat. "I don't see you as a tool."

"I know." She let out a long sigh weighed with the truth. Derek saw her as a person, and the Soul Charmer saw her (and everyone else) as pawns. Derek hadn't wanted her to apprentice under his boss. He hadn't wanted her to be any further involved in the soul renting business. So if he was suggesting he needed her help in figuring out the potential magicians from the fakes, it wasn't about turning her into a tool he could wield. She was 0-2 on being an asshole tonight. "Sorry. This whole thing has me on edge, and is making me a dick. I know you have my back, and if I can help us find out who put Cullen into this mess, I will."

"You're not a dick. Probably just hangry." He laughed at his own joke. A bold, throaty affair that brought a genuine smile to Callie's lips.

"That's the first time you've ever said hangry, isn't it?"

"It's a new fucking word. What do you want from me, doll?"

Everything. Her breath caught in her chest, and when she released it the gasp was soft but packed with power.

"Something super greasy for dinner and a promise that we won't end up bloody by the end of the night."

"Done."

They drove her car to their favorite greasy spoon, and were quickly sat at their table again—a booth in the far back of the restaurant. Derek could see the full perimeter of the diner, including the front and side doors. He was the most relaxed he could be in a public space when they were at Dott's. Callie supposed when people were always gunning for your back or trying to hide from you, having an even view of the landscape went far.

Derek balanced his menu on the edge of the table

even though he was going to order the same thing he always did. Short-order food done right didn't require a robust menu. Callie didn't have any allusions she'd do any different. Dott's still had their Dia de los Muertos wares out. She absently pushed the peppershaker from one hand to another across the table. The shaker was a black skull with orange flowers for eyes. Most stores and eateries were already shoving Christmas decorations in every corner, so she didn't mind. She'd rather have a couple skulls on the table in November than sleighs and crèches.

When their waitress arrived, she didn't bother pulling out her notebook and pen, and instead asked, "The usual?"

They each nodded to her. Derek handed the waitress his menu. Callie pushed the peppershaker back to the edge of the table and next to the white skull filled with salt.

"We need a plan," she said once the waitress had left and she had nothing to keep her hands busy any longer.

Derek's half smile tickled something deep in her chest. She scrubbed a knuckle across her sternum, but it didn't still the flutter beneath her breastbone.

"What?" she asked.

"We don't need a by-the-numbers list on this. The plan makes you feel better, but we won't know the next step until we have more information," he said this like it wasn't the first time they'd had this conversation. It wasn't.

Derek liked to improvise, but she wanted to mentally prepare herself for whatever was coming next. Dodging one problem after another wasn't the way to live your life. Callie wanted to believe this was a new situation, requiring a new plan. Or maybe she wanted to be a new person, one who *could* plan.

"This is different than finding marks who are dodging returning souls," she said.

"How?" There was no fire in his throat. He packed genuine curiosity into one word.

Callie, though, couldn't contain her fears. "Seriously? For one, someone died. For another, the Charmer has lost his fucking shit and he will blame someone. I sure would like him to blame the right person and not the one who goes up in flames around too many souls or the one who has been loyal to him for years."

"He's not going to risk you." If Callie's words had been a harsh whisper meant only for their table, Derek's answer was a quiet plea. The kind of promise best offered soft and breathy against a lover's lips. They sat on opposite sides of the booth, but the intensity hit Callie as though the words had been offered against her ear. Goose bumps prickled along her forearms. No soul renters were nearby; this was another kind of magic.

Her voice softened, too, but fear still cradled each syllable. "You saw my arms ready to go to dust the other day, right?"

"I saw it. I also saw your body heal. Like every time before. He's a shit teacher, no doubt, but he isn't going to risk you."

Callie folded her arms across her chest, tucked her hands in tight, and stared so hard at Derek he should have a shiner in the morning. She wasn't even sure what she was mad about. He wasn't saying she was wrong, and his grumblings about her working for the Soul Charmer *by choice* hadn't gone amiss. He wasn't about to miss the chance to encourage her to back away. So why was this yarn of rage coiling tighter in her belly each second. Her insides cradled and squeezed it, and refused to let it unwind no matter how much her brain was sending the 'it's cool, bro' signals.

"I just want to know what I'm getting into," she blurted. It was the most honest thing she could say in the moment.

A fleeting flash of pain rushed across Derek's face. A waterfall of resolve washed it away. Callie couldn't read whether he was thinking of her lessons with the Charmer, their relationship, or his own life. Not in that split second. She wasn't trying to add more guilt to the ever-growing stone on his shoulders. For someone who made little bones about working toward an end by any means necessary, he sure held on to the guilt of sin. Callie understood guilt, and the way it could rot your insides and hollow your bones. The weight constant and unyielding until you rammed it away in the back of your brain or did enough good to outweigh the bad. She mostly did the former, but would prefer Derek didn't have to do either.

The realization unwound some of the barbed ball of ire in her belly. She rolled her shoulders forward, as though to curl in a ball and disappear underneath the slick tabletop. She stared at the aluminum flashing around the edge, and resisted the urge to pick at one of the rivets. She ran the pad of one thumb over the nail of the other instead. While she sat there fidgeting and looking everywhere but at Derek, she gave him some actual truth. "I keep going into that damn shop, and thinking it will be better. That today he's actually going to show me something. Or that he'll finally hit fuck it and take the magic back. Neither happens, and I never know what to expect. I can take that from him because there isn't another option. That's his mystical motherfucker of a way. Solving problems outside of that place? Keeping shit from getting worse? We can do that. You and me. I'm not good at this stuff, and I need your help or whatever."

Now *she* didn't know if she was talking about finding the person who murdered Cullen, her relationship with Derek, or her train wreck of a life. All of them, she'd admit if she was being honest with herself. But being honest with Derek was enough truth for one day.

"I got you." His voice was soft, all the gravel shaken loose by a hearty sigh.

Callie dropped her hands into her lap, and then slowly raised her head to meet his gaze. "You do?"

"I ain't going anywhere, doll."

He reached one hand out on the table, palm up. His lifeline was deep and a smidge darker than the rest of his hand, like he'd run a knife across it to make a best friends pact as a kid and the scar had nearly healed out. Tiny lines crisscrossed the steady main tributary. Callie had to remind herself she didn't really believe in palm reading or she'd start to wonder which of those little lines was her in his life. She slid her own hand into his and quashed the worry.

"Good," she said. If she was in over her head with him, she didn't want to imagine how she'd handle this alone. Not just the Charmer stuff. She didn't like to talk about Josh with anyone who wasn't family, but she liked that she had Derek to balance her while she internalized all the shit of having her big brother detox on her couch. She liked having someone who wasn't a Delgado she could count on for once.

"You still want a plan, don't you?"

Her exasperated sigh must have spoken volumes, because Derek offered a half smile and then said, "I'm just screwing with you. Plans don't work because shit changes, but we can set expectations."

"Expectations," Callie tasted the word. It sounded good, but didn't erase the fiery threads scattered in her stomach.

"Yeah. Like who to look for, what we want to get out of 'em, and what we think they'll do."

"Sounds a lot like making a plan," she muttered.

They paused their conversation as the waitress brought their meals over. Once the plates were set, and she confirmed they had ketchup and didn't want any other condiments—despite the fact they never asked for any other condiments—the waitress scurried off leaving them alone on their end of the diner.

"So who are we looking for then?" Callie took a massive bite of her patty melt. It was almost hot enough to burn her mouth, but not so much as to deter her from scarfing it.

"There are three or four guys who work that area. Only two of them can actually do anything, though."

"And we know we need legit guys because Cullen had a rented soul."

"We know he's rented souls, but couldn't your cold fingers thing have been because he'd rented in the past?"

Callie considered for a minute. She dabbed a fry into the ketchup and ate it before answering. "No, I don't think so. He had those hash marks on his throat, but he still had his own soul in his body." She stopped and shook her head, as though it'd keep the memory from surfacing. "I know he had one, and I know that one was taken out from those wounds."

Her throat hurt, like the words had been excavated from it. She let her current French fry linger in the ketchup pool.

Derek leaned forward. His voice was barely a whisper, "Those wounds could have been a distraction."

She shook her head. She shouldn't be able to know, but fuck if the resounding shake of her sternum wasn't telling her she was right. "I don't know if it's the magic or what, but I'm not wrong here."

"Okay, then. Only the ones with power."

CHAPTER TWELVE

The corner hustlers with power looked a whole lot like the ones faking it.

"That guy? You're kidding." Callie looked again at the man Derek had identified as a soul magician. "He's wearing culottes."

Derek lifted one shoulder in a half-hearted shrug. "I don't know what that is, doll, but that's Jerrod."

"They're those ugly ass pants."

"You're stalling."

"I'm not." She was. "I just want to be sure that's the guy."

"That's him. You ready?"

She was supposed to say yes. They'd covered a rudimentary plan at the diner and this needed to be done. Her feet slowed, though. Derek eased his pace to match hers.

"Do you think he has souls on him?" Her fingers already itched, but it was imagined energy. The phantom twinge of remembered sensation reminding her the real thing could be a half block ahead.

Derek's hand slid from the small of her back to curl around to her hip. He tugged her closer until her shoulder was wedged underneath his own. A sideways hug that wouldn't catch the attention of anyone passing nearby. "He has to have at least one or two, but they'll be contained."

He spoke with such assuredness. She took one step and then a second, more confident one. "How much work does this guy do?"

"Not enough to open a storefront."

"Couldn't that be because he doesn't want a beat down?"

Derek feigned offense, leaving a gap between their shoulders. "What are you implying?"

"That people shouldn't cross the fucking Soul Charmer."

"Ain't that the truth. He'd be too scared to try that directly. Anyone with brains would be, but this guy doesn't have the chops anyway. He does low-level shit with bartered souls."

"Doesn't our boss barter souls?" She almost choked on calling the Charmer her boss, but every time she did so it got a little easier. That probably wasn't a good sign.

"If you want the fresh and pure, you have to go to our boss."

The sales-y vibes threatened to set her teeth on edge, but Derek pulled her back against his side and any unease dissipated. She was on the Soul Charmer's side officially, by way of blackmail and magical ties. She sure as shit wasn't going to say so aloud, though.

As they got closer to Jarrod, Derek slipped behind Callie. He put a few paces between them. As planned. He remained close enough to tackle anyone who was a threat or tried to run away because *she* was a threat— she wiggled her fingers at the reminder she was power- ful—but she was the one who would talk to this soul magician.

This was the plan. She repeated the phrase like some sort of daily affirmation bullshit her cousin Kris- ti would listen to before bed. Jarrod didn't know her face. At least he shouldn't. That meant answers might actually happen.

Wind whined a high-pitch warning as it whipped around the buildings on either side of the road. The gusts slapped her cheeks until they were warm enough to be emitting a rosy glow. Good. A flushed woman wouldn't scare this guy. Not at first.

The red high-tops Jarrod wore below the paisley printed culottes were in motion. Tiny dance steps to a beat only he could hear. Callie would have pegged him for another kind of dealer with those kinds of tweak rocker tendencies.

"Hey. Jarrod?" she asked when she was close.

He plucked a bud from one ear. Something bass heavy buzzed from it as he dropped it against his chest.

"I know you?" he asked as though he had learned the phrase from a movie, but believed it came off like he should not be fucked with. It didn't.

"Nah." She hated the naïve affect she put on. If she was going to convince him to talk about soul magic, he had to believe she didn't know anything. If she knew even an ounce about renting souls, she wouldn't be coming to a street corner hustler.

He gave her a skeezy smile, but she focused instead on the light freckles dotting the bridge of his nose. His blonde hair peeked out from beneath the ball cap he wore. She didn't recognize the logo above the bill. "Who told you about me?"

Ugh. He really was going to make this like buying drugs? Imaginary ants marched across Callie's skin. She wasn't a junkie, and she was better than buying bullshit from a corner dealer. She'd spent most of the day trying to forget Cullen's ghastly visage. Now the situation yanked that memory to the forefront of her mind hard and fast. She needed to remember why she was doing this or pride was going to punch her until she bailed.

"A friend. She said you could help me with, um, a soul." She whispered the last word like it was forbidden and she was thrilled to be breaking the rules. Internally she rallied with the confidence that she was *not this girl*.

"Oh you want to dabble in some extracurriculars without upsetting the big man? I got you." He sauntered closer, and slipped a hand into a front pocket of his pants. Any other random dude on the street puts his hand in that region, you bail, but where else is the guy going to keep his wares? Big bulky briefcases went out of style with the door-to-door salesmen. Though, given this guy's style choices, that might not have mattered.

"I—" Callie glanced up and down the street dramatically "—haven't done this before. How does it work? Like do I eat something? Do I have to bring it back or does it know to come back to you?"

These were the most idiotic questions Callie could think of, but Jarrod played them like they were serious and completely commonplace. That only made her even more concerned about the people who rented from this guy. At least people who left the Soul Charmer's store knew ninety percent of what they were getting into. That other ten percent was a big deal, but at least they had the general mechanics of renting down.

Jerrod nodded three or four times. It wasn't in time with his music, but like he was processing her questions. They shouldn't need thought, but she wasn't going to argue with the man's style. With each bob of his head he took another step toward Callie. Every inch closer he came forward, the faster the slicking of ice crystals and the snap of snow formed beneath Callie's skin. Colder and darker until he was standing a foot away and her fingers were locked in place. She buried them in the front pockets of her coat, but the stiffness told her they were blue. She shifted her right hand a little in the pocket, and her nail beds ached as she pulled them away from where they'd affixed themselves to the pocket liner.

Jarrod used rented souls himself. At least he didn't

have one lodged behind his breastbone now.

Callie could almost hear the Soul Charmer's derision at the realization. The Charmer didn't use his own wares. He'd told her he didn't know how hot dogs were made and so he could enjoy them. The opposite was true for soul magic. At the time she'd wondered if she'd eventually know enough to be even more disquieted by her one-time rental, but the Charmer hadn't taught her enough for that to happen.

"It's real easy. You give me fifty bucks, and I can put another soul into your body. You go sin all you want, the other soul doesn't care. You come back next week, and I take it back out."

"I heard you can get tweaked if you have one for too long," she said. Playing the ingénue wasn't a skill Callie could conquer for long.

Jarrod narrowed his gaze. Callie probably hadn't hidden her shock about his bargain pricing or his general lack of knowledge of soul magic.

"Don't worry about that." He didn't disagree though. So at least he knew a smidge about what he was doing to people. Fucking skeezeball. That made it worse.

"If one of my friends wants one, too, you got enough for her?"

That set him back into his King Shit confidence. "I've got all the souls in Gem City, baby."

"The Soul Charmer would disagree." Derek's bourbon barrel rumble was like a purr against Callie's back. She resisted the urge to press against him.

"Charmer's gonna gouge you for the same shit everyone else has." Jerrod was still hustling.

Callie was happy to drop the inexperienced guise. "We both know that isn't true."

Jarrod edged back a step, which put him closer to the building behind him.

Derek turned his head sharp and short to the right, an undeniable message to not even try to run. The asshole hooking kids on soul rental for cheap was not one to have the pride to stand his ground. Jarrod turned away from them quickly, but smashed his arm into the aging building behind. Derek moved forward in more of a bum rush than a step, and Jarrod was flattened against the adobe. The edge of his sweatshirt had a series of fresh, jagged holes where the wall's texture had captured the fabric.

"How many souls you got on you?" Derek asked through barely parted lips.

"None of your business."

"Wrong answer." Derek shoved the guy up against the building again. Jarrod *oof*-ed, but Callie was the one who staggered.

Heat seared her feet. The fire didn't hesitate. It clawed its way up her legs, filled her veins with flames, made her belly quiver with fear, and melted the ice on her fingers in a flash. "Soul," she managed to say before the fire began to roar in her ears.

It wasn't like this at the Charmer's shop. Yes, she'd burned, but only the parts of her closest to the soul. The black plastic pot peeked from the edge of Jerrod's sweatshirt pocket. The crack in its side obvious. The black, plastic shard on the ground below making it more so.

She heard Derek demanding to know how many souls Jerrod had stored on him again before the rushing of fire and the crackling of bones drowned all external sounds. She swallowed, and admitted to herself that if she could be a coward now and run, she would. Her knees were locked though. That hadn't ever happened before. The fire didn't disable the use of her limbs. Her body still functioned like it should. It was fear holding her still. The unknown. Derek was here, but he couldn't save her from this. Jerrod's eyes were so wide they could have overcome his whole face.

So the flames were visible then.

Callie couldn't stop the train of panicked thoughts charging through her mind. Could she burn to death? It didn't hurt, but she could feel herself falling apart. That had to be bad, right? The admonishments came next with curses to the Soul Charmer for doing this to her and not teaching her how to control it. The darkest profanity she saved for herself and her shit life choices. When she was certain her body would cave in like the oldest campfire log, the one dappled with blue flames, something rubbed against her.

Warm.

Heady.

Power and softness mingled in the energy dancing against her front. It roved from her left hip to the right ridge of her lower ribcage, and up between her breasts and then back around the nape of her neck. Everywhere the energy touched it pushed against her seeking entry, and in its wake it plucked the heat from her. Leaving a trail of dewy skin and heated streaks, but sucking the charred flames with it. The energy curled behind her ear. That's when she heard it.

The plea. It's so cold here. Take me home.

Callie couldn't be certain the words were spoken, but they reverberated against her sternum. The words didn't belong to her, but were meant for her all the same.

The soul.

Jerrod hadn't secured it in the vessel. Callie didn't know how to do it either, but the Charmer controlled when souls entered and left his jars. She could take the lid off and feel the magic, but the soul wouldn't escape without the A-OK from the boss.

The full-body torch-fest still simmered in the spots where the soul hadn't vied for entry, but with each pull of a breath she was steadier. The fire was there, her skin was surely flaking, but her mind was calm.

I'm not your home, she thought, but I can give you one.

Callie tugged the flask out of her pocket, ignoring the grey flecks of skin that showered to the ground as her fingers slid against the edge of her pocket. She opened the top, and brought the lip of the flask up next to her neck.

"Here," she said aloud. The hazy figures of two people—probably Derek and Jerrod—were in her periphery, but she ignored them. The shivering soul at her ear jumped forward and slid into the flask. Callie's skin regenerated in less than a second. Her body no longer flared hot nor was it overwhelmed with the shuddering of her insides. The flask, though, hummed beneath her palm and the soft, steady pulse of warmth the onyx gave sure sounded like a thank you.

Her bones were solid again, and maybe her gut was too. That quaking fear of how shit might go down poorly had quelled. Her vision focused, moment-by-moment, and the smug look on Derek's face almost made her laugh. This wasn't a situation for laughter, but he couldn't have been more chagrined if he'd thrown the deuces to the Soul Charmer.

Jerrod definitely wasn't thinking about laughing. He'd clenched his teeth together so tight the muscles near his temples protruded. Callie could have heard the grinding of his molars if there wasn't still a faint buzzing in her ear. The little bit of color he had in his face before had vanished. Even his freckles took on a more muted orange tone. Derek had let the guy off the wall, and she could see why. He teetered unevenly on locked legs. His pupils constricted more the longer he looked at her. The whites of his eyes were fading into the overall blanched nature of him and his fear now. Tiny dots of sweat started to pop along his forehead. The yellow light of the lamppost above catching them in a way that softened the image. Derek's right hand still gripped Jerrod's shoulder, because he wasn't one to place all his money on someone's fear keeping him close.

Callie stepped a little closer. Just a half step to

make sure her own legs were working and her body truly had healed. She was steady, but Jarrod flinched the way marks did when Derek pulled back to throw a meaty paw at their face. The ice seeped from her cuticles down across her nails. The freezing sensation started to snake up her forearms, but Callie still managed to reach back and tuck the flask in her back pocket without fumbling. It was likely the high of not crumpling into a pile of ash and shattered bones, but the frigid cold of her hands was more of a tool right now than something to fight. Her fingers began to lock up, but she would heal. They would move again once she was away from Jerrod, which meant getting answers out of him soon would only make her feel better faster. Side effects of soul magic on someone like her were definitely motivators.

"How'd you do that?" Jarrod choked out.

"Do what?" Callie stepped a little closer. She lifted her hands so he could see the ice crystals building a lattice around her arms. The blue tinge to her skin was unmistakable even in the warm glow of the street lamp. Jarrod's chest rose and fell too fast, not getting enough air in or out.

Derek's fingers flexed on the other man's shoulder, digging in. Jarrod wasn't going anywhere.

Before Jarrod could bumble through a response, Callie said, "You talked a big game about being able to rent me a soul. Shouldn't you know exactly what I did?"

She bore the confidence of someone who found rogue souls all the time and captured them with deft skill. She wasn't sure who this person she was pretending to be was, but she might be a little high off that soul. When she'd rented from the Charmer she hadn't felt a damn thing, but now there was a wave of power crashing against her heart and she wasn't going to miss her opportunity to leverage it.

She met Derek's gaze. Her silent question was quickly answered both by the warmth in his eyes—something only for her—and the subtle lift of his chin. It hadn't been in the plan, but she was going to control this.

"We don't have to talk about how you work soul magic." She tried to keep the singsong out of her voice, but the taunting tone tickled the back of her throat regardless. Jarrod's body began to ease, but Derek gave his shoulder a quick squeeze and the tension was back.

"You—you—you're like him." Jarrod's fear was so overwhelming Callie almost didn't realize he was comparing her to the Soul Charmer. She fought the pitch of her stomach at the resemblance. For now it was a good thing to be that sketchy fuck's contemporary. It made her scary and powerful in Jarrod's mind, even though she was neither.

"And you're not, but that hasn't stopped you from trying to do his work. So, I want to know if you ever gave a soul to a kid named Cullen."

He flinched again. "What you want to know about Cullen for?"

Derek shook him by the shoulder. Jarrod was a head shorter than Derek, and all skin and bones. The simple move flapped Jarrod's body like the fabric of the culottes.

"Right. Um. Yeah. I've helped the kid out." Jarrod didn't look at either of them as he spoke, which was a downright challenge given the way the two and an adobe wall framed him in. He peeked over Callie's shoulder, but she wasn't going to take her eyes of this guy for even a second. The fine layer of ice had begun to cap her shoulders. She couldn't keep this up much longer. Her arms were close to being fully locked, and when their mark realized she was immobilized, it wouldn't do anyone any good.

"Why didn't you want to tell us that?" Derek asked, never bashful about cutting to the center of the issue.

"Heard you've been beating down anyone selling souls."

Callie stilled her features. They hadn't been after a competitor since Tess disappeared.

Derek didn't refute it, though. "And yet here you are selling souls. So, real answer this time. Why didn't you want to tell us about the kid?"

Jarrod tilted his head so he could look at Derek, but as soon as his tiny pupils caught the gaze of the big guy holding him he quickly looked away. "Just lots of people are interested in that kid. All right?"

It was most certainly not all right, but it might be helpful. Callie refocused. "Why'd they want to know about him?"

"They just wanted someone who rented from both of us."

"Of who?" Derek asked.

Jarrod looked to the cracks in the concrete by his feet. "You know, your boss and me."

Not even in the same league. The Soul Charmer wouldn't have been caught like this. He would have stolen any shakedown artists' souls and let his power crumple them. Not that she and Derek were shakedown artists, Callie reminded herself. She was getting answers for a murdered teenager. For once she was on the side of the angels, but with a toe still in the Soul Charmer's swamp waters.

Callie couldn't help herself. "And you gave them a seventeen-year old kid?"

At the same time, Derek asked the more useful question, "What did they look like?"

"Short, stocky dude and a too skinny girl." Jarrod answered Derek. Probably because her question would make him think about what a shitbag he was.

"How old? You catch names?" Derek asked and then tweaked Jarrod's shoulder a smidge. The mark didn't whine, but his lip curled until Derek eased the pressure.

"Young. The girl was barely legal. The guy was probably her age." He gestured toward Callie. She was tempted to touch her hardened ice hand to his. Could she transfer the cold to him? Why did she want to find out?

She held back. Her arms ached, but she couldn't be sure if it was from the deep freeze happening or from the lack of action. "Names," she demanded.

"I don't know."

She touched him then. She shouldn't have. The second the pads of her fingers touched his free shoulder, he yelped. The cry was howling, and it banged against the nearby lamppost and the dumpster a few yards away and then the windows recessed into the storefront another block down. The cry carried. It was the kind of noise that got the cops called. Even downtown. It was the kind that brought eyes in their direction and nearby friends running. It was sure to bring the exact attention she and Derek did not need. Callie twisted her hips away from him quickly to pluck her immobile arm from his. Fresh holes dotted his sweatshirt where she'd touched him. The fabric clung to her hand, and she tried to ignore that.

Derek didn't admonish her. Not even with his eyes when she met them a second later. Faint lines had formed at the corners of his, but she read the flicker of worry in his gaze as pure concern for her and not for the job. She trusted what she saw, and the realization made her suck in a quick, heavy breath.

"Names." Derek repeated with a harshness that required urgency. It wasn't a question.

"I don't fucking know, man. I think the girl called the guy Dee or Gee or something like that."

Derek edged close enough to almost be standing on Jerrod's toes, and arced over him. If anyone knew how to play size to his advantage, it was Derek. The man was fucking *imposing*. "Dee or Gee? You can do better."

The clatter of sneakers against pavement grew louder at the corner. Callie checked the side streets, but didn't see anyone. That didn't mean much. The roads downtown were ancient, narrow, winding and with a lot of sharp turns. She couldn't see jackall, but as the sound carried out, it surely carried in. She caught Derek's attention and jerked her head in the direction she thought people were going to enter from.

His growl wasn't likely for her, but she rolled her eyes anyway. Maybe the ice was getting to her. She needed distance from Jarrod either way. The ache in her chest from the prolonged cold was becoming more and more tangible. She wasn't superhuman or invincible. She wanted to heal, and she wanted to do it soon.

"Anyone else comes around asking about Cullen, you keep your mouth shut to them, and you find me. You feel me?"

Derek didn't have to threaten the guy. They'd already put Jerrod completely on edge. "Yeah. How do I find you?"

Derek released the guy's shoulder, and took a step backward. Callie started her shuffle away, too, not ready to give the guy her back. The itch of warming skin began to ignite at her shoulders as the ice began to fade. Unlike real ice it didn't melt or soak her clothes. It just disappeared until her skin was back to its standard brown.

"Don't ask dumb questions," was all Derek said. He slipped his arm around Callie's shoulders. His body heat didn't actually increase the thawing process, but it sure as hell made her feel better. She curled in, and they disappeared down one of the darkened side streets.

When her arms could move again, she lifted her

right hand to touch the one Derek had placed over her shoulder.

"Was that worthwhile?" she asked.

"Pretty sure you became the soul whisperer or some shit, so I say yes."

Was she supposed to laugh at that joke? The confidence high she'd worn earlier had dissipated, and now she was struggling to remember which way was up. "Let's not talk about this here."

He nodded, understanding that meant 'give me time before we talk about the magic bullshit.'

"Do you know a Dee or a Gee that gives us a clue?" she asked as an additional diversion.

"I've got a couple ideas, but neither of them are good."

"That's okay. Our plans never work out anyway."

He squeezed her a little tighter. "When we skip the plan you get extra badass, doll. Ditching plans looks good on you."

She hated that he was right.

CHAPTER THIRTEEN

Callie asked Derek to drive them back to her place. The lingering sensation of her skin dancing made her squirm. The hum of energy in her ears wasn't real. At least she didn't think so. She shoved a sleeve of her coat up to expose her forearm, but it didn't show any trademark chill bumps. The sickening pull, tug, and whirl of her flesh being plucked continued to stab at her mind. She ran a palm over her skin again, for good measure, but it was clearly where it should be and not swirling, detached above the muscle.

The flask was nuzzled against her hip. She pulled it from her pocket and placed it in the center console. It didn't fit in the cup holder, but teetered on a small ledge behind it. Her body was too tight, but it no longer bore the about-to-burst-at-the-seams sensation. So that was a plus.

"You good?" Derek asked. The gravel was gone

from his voice, but a deep groove furrowed between his eyebrows.

She rolled her head from one shoulder to the other, trying and failing to ease the tension still bracketing her neck. "Yeah."

He knew it for the lie it was.

"Magic can fuck you up." It wasn't clear if he was talking about the way her body belonged to the magic when that soul had shimmied its way up her torso, or the way it lured in people and got them hooked on freedom, on the high of believing they were able to do almost anything without consequence. Or maybe he meant the way that soul magic led to bad decisions. All of it was true.

"I don't know how to feel." Not a lie.

"Who says you have to?"

She audibly exhaled, but the air carried an undertone of approval. Damn, she was starting to communicate more and more like Derek.

"People get high on soul rental in a lot of ways, doll."

"I'm not high," she snapped. She didn't know what she was, but it wasn't a delightful buzz.

"Didn't say you were. Just you've seen it. Some people are squirrelly. Some use constantly and get that white-eyed ghost shit going on. Some use once and try to return it early swearing up a fucking storm that the soul is trying to take over their body."

The rogue soul earlier hadn't been looking to take

Callie over. It'd wanted a home, but the request made her think it wouldn't have turned her into a pod person or anything. Not that renting souls gave her any sensation at all. She'd done it once, and other than the fact she had seen the effects—zigzagged fingerprints and such—she still had been regular Callie. Albeit a regular Callie who had been super stressed and squicked to the ends of the Earth for letting the Charmer stick *anything* in her body. She swallowed hard to dislodge the stone forming in her throat.

"Okay," she said without hiding how royally fucked everything had become.

Derek kept his eyes studiously trained on the road. "It's probably the same for people like the Charmer."

"I'm not like him."

"Didn't say you were. Just saying I know that souls affect him more than he lets on. You aren't the same as him, but magic is fucking magic and it doesn't help us to pretend otherwise."

The bubbling ire in her belly urged her to disagree. To spew the anger and the disgust for being lumped in with that asshole. She'd spent the better part of a decade trying to distance herself from unsavory types. Every time she made progress, she tumbled back down the hill. To the slums and across the figurative tracks. She'd be back with the junkies and the con artists and the people willing to sell anything. Earning money honestly was paramount. Avoiding the people who didn't was equally important. The Soul Charmer was conniving and used people to get his ends, but at least he actually exchanged legal goods for money. She didn't know how long that would be true. You can only get away with selling goods that change people's DNA for so long before the government gives it a big, red "HELL NO" stamp.

The fire in her gut didn't reach her voice, though. Derek wasn't the bad guy. She was mad at the situation, at the world, at the fact she didn't know what was wrong with her body and why it had prickled with the same askance of the rogue soul after she'd already given it cozy, temporary digs inside the flask. She was not actually mad at Derek. Sometimes it was hard to remember that when he had so much insight into the Charmer and she had so little.

She sucked in and then exhaled a few breaths before saying anything more. Derek didn't push. She was grateful he could read her well. "What do the souls do to him?"

Derek eased his shoulders down and backward. She hadn't even paid attention to the way they'd tensed while her brain was chugging through all the anger. "That's a broad question, doll."

She almost smiled. "I've got a lot to learn. Big questions are kind of how it works."

"He doesn't let anyone see him capturing souls outside the body, but he does. That's what you did earlier, right?"

"For someone who can't sense the souls the same way I do, you sure do know what the fuck is going on." She'd meant it as a joke, but the pang of truth crashed in its wake.

"I watch him, but I watch you more."

That *did* make her smile.

"You lit up, which is normal around open souls—at least in the jars—or when there are lots around. So I kind of figured it out."

"Fair enough. What happens to the Charmer?"

"Like I said, most of that shit is private for him. But I have seen him hunched over broken glass in the back corner of his workroom before."

"Like he was going to be sick?"

"Like he was a fucking dragon making sure his pile of gold was intact."

"Oh."

"Yeah. He damn near dislocated his shoulder reaching to a nearby shelf to get one of his jars."

Callie could picture the Soul Charmer, all slime and serpentine energy, bending and breaking to keep what was his. It was the reason he'd been so volatile when they'd found Cullen. It hadn't been that a person had died. Not for the Soul Charmer. He'd been angry someone had taken what was his and had disparaged his place with a corpse.

Derek parked Callie's car in the lot outside her apartment, but he didn't turn it off. Neither he nor Callie moved to exit, either.

"Did his skin—" she couldn't ask about the perception of pinching and pulling all over her body, because no one could *see* that. She was a little crazy for holding on to it, but she had to know more. Had to know if this was normal. She stuttered through the rest, "—did his skin change at all?"

"You mean burn until it was black and falling off?" The pang in Derek's voice had Callie's sides clenching like a mighty blow was about to land hard against her liver.

She nodded, unable to risk sending either of them into a darker place.

"No. He didn't burn, but his teeth were gritted."

Callie nodded again, though it was mere acknowledgement. Derek rested his hand on her thigh, just above the knee. His hands were always so warm, and she let his touch soothe her. It was the delicious warmth of sunshine and towels fresh from the dryer and the reminder of how she was little and special when he wrapped his arms around her

"I think he learned how not to burn?" The question in his voice was more hope than fact. Callie let it ease her worry, though, for a moment.

"I want to know how to do that."

"You controlled it tonight. That's got to be a start, right?"

Had she, though? She had been unable to move until the soul had pleaded for a safe space. If she'd funneled it into the flask sooner, she could have avoided the fire and the ache and the shuddering cracks throughout her skeleton.

"Maybe."

Callie had considered asking Derek to take the flask back to the Soul Charmer on her behalf. He'd done so in the past, but it was no longer fair to ask. Avoiding the Charmer used to ease her worry. It had kept her from getting pulled in deeper into whatever crazy-ass shit he had going on. It was different now. If Derek got pulled into the aforementioned crazy-ass shit, she was in it, too. The two shuffled up the stairs to her apartment, the flask kicking new, uneasy energy ripples over her body. She turned her mind to Derek instead of letting the sensation set her ears ringing and her teeth on edge.

She and Derek hadn't discussed what their connection meant—Callie preferred it that way—but somehow in the last few weeks they'd become an unspoken package deal. She'd seen the way his tough, aquiline nose and sharp cheekbones had lost their tough-guy power, and shifted gaunt after returning from "disposing" of Cullen. Her knees bucked at the memory. She set a hand on the rail to steady herself. Derek's hand cupped her lower back.

"All good, doll?"

She nodded. She wasn't sure which was more unnerving right now: the constant pull barely beneath her skin or the memory of how a task for the Soul Charmer could send even Derek Shepherd into anguish. His stoicism constantly awed her. When they'd first met, she'd been certain he was an unfeeling thug who beat people up for a living. He wasn't. Though he had no compunction about punching people or generally doing whatever it took to get the job done, he was more than that. He had standards; he didn't punch people who didn't deserve it. It's not like people who skipped out on returning rented souls were the upstanding sort. There wasn't a pure reason to rent a soul. If you were bartering with the Soul Charmer, you weren't up to anything good. Fuck. Even when Callie rented from him it wasn't for a noble cause. She did it to save her brother, yes, which sounded great late at night when she lay awake in bed pretending she was a better person. Saving Josh had been the right thing to do. Family first. But the soul she'd rented was to keep her DNA a secret as she stole research from the police on the behalf of a mobster who was one-hundred-percent a murderer and had no problems with whipping out a knife against anyone. He'd probably threaten to cut a kid and not even lose a second of sleep over it. Callie had found a dead body, and couldn't sleep at all thinking of the myriad ways her day could have been different and how it could have changed the outcome. None of it mattered, though. Cullen was dead. The people who had done it were out there, probably laughing at how riled the act got the Soul Charmer. Callie and Derek were the ones left cleaning it all up.

She'd complain about how she'd gotten involved in this shit, but the truth was Callie had spent her life cleaning up other people's problems. She'd taken care of Josh on and off. She'd cared for herself. She'd hid her mother's crimes. She'd cleaned up after any Delgado who had her phone number. It's what she did. No wonder the Charmer didn't want to let her go.

Derek nudged her side lightly with his elbow. "You going to open that?"

Magic might be melting her mind. She dug out her keys and unlocked the front door. Derek didn't say a word, but smiled like he could see the cogs and wheels in her brain spinning at peak speed. She shook her head both to avoid eye contact while she pulled herself together and to dislodge any lingering thoughts of Ford, the Soul Charmer, or what either of them could convince her to do with the right threat.

"Where's your brother?" Derek asked with lightness in is voice that suggested he did not mind at all that Josh wasn't currently affixed to the couch cushions.

Callie opened her mouth to say he was probably in the shower, but she didn't hear the water running. The pipes were old by desert standards and the walls were thin. If the water had been running, she'd know. "Hmm," was all she could muster.

Josh's pillow was still wedged in the crook of the couch at an angle he'd perfected for optimal sofa sleeping, but the blanket she'd placed on him before leaving earlier today was folded and resting on the coffee table.

Derek moved to the kitchen and plucked two brown bottles from the refrigerator. He'd stocked beer in her place. She'd told him she never kept any here because that would make her a lush. It was only a half-truth. While she didn't want to fall into the habit of soaking her sorrows in beer—it was a family pastime—she also didn't have the extra cash to keep booze in the house. If she had to pick between bread and beer, it was going to be bread every single time.

He popped the caps. She was still standing next to

the couch when he brought her the drink. She accepted the cold bottle, and took a quick pull from the top. The couch offered her no clues, though she continued to stare at it like it would suddenly expel Josh from its depths. He'd been asleep on it for so long, maybe they had fused into a man-couch hybrid. A *mouch*.

"He left a note. I think." Derek was a few feet behind her, and she hadn't realized he'd moved. She needed to get her head straight before something wicked caught her with her guard down.

Callie moved next to Derek at the small counter near the kitchen. It shared one side with the kitchenette, but jutted into the living space. There was just enough room for the two of them to stand next to it, which was probably its intent. Sure enough there was a small note resting atop the Formica.

Josh's handwriting was dubbed chicken scratch by the kindest of teachers. He'd done his best here using all block letters, but any untrained eye would have difficulty reading it. Callie could read it better than even Zara.

"You've got to be kidding me," she muttered.

Derek edged close enough for his arm to brush hers. He didn't say anything, but the hint of support was enough to get her to explain. "He went to Mom's house."

"Why the fuck would he want to go to Zara's place?" He left off the obvious reasoning that Zara was batshit.

"He's her favorite."

"I doubt she has a favorite."

Callie kept her eyes on the scrap of paper and Josh's handwriting. "No, she does, and it's him."

Derek pulled her against his chest. He hadn't divested his jacket yet, and she buried her cheek in the notch of open skin between the notches of worn leather. The lingering hint of Irish Spring uncoiled some of the anxiety in her chest.

"Didn't mean it that way, doll. Your mom looks out for herself above everything else. She's her own favorite."

He wasn't wrong. "She isn't good for his sobriety." The words slipped from her mouth on with a long sigh. Keeping everyone else's shit together was exhausting.

"She..." Derek started but didn't finish.

"He said he's going to help make dinner over there tomorrow night, and we need to come."

Derek pulled back just enough to get a good look at Callie's face. His eyes flickered over hers.

She spared him. "Yes, really."

"Didn't Zara threaten you last time she was here?"

Callie couldn't muster the anger that was clearly washing over Derek. His reaction was correct. It was honest and real. It was the appropriate response to re-engaging with her mother. It was the right way to feel after the person who had raised you sided with the bad guys. She'd stormed into Callie's apartment and demanded that she find Tess—the Charmer's rival at the time. She hadn't cared about how her daughter had become involved with soul magic, or how she knew the Soul Charmer or Tess. Zara wasn't concerned that Callie's hands froze over when she was near a soul magic user, but also didn't want to admit that she was one. Zara cared about herself and used anyone she could to achieve her goals. She could con a priest, if properly motivated. It was this complete understanding of how her mother worked, of how Zara saw her, that allowed Callie to bypass the fury that should have scalded her veins. Callie had never been more than a means to an end for Zara, and she was grown enough now to understand that.

"She did. She also was certain she would find someone else to siphon her soul after Tess skipped town." They shared a knowing look that said they both suspected Tess was more permanently relocated below the earth than gallivanting in the mountains, but some acts shouldn't be spoken aloud.

"I haven't heard of anyone else pulling pieces of souls like Tess had. The chakra massage place closed down."

Tess had offered a different service than their boss. Instead of bartering for a bonus soul, Tess's customers came in for new age healing and had small pieces of their souls ripped away in the process. Apparently it created a similar high to frequent soul rentals. While Callie wasn't much for being the Charmer's minion, at least he was upfront about his slimeball ways.

Callie shrugged and tried to ignore the simmer of souls she could sense from the flask. "Tess's disappearance wasn't kept quiet. If I were someone working any kind of legit soul magic, or anything where I took souls instead of placed them, I would be fucking shitting myself in fear of the Soul Charmer."

"Scorched Earth is his style." Derek took a long drink from his beer. He'd earned a little booze to quell the memory of the fire and brimstone working for the Soul Charmer required.

Wasn't that the truth? Hell, Callie often considered kicking herself for the daredevil dumbassery of choosing to apprentice for the Charmer. She didn't have the energy left to deal with soul magicians would who burn the world to the ground to get vengeance or brothers who made poor decisions and left her to fix them or mothers who damned their own kids. Nope. It was close to eleven, and she was done for the night. She dropped the flask onto the counter. The black inlay made the off-white paper of Josh's note look pristine. She wasn't going to contemplate if it actually made a difference.

"I need to shower and sleep," she said more to hold herself accountable for basic tasks of self-care than to inform Derek.

"I'll clean up out here, and meet you in there."

She hadn't been sure if he was going to stay. Her body and brain were tapped, and the thought of processing what he needed from tonight was a bit overwhelming. "You know I'm getting up at four to go to work, right?"

He donned a roguish grin and wore it like he was always a little coy and a little rough. It softened the hard veneer she'd been shellacking around herself.

"Nothing new to me. I don't want you here alone."

"Josh might come back," she said. She wasn't out to deter him, but part of her needed to hear what he'd say.

He slid off his leather jacket and folded it over the back of one of the dining chairs. His shoulders might have become even broader freed from the leather layer. "Even more reason for me to be here."

She wasn't about to disagree. Loyalty and protection were paramount in the Delgado family, and she was starting to think Derek might earn an honorary title there. She tipped back her beer, and finished the last few gulps. She dropped the bottle in the bin.

"Works for me."

Derek took the flask from the counter and tucked it in his back pocket. Callie struggled to keep from asking him what he was doing. It must have shown, because he said, "In case your brother does come back. We don't want easy-access souls to fuck with his sobriety."

She was pretty sure he was more worried that Josh would hock them for cash or absorb them before getting high again. Callie doubted her brother would know how to get the souls out of there, but she didn't disagree he'd be drawn to a flask. Her emotions were too muddy to unpack that right now. She gave Derek a half nod, and headed to the bathroom.

Shower, sleep, and the steady strength of Derek at her side all night would help her reset.

It had to.

CHAPTER FOURTEEN

Callie was good about turning off her phone at work. Well, the volume anyway. Her job in the kitchen at the retirement home may not have made the same difference as she had back in her medical assistant days, but that didn't mean she shouldn't give it the same attention. Being focused and on time were two of the things Callie could consistently do, and so she did. The loyalty was rewarded with some flexibility when Josh had been kidnapped—though she hadn't told her boss that was the reason.

Today, though, she hadn't flipped the switch to silent on the side of the device before walking through the door. It chimed as she was shoving her purse and coat into her cubby of a locker. Anyone who would text her at 5 a.m. was not someone she wanted to talk to. People usually called in the case of emergencies, but with her brother working hard to get clean and teenage soul rental users being murdered, it was probably worth double checking.

She opened the message. Zara. Nope, not an emergency.

"Come to dinner tonight. Or else. Josh will. Be mad." The punctuation was a problem, but Callie wasn't completely convinced it was a mistake.

A half-second later another message pinged through. "Please."

Callie rolled her eyes, and squeezed the phone in her hand. The urge to chuck it and Zara's polite bullshit against the back of the metal cabinet gripped the base of her spine and shook until Callie's fingers twitched. She opened her palm over her purse. The phone plopped against it, and then dropped to the metal bottom of the bin with a finite clink. It could wait there until after her shift. She'd like to think she was punishing the phone, and it could ruminate on the error while she worked, but the truth was she needed time to figure out how she was going to behave. Distance from Zara was for the best, but not when it hurt Josh. If she spent enough time thinking on Zara, she'd come up with a reason seeing her was a good idea.

Callie closed and locked her cubby, and then grabbed a hairnet from the box next to the door. She pulled it on as she walked into the kitchen, and pretended that plastic weave would keep the bad thoughts away. Zara wasn't going to be deterred by a net. The Delgados didn't give up on anything that easily.

"Callie, my girl! Ready to cook?" Louisa was the most morning person to ever morning.

Her enthusiasm was somehow infectious, though. Callie's begrudging smile only encouraged the woman, but it couldn't be helped. "Yep. Same as every other day."

"There should be fresh tortilla dough in the refrigerator. I had Ana make it last night."

Callie headed toward the walk-in. "How many tortillas do we need?"

"The whole batch."

She'd been hoping for a number so she could tally her progress, but asking for more information from Lou meant getting more tasks. She might be in a better mood around her boss, but that didn't mean she wanted to double her work. She found the dough, and moved to set up the machine they used to heat and press each one. Hot, freshly pressed tortillas were one of Callie's favorite foods. Simple and with fresh ground corn meal used? Delicious. It made the task of crafting them both her favorite and a bit frustrating. It wasn't a one-for-them, one-for-me task, but she'd still test the first one off the line to make sure it was good. Kitchen staff perks.

Making tortillas through a press was not the most interesting of activities. Callie would have preferred to do them one-by-one to be more engaged, but in the name of efficiency and getting enough crafted for the home's residents, the press was the way to go. She plopped the little balls of dough onto the entrance in a metered fashion. The Cedar Retirement Home kitchen was a time vacuum on mornings like these. It was early enough that the nursing night shift was still on task, which meant a lighter crew. Lou had dialed the radio to a classic rock station, and Callie didn't hate it.

The two worked in relative silence, and Callie let her head bob to the beat of some blues-based guitar riff. She focused on the mundane task and the kind vibe that hovered in the room, and pushed her worries to the back corner of her mind. An hour passed, and soon they could hear the opening and closing of locker doors tapping off beat from their music. The employee locker room adjacent to the kitchen was for all employees. Their shift change meant they were only two hours from serving breakfast. Luckily, that meal was the easiest as many of the residents were eggs-and-toast diet folk. Their current work was all for lunch and dinner.

"You need a break." Louisa didn't make it a question, and Callie was too smart to argue.

"Okay." Callie hit the stop button on the machine, and waited until the last tortilla fell from the other side. "Back in fifteen."

Lou was funny about breaks. The kitchen staff wasn't overwhelming. Jenny wouldn't even be in for another hour, but Callie appreciated her boss's sense of fairness. She wanted to be certain Callie got everything the employee handbook promised. Normally, this was nice, but right now, she didn't want to go back to the real world.

She popped into the employee lounge and checked her locker. She had two missed calls and four text messages. The calls were, unsurprisingly, from Zara. Her mother knew damn well she worked in the mornings. She hadn't left voicemails, which was for the best.

Hearing her mother's inane commentary on Callie's job, social life, and consistent failure to meet familial obligations was not something she needed today. Besides, she could run through the conversation on her own. Instead Zara had texted twice following up on the dinner invite.

Zara's first message was standard guilt trip, and pawning Josh's wellbeing onto Callie for the thousandth time. *"Don't disappoint your brother. This is a difficult time for him."*

She iced her guilt cake with one more blow: "Kindness to your family is essential if you wish to rise to Heaven."

"Lovely," Callie muttered to herself. This dinner was fucking real.

"Everything okay?" a bright, high-pitched voice asked from behind her.

Callie looked over her shoulder to meet one of the caregiver's eyes. Callie had met her before, but her brain couldn't pull her name to the forefront. Something with a B, maybe? "Oh, yeah, just trying to organize a family dinner thought text messages." She did her best to keep the tone light, to make it sound like she wanted to have dinner with her family and was merely caught in a group text message tsunami.

"Been there. I'm sure it'll be worth all the organizing," the other woman said. She waved a hand as she left the room, "Have a blessed day!"

Callie was good at faking normal conversation. She could pretend to have the same prosaic problems as the people who came from stable homes, never scrounged for money, and never had to worry about their family members stealing from them. She could blend. Emotional scars could be concealed if you had the right tools, and she did. She wasn't certain it was a skill she should be proud of. She didn't want to have to pretend her problems were light and airy. She was sick of the slashing wounds of real family distress, and the unyielding ache of problems that couldn't be solved.

Once she was alone again she read the other two messages. These were from Derek. She smiled big and goofy as her heart warmed for a second upon seeing his name on the screen. She mentally shook herself. She wasn't a woman who went all weak in the knees. It was easier to pull herself together once she'd read the messages.

"Charmer probs. Again. Not like that, but complicated."

"Get here as soon as you can after your shift. - D"

At least he knew she was at work. Derek texted about big, scary shit in the most cryptic way he could, and still took into account her work schedule. Zara whined about a meal no one wanted to go to while forgetting that her daughter had to earn money an honest way by working. Not everyone came away from the collection plate with a fuller wallet. Callie read and re-read Derek's messages. She was fairly certain he was telling her there was another *something* happening at the Charmer's that would have the gnarly old man up in arms, but his "not like that" had to mean not a kid again, right? Or maybe no one died?

How had "no one died" become her gauge of if a situation was going to be scary as fuck? Callie had officially crossed to batshit territory again. How was she supposed to go back to pressing tortillas when something awful had happened at the Charmer's shop and Derek was the one holding the bag until she arrived?

Double lives were bullshit.

She did go back to work, though, because cash was spread thin and if there was anything she'd learned from her youth it was you did whatever it took to maintain the essentials. Food and shelter were actually not as easy to come by as the asshole soul users with carpet-like green lawns would have believed.

For the next hour the only sounds in the industrial kitchen were those of wooden spoons rhythmically colliding with stainless steel mixing bowls, the soft sizzle of eggs atop the griddle, the guitars on the radio, and Callie gnashing her teeth.

Louisa returned from the big walk-in refrigerator with a bin of green hatch chiles. She set the box on the counter and pulled a large knife from the block. A smaller, paring knife would be better, but Callie wasn't about to critique her boss.

Louisa broke the silence. "Your brother. He still clean?" She poked the tip of the knife into the pepper near the stem.

"I sure hope so." Understatement of the year.

"Michael..." Lou started, but her voice faded into a long sigh. The hum of the radio behind them almost overtook the room. Callie focused on its words and not the ones she and Louisa were avoiding.

The other woman slammed her knife hard against the wooden block beneath the pepper. She was dicing with fury now. Callie completely understood. She hadn't needed to use a knife this morning, and that was one hundred percent for the best. Was it shitty to be happy she wasn't the only one with drama smashing in from every side?

After a few solid thwacks from the cutting board, Lou was ready to talk. "Spends all his time downtown." Louisa was a petite, plump woman, but she hurled the derision and disgust for downtown with the vigor of a world-class shot-put athlete.

Callie tried not to think about how much time *she* spent downtown. She dropped another ball of dough onto the tortilla press, and focused on the soft sizzle instead of the way her insides squeezed in preparation for another blow.

"He won't even go to church. He's been to church at least once every week of his life. That's at least fifty-two times for twenty-eight years. I can't do the math, but you don't just stop your faith like that."

Callie's mother had once said something similar to her. Only her mother was concerned about the way it looked to have her daughter skipping any masses. Callie kept up the face, but the rejuvenation she was supposed to get within those hallowed walls with the multi-colored light streaming in through the stained-glass windows evaded her. She was broken in a way that made her pure by the Soul Charmer's standards, but probably not the right kind to be in the Cortean

Catholic Church's good graces. Not that she was going to inquire one way or another. Lou's son may have never been faithful. Or maybe he'd lost his way. It didn't matter, because Louisa was bone-deep worried about him and Callie understood that kind of fear.

"He'll find his way back. He always does," she said. Louisa had said it to Callie not long after she'd started at the retirement home. It was just after Josh had punked out of rehab, but before he'd stolen Zara's television.

"I don't know." Hesitation shook Lou's voice. Her knife blade skidded across the block, completely missing the current pepper. *That* got Callie's attention.

Lou stared at the green pulp on her right side of the chopping block. "Father Domingo prays for him. He even said we might want to visit that heathen soul man. To protect Michael."

It had previously made Callie uneasy that the Church offered backdoor approval for soul rental. It isn't like God gave the priests quotas to meet every month, but that's how they behaved. Like it was all about the final score and not how you got there. Still, she hadn't ever heard of a priest recommending it. Usually it was more a blind eye situation. Turn the other cheek or some shit.

"You don't want to do that." Callie tried to keep the panic from her voice. It hurt her enough to know that her mother and brother had both used soul magic in some ways, because unlike the public she knew the consequences were real. A news expose on people getting addicted to the sensation, and delving into the possibility that the white-eyed glaze of a frequent user was akin to that of most opiate addictions had made people talk. It hadn't stopped them from renting souls. The thing was, the addition was only part of it. Using once had an effect. The kind of effect that permanently changed someone. Tiny pieces of your own soul were ripped away with every extraction of a rented one. You became less whole every single time. A hard pang resonated behind Callie's sternum. The same spot the Soul Charmer had placed and removed a rented soul from her body.

"Well, of course not," Lou said with enough vigor that Callie knew the woman had rolled her eyes.

"Of course. Good." She couldn't tell Louisa the full truth of why renting was the wrong path. Sharing what she knew was a good way to get herself dead. Seeing as she was spending her days avoiding mobsters and letting her body freeze and burn, she really didn't need another threat of death in her life.

"I worry about his soul." In that moment Callie knew that Louisa was considering soul rental. The realization she might have to hunt down Lou's kid to get back a soul pressed hard against her ribs. She sucked in a deep breath and held it to combat the tightening around her torso.

Louisa dropped the subject, but for the rest of her shift that side stitch snapped at Callie with every breath.

Double lives really were bullshit.

CHAPTER FIFTEEN

Callie sped to the Soul Charmer's shop as soon as her shift at the retirement home ended. Her thumb had hovered over the call button on her phone the whole walk to the car, but she'd resisted and dropped it back into her purse. Derek wasn't going to tell her anything over the phone. Whatever had gone down, it wasn't something to share with others—especially not any police officials who could easily have access to open lines.

Callie shook her head. Being worried about being overheard by the cops wasn't a new thing for her. When your mom conned tourists on the regular and you shoplifted to eat for most of your childhood, you got good at avoiding law enforcement. She'd thought she'd moved past it. Legit job, food obtained legally, a car that was hers. Instead she had adult problems that meant distance between her and any police officer was essential. She'd stolen from the cops, worked with a mobster, and probably was an accessory to some serious shit at the Soul Charmer's. To think her biggest concern used to be how to keep Josh in rehab.

Callie parked two blocks from the shop. The streetlamps weren't lit, but she still stayed near one. Eventually the sky would darken, and she'd want that halo over her car. It was a POS, but it was her POS. Sometimes a sense of security was enough to get you by. She still wore her light blue scrub top from work, but found a black hoodie in her backseat to pull over it. The sun was out today, making it bright but cold. Mother Nature playing tricks. She hurried down the block ignoring the brittle air snapping around her, and hooked a right into the alleyway that led to the Soul Charmer's abode.

Tourists mingled on the street. Hustling from one artisan's shop to another and discussing the statue of St. Catalina they'd seen near the cathedral and their hotel's former life as a monastery. She was glad they didn't notice when she turned into the alley. She didn't want them to follow. Didn't want them to discover the Soul Charmer. Didn't want them to think it was another quirky Gem City destination like a balloon festival or a glass blowing exhibit or trying posole for the first time. Renting a soul wasn't an act to be scrapbooked. The Charmer didn't sell postcards, but she wouldn't put it past him to spin a tale about the ancient culture that the conquistadors brought to the area at the same time as the offshoot religion that dominated the desert.

Tourists had a habit of getting Callie riled. They

found beauty in the mish-mash of her community. They thought they seedy streets she avoided—the ones that brought back bad memories and yielded the deepest scars—were "authentic" and the people were so "real." A coil of concern wrapped itself around her neck. If Derek wasn't inside she was liable to do something dumb. She was on edge, and the chances that she'd either offer to do more work (for free, no less) or get in a verbal sparring match with the Charmer and end up with her head frozen were significantly higher when Derek wasn't there to even the ambiance.

She took her phone from her pocket, though, and shot Derek a quick text. "There in 30 sec."

Her phone chimed a second later. "We're in back."

She hoped that meant they were in the Soul Charmer's workspace and not the crumbling back steps that led to the shop's side door. That's where they'd found Cullen, and she really wasn't up for another visit there yet. There was a reason she'd chosen the front entrance to the shop, even if it meant sharing the roadway with the gawking masses and the possibility of anyone spotting her heading into alleys with broken concrete, broken bottles, and broken dreams—the kind of alleys where souls were exchanged.

Thankfully the men were in the back workspace. The Soul Charmer called it his office, so Callie refused to use that word. It was petty, but when the balance of power is so uneven, one must take the wins when they can. The Soul Charmer sat on a stool next to the large oak desk that dominated the back half of the sterile room. He wore purple pajamas today. His arms were folded across his chest, forcing the sleeves to slide back revealing a series of thick gold cuffs on each arm and an arc of black outline. Callie almost thought she saw a drawing of a bird on his forearm before the Charmer huffed and the sleeve fell back over it.

Derek's palms were planted on the desk, and the strain in his forearms suggested his entire body weight was crushing forward.

Callie wasn't sure if she should speak. They both exuded enough tension that it had to be collecting near the ceiling. It'd hit an evaporation point and come tumbling back down upon them all within drops of anxiety, if she weren't careful. She took a couple steps forward, intent on touching Derek's back as way of greeting.

The Charmer spotted her first though, because of course he did. "Took you long enough!"

Callie unzipped her hoodie enough to display the scrubs beneath it. "I came straight from work."

"This is your work," he said, as though he wasn't listening.

Callie was ready to tell him exactly how employment worked and the requirement of recompense for one's time, but Derek turned to her then. The pain on his face did more than conjure sympathy in her heart; it unsettled her through and through. Derek was the steady one. The rock. Sure, shit had been shaky since they'd found Cullen, but...

"Not another kid." Her voice was almost a prayer, and she barely recognized it.

"No." His tone was all stone-and-sandpaper.

"We don't know that," the Charmer corrected. He was clearly in a pissy mood and determined to make sure everyone else in the room felt at least five times worse than he did. "We don't know who that skin belongs to."

It took Callie four tries before she got the question past her lips. "Skin?"

Derek's shoulders slumped. He was silent, but the soft slip of his shoulders told her more than his words would be able to. He inclined his head toward the desk, and Callie's toes curled like they thought to root her to the floor through her shoes. Her knees ached from the internal war. Her brain urging her to step forward and face the problem head-on, and her heart holding her back saying she had enough horror to bear for a lifetime.

At least it wasn't a body. She'd have seen that as soon as she'd stepped into the room. No corpse was a good sign. Or it would have been if Derek wasn't wearing his fuck-my-life face and the Soul Charmer— a master of magic who could literally take people's souls away—wasn't pouting like a four-year-old denied a cookie. Derek turned his attention back to the desktop, and Callie did the same. A slice of silver lay at the center.

A knife. Whatever metal it was, it wasn't stainless. It was marred with blood and something thin, wrinkled, and in a soft brown color flapped over the tip of the blade. Callie stepped closer, her brain winning. She'd heard them say skin, and the material at the end wasn't far in color from that of her own skin, but it didn't look human or real. The blood was real. It was a darker red, as though the hours had passed aging it quickly, and the subtle tang of rust caught her when she moved closer. She didn't have any real experience with flaps of skin separated from their bodies. Even when she worked emergency room shifts at the hospital, skin had usually been peeled back or sheered away. She hadn't ever seen it completely separated. It wasn't an experience she'd recommend. She handled gore better than most, but bile burned the back of her throat regardless. She pulled away and turned her head toward Derek. He was safe to look at. He was whole, and solid, and hers. He nodded at her, and she tried to not worry about the grimace plastered on his face.

"Where did this come from?" she asked as if solving a problem would actually distract her from any of this.

"That's the question isn't it?" The Soul Charmer sneered.

Derek answered her, though, "Out back. Same place we found the other one. This time they left just the knife, though."

"Why would they do that?"

"To let me know they're coming for me. Fucking no-talent garbage. If they could truly take me on, they wouldn't do it through taunts outdoors. I am goddamn above that," the Charmer sneered.

She'd meant why would they leave the knife instead of the body, but now wasn't the right time to correct her boss. He was offended, which wasn't a surprise, but his voice had scrabbled up half an octave.

He probably hadn't noticed, but Callie knew fear when she heard it.

If the Soul Charmer of Gem City was scared, Callie was fucking terrified.

The grimace hadn't disappeared, but Derek took a side step closer to Callie and shifted into solving mode. "Why the knife? It's kind of a wuss move, and what if one of our regular dumpster divers had found it?"

"Is the knife supposed to be a threat to us? Like letting us know he or she wouldn't have a problem using one?" Callie asked.

The Charmer rolled his eyes. Fucker. He wasn't even contributing. "He dropped a dead kid outside, Calliope. We already knew he was fine with killing people."

Callie made a low rumble of objection in her throat, but didn't bother trying to argue.

"That knife has fresh blood on it. He's telling us he killed someone else. Or cut someone else," Derek said to them both, but he kept his attention on Callie.

She followed him. "Which means he probably stole another of our souls."

"My souls," the Charmer corrected.

"Either way, someone is deliberately stealing your souls and wants your attention," Derek said.

"But why do they want his attention?" Callie asked.

It didn't make sense. If someone was trying to collect power or better souls to rent or was merely a rival business, why tell the Charmer? What was the point of letting him know his shit was stolen? It's not like when someone broke into your car and took your radio they left a sticky note with a "your radio has been stolen" message. You see it missing and get the point. There were only two reasons to sign your work: you have a huge ego and are ready to rub your conquest in everyone's faces or you want to get caught.

"Whoever it is wishes they were powerful. They aren't. They can't get the pure souls like I do. They can't get the supply needed to tend Gem City. They want to feel important by stealing from me." The Charmer was almost calm. His even, sweet tone was eerie and a wave of goose bumps rose from the base of Callie's back all the way to the nape of her neck in a fever-chill rush.

"How do you think they learned to steal the souls?" Callie's words were already tiptoeing backward as they left her mouth. She shouldn't be going there.

"Taking them out is the easy part." The Charmer dodged the question. Curious.

"Tess knew how to do it. So others could learn, too, right?" Derek asked.

"She scratched the shit out of people. This—" Callie pointed to the five-inch knife on the table and the small blood pool beneath it "—is precise. This is cold."

Cold was the word for it. There was something distant about the way whoever was going after the Charmer's customers was doing so. It was clinical and deliberate, but not with the heat of dealing with life. Callie had experienced the energy of a soul last night. The power, the organic fire borne of it. She almost understood Tess, and the reason she'd claw to get to the soul. She could sense and feel it. "Do you think this person can actually feel the magic, or are they following a textbook or something?"

That got the Charmer's attention. He stood, and cocked his head at Callie. "Interesting."

"Are you holding out on me? Is there a textbook?"

"Child, there is not a textbook in which one can learn mystical skill."

Oh.

The Soul Charmer cocked his head to the left and then the right. "But there may be rudimentary notes made by my predecessors."

Callie mouthed "predecessors?" to Derek, and he subtly, but sharply shook his head no. That was enough to keep her from stepping into that quagmire.

She was going to ask more questions—about the blood, about the purpose, about what the others could be doing with the souls—but the Soul Charmer's cheeks were already dappled with a rusty pink. When he was mad, his face popped with ire. Good thing it took quite a bit to get him riled. So, instead, Callie asked the one question she couldn't continue the day without knowing. The golden question. "Could this be Tess?"

The Soul Charmer and Derek shared a long look. Whether it was full of secrets or betrayals she wasn't certain. Derek finally said to the Charmer, "I don't talk soul magic with her."

That was a lie, but Callie wasn't about to correct him. Not with so many jarred souls within grabbing distance ready to be released and turn her into a human kindling.

The Soul Charmer answered her, "Tess has been taken care of. You should remember you were instrumental in getting information from her before others took care of seeing she would not return."

It sure sounded like the Soul Charmer was saying he killed Tess. Made him a bit of a double-standard guy on acting like he was above whoever was leaving bloody bits at the backdoor or better than the mobsters like Ford that the Charmer loved to tout weren't worthy of his time. He hadn't *actually* said that Tess was dead, and whatever other possibilities the Charmer could come up with to detain her permanently, Callie didn't want to know them.

"Okay, then, so not Tess. Got it." She said just to make sure no one was going to give her details on how they were keeping the woman who tried to steal the Charmer's business at bay. Word had gotten out about the consequences of crossing Gem City's premier soul magician. So why was someone already jacking their goods again, and hurting (mostly) innocent people in the process?

Callie let out a long breath, and wiggled her toes back to feeling. Sometimes people were egotistical assholes who left taunting messages when they looted your car. They were the kinds of people she didn't mind Derek punching in the face. From the way things were going, though, it was going to take more than a steady right cross to solve their problems.

"You said you were going to find out who did this.

So. Who is it?" The Charmer asked like he hadn't been present for the first half of the conversation. He'd be doing this more and more the last week or so. Scary powerful dude plus distraction equaled a whole lot of worry.

"If we knew that we wouldn't be here," Derek said.

"And we wouldn't all be staring at a bloody knife." Callie didn't want to mention the skin, because that meant thinking about whom it had belonged to and wondering if they were still alive.

"Have you done anything? I can't have people thinking they can threaten me without repercussions. Enemies will be burned." As if to emphasize his message, the Charmer snatched two of his jars from the shelving on the wall to his right. Callie took a couple steps back and angled her shoulder behind Derek's. She was not too proud to duck behind him if the Charmer decided to unleash some souls right now.

"Always." Derek's steady gaze underscored the word. Callie wasn't sure she wanted to know what secrets where buried in that look. He softened and continued, "We have a good lead. We're going to check it out tonight, but came here first because…" he pointed at the weapon on the desk.

Callie wasn't sure their lead was all that good, but any lead was better than no lead. "I told you we'd find out who did this, and we will," she said with the kind of confidence she'd seen in action movies. She doubted she'd actually ever be a yippee-ki-yay-motherfuck-er level of badass, but if she could fake McClain-level bravado, maybe she could at least keep her head above water…and attached.

The Soul Charmer grumbled, but didn't open either of the jars. Callie had wondered about her training session for today, and if she should tell him about what happened with the broken jar and the escaped soul last night. She didn't want to stay in this room any longer than necessary. The tile floors reflected the bright tube lights overhead. It was almost enough to make her believe this place was clean. It wasn't, and she wasn't, and the longer she stayed in this room the more filth would coat her. She needed to do something good, something honorable. Finding the person who was fucking with the Soul Charmer wasn't that, but finding the person who killed Cullen and maybe another of the Charmer's clients was close enough. She'd pretend she was only doing it for the kid, and maybe after a hot shower she wouldn't feel like she was swaddled in sludge. She might be able to breathe and think and actually do some good.

The Charmer grabbed Callie's flask from the corner of the desk—she hadn't even noticed it there. Derek must have brought it in for her, trying to spare her *this*. When the Soul Charmer's knobby fingers touched Callie's as he handed over the black and silver vessel, sparks flickered beneath her flesh, visible and golden. The stone inlay hummed in her hand.

"Pay attention to every person you talk to. You can feel them," he said between barely parted lips. The words hidden from all ears but hers.

His cryptic double-speak usually got her to ask questions, but today wasn't a day for questions. He was handing her a soul magic tool, so he probably meant souls. She was going to take it at face value, and get the job done. She could worry about subtext when people weren't dying.

He pulled away, and then spoke to both her and Derek. "Go. Find the people who did this and bring them to me."

Because he would want to be the law here, and the Soul Charmer was a far bigger threat than any police officer she'd encountered.

At least they had rules, ethics.

The Charmer had none.

CHAPTER SIXTEEN

One of the downsides to taking Callie's car in lieu of Derek's motorcycle was it allowed for more conversation. It wasn't that Callie didn't like talking to Derek. Quite the opposite, but when they were traveling somewhere it was usually to do something intrinsically dangerous and the quiet allowed for significant discussion of the lack of plan for said situation.

A Delgado family dinner definitely dropped into the dangerous column.

"The Charmer's eyes would pop from his skull if he knew we were going to my mom's house for dinner," Callie said, trying a fresh angle to avoid this dinner. She'd already lamented fatigue and feigned illness.

Derek lifted a shoulder in a half-hearted shrug. "He wouldn't be happy about you seeing Zara. Sure."

"No, he needs us finding the person targeting him." *I need to find the person who killed Cullen*, she added to herself, as if catching a murderer would absolve her guilt. Being back working with the underhanded sent her self-worth plummeting, and didn't do a damn thing to help her almost-empty bank account.

"Maybe we'll get a lead." Derek didn't even bother pretending this was a real argument. Wrinkles formed at the corners of his eyes as he tried to hold back a grin.

"Yeah, because Zara was so helpful last time. I think she threatened me instead of helping me. Or am I remembering that wrong?" She wasn't.

Derek's hands tightened on the steering wheel for a fraction of a second. When he loosened them, he said, "You need this."

"What? Delgado drama is not what I need." It was an inherited trait like her dark hair and her increased odds of alcoholism.

"If you're worrying about Josh, you aren't able to focus." Derek's requisite rumble softened and hewed until his words were more rasp than voice. "That's not a bad thing. While I don't think either of them deserves your time, you're fucking loyal. If spending an hour at Zara's place and eating a meal will ease that tickin' brain of yours, we should do it."

There he was, her Derek. More considerate than she deserved. She should probably thank him for the constant kindness. He was good about knowing what she needed and reminding her to take care of herself instead of everyone else first. She wasn't raised that way. Family first, but Derek was starting to convince her that doing what was best for herself put him in a better place, which was kind of like putting family first if you squinted.

All she said was, "Fine," but the undercurrent of "thank you" and "you're right" were pronounced enough that he replied, "You're welcome."

A few minutes later when she knocked on her mother's front door, Callie was almost excited. They hadn't had an outsider at a family dinner in years. Josh had brought a girl home once. He didn't do it again. Callie frowned, but then shook it off. If Derek could handle her brand of fucked up with fire and bad decisions and blood, then he could take Zara's bullshit for an hour. He was made of steel and rebar. He could withstand Zara's offensive guilt attack.

Callie shored up her own internal shield as the door opened.

Her mother was wearing bright summer colors and sheer fabric as though she was defying the November weather. She waved them in, silver rings clacking against the doorframe as she held it open for them. "You didn't say you were bringing someone," Zara said as way of greeting.

Instead of dwelling on the cutting way she referenced Derek, Callie focused on the simmering heat creeping into her fingertips as she stepped through the doorway. Great. Her mom was still using soul magic. Even with Tess gone, her mom had found a way to escape her guilt or get high or whatever by borrowing another's soul. Guess she hadn't paid attention the last time Callie warned her against it. Maybe that was her job in this family. Callie was the foreboding one. The mother hen. The one who warned them against the coming consequences. The protector. They all ignored her like she was the weatherman predicting rain on a Saturday.

"I didn't tell you I was coming either, but you still expected me." Callie said as she rushed into the living room, putting necessary space between her and Zara. Heat blazed brighter in her palms as she passed her mother. At least it was only a single bonus soul her mom was toting and not a pack of them. Damn it. She wasn't trying to start this dinner being the bitch. She quickly added, "This is Derek."

Derek stayed close behind her. She was grateful for his calming presence. Only that innate "I've got your back" warmth kept her from darting a panicked look backward.

"That guy is with her all the time, Mom. Practically lives with her." Josh appeared in the adjoining kitchen a moment after his words. He was eating a candy bar. Callie wasn't going to let Josh shame her, and, really, all she could think was 'at least he's eating again.'

Derek spared her the need to bicker. "What are we having?"

Zara closed the door and moved toward the kitchen. Callie took an involuntary step back, and Derek edged between her and her mother. Zara glared at them. "Quit being melodramatic. Today is about Josh," Zara muttered to Callie.

Then she answered Derek, "Tamales."

"Pork or beef?"

Zara paused, reassessing him. "Pork."

Derek's pleased grunt was genuine and translated well to everyone in the room.

They followed Zara into the kitchen, where she busied herself at the counter moving the husked deliciousness from a pan to a long silver plate. It was rounded, shiny, and a new acquisition. It was too big to be something her mom pocketed, so she must have fuzzed a tourist recently to have cash for it.

Callie didn't call Zara out. There wasn't a point, and somehow in this household the Delgado "family first" mantra had morphed from care and welfare tasks into keeping secrets, occasional abetting, and a fuckton of looking the other way.

Derek, though, didn't know these rules. Hell, he probably didn't know there was a story and a mark and a sad man going back broke to his wife in Pueblo behind that dish. "Is that one of those plates they make out of sand at that factory at the edge of town?"

Funny how the fancy shit was always crafted in industrial complexes next to body shops and junkyards. That's how they made all the money, Callie guessed.

He was clearly trying to make conversation, but Zara shot Callie a glare that scorched more than her soul sensing hands had all day. "I think so. Found it at the outlet in Pojoaque," her mother answered the question and made it almost believable because—as she so often preached—holding a good face can get you through anything. Callie'd rather look perpetually pissed and avoid the kind of confrontation Zara's skills demanded.

Callie grabbed a couple beers from the refrigerator,

popped the caps, and handed one to Derek. She took a drink from the other.

Conversation continued stilted and awkward as Zara put the finishing touches on the rice. Callie and Derek stood near the china cabinet. It held a mish mash of plates collected over the years. All antique, none of it ever used in this house. Zara liked the way it looked though. Josh cuddled Zara's cat in his lap, and Frankie's purring ruminated throughout the small kitchen and dining space. He sat at the table, which had been set for three, but had four chairs.

"You guys working on anything cool?" Josh asked as if he was in the loop on her gig with the Soul Charmer. All her brother knew was Callie reacted to people who had rented souls and that she worked with the Charmer at night. He didn't know about capturing souls that were due back to the soul emporium.

His attempt to dig into what was happening with the Soul Charmer ground against her back teeth. "Nothing you need to get involved with," she said with the protective tone that Derek had mentioned on more than one occasion should have come from the older sibling.

Josh slunk back into his chair. His gaze turned to the cat, who he was petting with more focus now. "You don't have to be a—"

"Actually, maybe you can help us." Derek cut him off with polite diversion. Why couldn't she have considered redirecting the conversation? Oh, right, because family had a way of getting under your skin and regressing your brain back a decade.

"Whatcha need, boss?" That easy canter returned

to Josh's voice. The slick act was the same one that worked on their mother. Callie's ears buzzed upon hearing it leveraged on her lover, but she kept her mouth shut.

A pan clattered against the cooktop across the room. Zara didn't say anything, either, though.

"We're looking for this guy, but one of our guys could only remember his name as Gee or Dee. Any ideas?" Derek's normal gravel-spit tone had been replaced with the smooth, steady ride of fresh asphalt. The power in his inflection shifted to the mid tone. So much strength in such simple words.

The pilot light blazed within Callie's center in seconds. Why would her brother know someone associated with Cullen's death? Why should Derek even think Josh would know these kinds of people? Her brother wasn't involved. That fire, though, never reached her lips. Maybe it was the even keel Derek applied to his words, or the light touch of his palm against her thigh—a private quell for the anger he'd known would flash through her.

Josh cocked his head. He wasn't looking to where Callie and Derek connected. Hell, he wasn't looking at his baby sister at all. He was doing that inward search thing that made his brows pinch and his lips twist. A moment later he said, "You mean Little D?"

"Well, that's an unfortunate name." Zara's snickering was apparent from across the room.

"Mom!" Callie chided.

"Well, it is. Who would want to proclaim such a

thing?" That was the real Zara. Not the one who shuffled to church twice a week. Or the one who worried about her son. The real Zara was the one who made dick jokes. In the midst of her children talking about *maybe* something criminal, but definitely something involving a man she had previously vowed her disdain for: The Soul Charmer of Gem City.

"Who's Little D?" Derek asked as if he hadn't heard the side exchange. The slight squeeze of her leg suggested otherwise.

Josh deliberately avoided looking at Callie. "He's been around for a few months. Helps out whenever needed. Good dude."

Helps out with drugs. Callie fought the urge to say so, because they were supposed to be here for a family dinner and calling out your newly sober brother for telling your boyfriend about his drug hookups was probably a party foul.

"Right." Derek scratched at the stubble peaking at his chin. "He a lanky…guy?"

Should she bother telling Derek that her mom wasn't going to care if he swore? Nah. He was doing his best to get info and pull off the meet-the-family thing. The less she corrected shit, the better.

"Yeah, yeah. He hangs out with Horan's crew by that open parking lot near the plaza." Josh returned to looking at the cat. Because that lot was the easiest place to find meth in the whole city. *She'd* never done it, but even without Josh, she would have known that was the place to score.

"Thanks, man," Derek said. The double squeeze he gave her leg then suggested maybe this was actually useful. She was glad, because watching them talk stressed her the fuck out.

"So I hear you have news, bro, what's up?" Callie redirected the conversation to her brother, because she knew how to talk to him without getting drenched in guilt or having anger corkscrew through her.

He grinned wide. All teeth and dimples and wonder. "I got a job today."

"That's awesome," Callie said automatically, though her brain stuttered. She wanted to be excited for him, but this dinner was requested damn early. He couldn't have gotten a job before six in the morning. Maybe he had interviewed yesterday?

"What's the job?" Derek asked with zero inflection. He used this voice on his first go at defaulting soul renters. So she wasn't the only one thinking this sounded sketchy.

The beaming joy on Josh's face didn't falter. "Construction. It'll be hard work, but it'll be good for me. You know? Callie tell you I used to build stuff?"

"You built a spice rack once." Her lips tugged at her, the desire to smile, to enjoy this beginning to fill her.

"It was a damn nice spice rack, though, right?" He laughed, because it had actually been a tiny spice rack.

"Do you still have it?" Derek asked Zara.

"What? No. What do I need a spice rack for? Fresh herbs only in this house," Callie's mother said.

"She means she never cooks unless I beg her," Josh said, conspiratorially.

Zara snapped a kitchen towel at him, and Callie sucked in hard at the pang of jealousy flicking against her temples. They'd always been like this. Playful and smiling. She'd never had that with Zara. She'd never be the favorite. Hell, even the cat liked Josh more than her and she'd rescued the damn thing.

Derek's palm found the hollow of Callie's lower back. He didn't move it at all, and the others couldn't see it, but he pressed hard enough to remind her she was grounded. If Josh and Zara had roots together, he could still be here for her. She wasn't alone. It didn't stop the irritation of jealousy from snapping at her, but it nudged her away from fixating on what she didn't have. Maybe that was enough.

"If your sister hadn't been keeping you locked up, I would have had reason to cook sooner," Zara said.

Callie bit her lip. Thanks, Mom.

"Are you two going to sit down or what?" Zara asked, and Callie had to admit it would have been rude in another situation. She just hadn't planned how to actually sit at a table next to two soul magic users and be able to actually use utensils.

A tiny part of her prayed that if she sat equal distances between Zara and Josh that her bonus soul and his slightly shredded one would even out, but she'd been in enough public places to know it didn't work that way. Her skin flared between the two and it was worse.

"Remember me telling you I couldn't get too close to people who rent souls?" Callie was trying to dance around their last encounter, which involved lots of screaming on Zara's end and a door slammed to punctuate the whole ordeal.

Zara rolled her eyes. "You've been hanging out with your woo-woo cousin too much. You're not magical."

Zara waved her hands to exaggerate how "nonmagical" she found Callie. Her mother then took a couple steps toward them, and stood next to Josh's chair, before continuing, "No one here is renting souls."

"I can feel it, Mom," Callie said plainly. The mild heat in her palms wasn't visible, though.

"Today is about Josh. Why are you ruining it by accusing your family of being tainted? And in front of a stranger. That's not how you rise to Heaven."

"He's not a stranger. Just because you haven't met him doesn't make him a stranger to everyone else."

Callie's mouth was open and ready to continue mounting that high horse, but her mother rushed forward until her nose could have brushed Callie's chin. "You know better than that, Calliope. Delgados come first, and no matter what he isn't one of us. You need to be focusing on your family instead of adding to the tally of sins you need to confess for. The number of sins that involved you with your pants off has to have reached the double digits at this point."

Callie had never been a violent person. Even as a kid, she'd preferred to stay hidden rather than take consequences head-on, and in her neighborhood and her home that typically meant she avoided getting the shit kicked out of her.

She was different now, though. It wasn't a good thing. Fuck, there was no question the boiling rage choking her now was a bad sign. The rope whipping flaming loops around her brain was far more painful than the simmering heat in her palms. Her mother had a single rented soul in her body, and, while uncomfortable, the heat in Callie's palms was bearable. The urge to slap her mother across her face, though? That was another story.

Callie was above hitting her mother. Trying to shame her for sex was a cheap shot, but it worked in its way.

"I told you the extra soul in your body was a problem for me. Why are you in my face?" The ice-cold tone should have warned Zara that bad shit was about to go down. Deadpan Delgado always equaled pure rage or retribution on the horizon.

Callie took three swigs from her beer. The bottle was heated in her hand.

"And I told you that you were full of shit with that magic stuff. We don't believe in magic in this house. You pray. You repent. You rise. You've always wanted to ruin everything for everyone else in this family. It isn't about you."

"Couldn't agree more," Callie muttered. She slammed the open mouth of the beer bottle against Zara's sternum and sent out a silent call for anything or anyone that didn't belong to hop on out.

Callie watched the iridescent light stream into brown glass. The way the wicked grin on her mother's face fell as the rented soul was sucked from her brought Callie a cruel kind of joy that she would be haunted and disgusted by for years to come.

Zara staggered back. She wasn't injured. Callie could feel her mother's tattered soul still buried within Zara's chest. Her fingers didn't freeze this time, though, because the bottle was burning. The glass glowed with red undertones. Flames burst from Callie's palm and forearm. The bottle shattered. The beer that was left sizzled as it sprayed on to Callie, the glass littered the floor, and the soul inside sought refuge.

It was a live wire snapping forward toward Zara and then backward again in Callie's direction. It coiled around her leg, like a snake inching up a small tree in the name of meatier prey. Where it moved, sparks followed. Callie's legs locked. Fuck. She had not thought this through. This was the kind of consequence that she couldn't dodge. This was immediate comeuppance, and it was brutal.

Callie was locked in a pillar of fire and fear. Her legs were solid, but her brain was certain her bones had gone liquid and were pooling on the linoleum floor. Her fingers were black beneath the flames, and were set in an awkward claw curl. Like she were a wicked witch offering an apple and not an apprentice soul magician losing her fucking shit all over her mom's kitchen.

Derek grunted and hissed to her right. She couldn't turn her head to look at him. The soul etching up over her hip had her attention. If she stopped denying it for a moment, she feared it'd find a way into her body. She was a one-soul type of woman.

Derek moved in front of her and carefully dropped the flask—her flask—into her charred and gnarled hand. He tapped out the flames that leapt to his forearm. The acrid scent of burning hair began to overwhelm her. It wasn't hers. The onyx inlay of the flask began to suck some of the heat from her hand. Not enough to remove the flames all together, but enough to give her a tiny bit of dexterity.

She tilted the opening of the flask toward herself, and then called out to the soul. "In here. You will be safe. I can find you a home." She couldn't be certain if she'd spoken aloud or if she was simply thinking really hard, but the soul zipped across her stomach, up between her breasts, down her right arm and straight into the flask. Once the soul was inside, the flames disappeared and Callie's skin returned to the soft, healthy tone it was supposed to be.

CHAPTER SEVENTEEN

Wielding a beer bottle as a weapon before the meal was even served was fucked up, even for Callie's family. The immolation and magic that followed only served to further sear the event in everyone's memories. At least Callie didn't have to worry about accusations she was faking reactions from her mom anymore. The blotchy color on Zara's cheeks made that one clear.

It's difficult to sit down for tamales after a forceful soul extraction from your mother. The masa and pork would have smelled amazing, but Callie's nostrils still held the echo of sulfur and singed skin. She cracked the window in her car, as Derek drove them away from Zara Delgado's house. The crisp air couldn't cut that olfactory memory.

A band of white had risen around Callie's wrist. She hadn't noticed it until they entered the car. It'd puckered and crusted like a barely toasted marshmallow, but it didn't hurt. She ran her thumb over it, and found the skin smooth. She tugged her sleeve down to cover it. Weird inch-wide rings on her wrists were more than she could handle right now.

"What now?" Derek had done a good job pretending Callie hadn't lost her mind. He hadn't flinched when he escorted her out of the house with a distracted wave toward her family. His arms had been steel bands holding her upright and steady. Her legs worked fine. Her skin was back to normal outside the stripe she was ignoring, but her heart was squeezed so tight it was certain to implode. The guilt poured over her with the thickness of shimmering oil. The spatter was in her mind, but it didn't sting any less. She'd attacked her mother. She'd used soul magic. She'd brandished a fucking beer bottle like an asshole in some shit bar who had too much to drink and too little sense. She wasn't supposed to be one of those people. She'd gotten out. She'd gone straight. She was honest and upright and a protector. What kind of person does that to family? Maybe there was a reason Zara liked her least. Josh had stolen her television in the past, but he'd never sucked a soul out of her body. On the scale of things to steal, elusive and surreal energy stored behind one's sternum was probably more invasive than the device used to watch sitcoms. Though, they could cost about the same. So, there was that.

Derek's arm rested heavy on her shoulders. Solid and real and a steady lifeline of body heat. No fire. No anger. Just consistent presence. His hand curled around her far shoulder, and he gave her a little tug toward him. Not enough to move her, but enough to make her feel wanted.

"You okay?" His voice was gentle, but he wasn't good at hiding his worry from her right now.

She wasn't, but he'd known that tonight would haunt her. He'd seen just enough of her scars to know she could wear guilt better than most. She nodded, though, to acknowledge she'd heard what he was actually saying.

He pulled to a stop at the next intersection. Traffic was minimal, with no one behind them. "What do you want to do next?"

"Bury myself in a hole?"

"Not an option. Try again."

"I could use several days in bed. You could join. Does that work?"

"Tempting, but no hiding." He wouldn't shame her. He wouldn't hold what he'd seen for use in a future fight.

The fact he was asking her what she wanted was big. Derek liked to set the schedule. Sharing it said so much. They had so many obligations hanging over them, and Callie had a feeling the Soul Charmer's pressure on Derek was greater than she'd seen. He'd been popping off on tasks every other day. The Charmer had to be squeezing him for *something*. "I'm not ready to see the Soul Charmer. I've got questions, but…"

"But you don't need him digging into your heart right now?"

"Exactly."

"Are you up for tracking down Little D, then?" He flipped on the turn signal indicating his intention to head toward the Plaza.

"Yeah, but that name really is shitty." Her attempt at humor was shaky, but it eased some of the tension between her shoulder blades.

"People never get to pick their own nicknames." Derek hit the gas and they were on their way to finding out who had killed Cullen.

"Did anyone ever give you a nickname?" She almost smiled. Focusing on a problem to solve and on the man next to her made it a whole lot easier to shove her stack of guilt to the back of her brain. It wouldn't wait on that shelf forever, but if she could get an hour or two before being bowled over by regret, she'd take it.

"If they did, I wouldn't tell you," Derek said.

"Why not?"

"Because no one picks their own nicknames. It sucks. Why, did you have a good one?"

"I had a teacher who called me Delgado."

"That doesn't count. That's your actual name."

"Are you really going to hold out on me? You saw a whole lot of embarrassing awful shit on my end today." She played it like a joke, but that spike of truth beneath the words rang loudly.

He grumbled, low and throaty, but then with a similar rasp said, "Short stack."

"What?" Callie eked between bursts of laughter. She needed it. She let the humor fill her lungs until they pressed hard against her ribs. The ache was welcome.

He scratched at a nonexistent itch at his temple, but still answered her. "I went through a pancake phase when I was eight. It's all I would eat."

"Pancakes, that's it?"

"Well, at the time I hadn't had my growth spurt, so I was short and stocky. Mom's little short stack." He rolled his eyes, and Callie laughed more.

"I can't picture you as a short stack, but I can make pancakes some morning."

"No. I burned out on them. Cereal's just fine, doll."

"It's been decades. How are you still sick of pancakes?"

He offered her a half smile and a partial shrug. Fair enough.

The lampposts on each side of the street started to shrink from freeway-style arcing lights into iron posts. Buildings grew closer and closer with each block they passed until the adobe between one home and the neighboring storefront blended in the diffused light. They'd be at the plaza soon, and the realization she was going to have to get shit done hit Callie again. That adrenaline pickup squeezed her lungs, but also nixed the lingering guilt apnea.

She didn't know how she was going to fix her relationship with her mother—or if she even *wanted* to—or how she was going to smooth the inevitable rough words with Josh, but finding the people who killed Cullen and left him for Derek and her to deal with? That she could and would do.

"What do you know about this Little D?" she asked. She didn't even snicker about the asshole's nickname this time.

"Low-level drug dealer as far as I knew."

"Guess he branched out."

"Guess so." Callie didn't know one way or another, but if this guy had gone to Jerrod to find people desperate enough to rent souls from a hack, he was doing it for a reason. That reason was probably cash. Or drugs. Either way, she doubted his loyalty. Anyone cold enough to kill a kid didn't have moral high ground.

"You think he's still selling on the plaza if he's moved up to hit jobs?" Callie was surprised how much vitriol had leaked into her voice. There was a tiny pocket of her brain that ached for retribution when she saw such atrocities. In the past she'd reserved those feelings for protecting Josh, and her cousins, and her aunt. She'd seen the ghastly shift of Derek's face the night they'd found Cullen's body, though. That was what she needed reparations for.

Derek inclined his head. "Cash is cash."

She guessed that was true. Desperate people do desperate things. "It had to pay better, though. Why else would he do it?"

Derek's lungs may have been laden with lava rocks for the slick, heavy, rattle beneath the sigh he offered in response.

"Sorry," she muttered out of habit instead of real emotion. She was sorry a kid was dead, she was sorry they were the ones who had to deal with it, but she wasn't really sorry for trying to understand how it'd happened.

She understood better than most that there often wasn't an easy answer as to the why of it all. Shitty things happened. To good people. To bad people. Shit was not discriminating between those rising to Heaven and those lingering below despite what Father Domingo wanted her to believe. The universe gave zero fucks when it came to meting out the awful. So, yeah, there probably wasn't a good answer as to why Cullen was dead. There was no such thing as an honorable death, especially not among teenagers. Even finding the man who did it, or the one who orchestrated the kill, wasn't going to change the fact a boy was dead and she and Derek would be forever scarred for having been a part of the tale.

"Mhm," was all Derek said, but his shoulders sagged and his hips slid forward on the seat a smidge. He was doing his best to hold it together, too. His knuckles were gilded in a flash of golden streetlight through the windshield. Maybe wearing your scars on the outside did a better job of concealing when your insides were breaking at the seams. She'd done shoddy patchwork to keep her darkness, her fears on her inside—the holes and tears covered with the emotional equivalent of red twine and grit.

This time it was her turn to reach out to him. She brushed the backs of her soft knuckles against his jaw.

The rasp of his scruff against her skin filled the car for a half-second, and they both let the tension ease at the sound.

"We're almost there," she said, her voice low.

"You wish we weren't, doll?" His husky laugh sent a delicious plunge of heat through Callie. The kind of heat that made her forget what souls could do to her body, because her mind was flitting to the things Derek could do to it instead.

Her response was unintelligible, but a definitive yes. Derek's arm was still around her shoulders. He parked the car a few feet away from a lamppost, and then pulled her closer.

Derek groaned, and it wasn't the rasp or the grated gravel grunt he'd used in public with others, it was a call of pure pain and stunted purpose. "Woman, you wreck my brain."

She walked her fingers from the line of his jaw down the side of his neck to tug the edge of his black tee away from his collarbone. Callie leaned in and kissed the newly exposed skin. She pulled in a long breath filled with the signature Derek scent of crisp soap and worn leather. "Pretty sure it's not your brain that made that sound."

"Fuck." Derek slid his hand from her right shoulder up to the nape of her neck and pulled Callie in hard and fast for a matching kiss.

Callie kept herself from clamoring into Derek's lap. They were downtown in tourist season—fuck when wasn't it?—and almost under a spotlight. Her lips parted automatically, though, and the heat and desire coursing through her combusted when Derek's tongue met hers.

Their kiss lasted less than a minute, but both were panting when they pulled apart. Callie's forehead was dappled with sweat, and she was pretty damn sure the rest of her body was in a similar state.

"We can't do this right now," she said in a rush. Her brain restarted and already backfilling with guilt.

He pulled her close again for another, brief, scorching kiss.

"Disagree," he said against her lips.

Her hands were twisting his tee shirt. She released the fabric and pressed her palms against his chest. She pushed herself away. "Not now."

He didn't argue or try to pull her close again, though his lips remained parted as though he was imagining putting them back against her body. "What do you need?"

"This will feel great."

"Amazing," he corrected.

"Yes. That. But I'm not going to sleep tonight thinking about all the shit we haven't solved." The crushing anxiety from what happened at Zara's house was unavoidable, but she couldn't do anything about that part.

"You don't want to go back to the Soul Charmer without more info." Derek didn't pose it as a question. He was right.

"That, too. We can't keep going on without him making a strong front. The sooner he can stop this person, the less kids die, the less what-the-fuckery you and I are involved in."

"Shit ain't going to get easy just because the Charmer gets his pound of flesh."

"Maybe not," Callie admitted. "But I'm sure a lot more comfortable with him teaching me how to use soul magic when he's not amped up to tear down the world."

"True enough."

Derek looked her up and down, lingering on her chest long enough that that familiar rush of heat crept up her neck. "Later." She was ninety percent sure he said this to her boobs, but they were on board so she didn't call him on it.

"Yes. Definitely. Later."

He sighed. "Let's find Little D, get some fucking answers, and get back to the part where I make you naked."

"It's probably good that the Charmer doesn't know how motivated you are by a pair of breasts."

"They are fucking nice breasts."

Callie was still laughing when they got out of the car, after she'd bundled up tight against the November wind, and after Derek threw an arm around her.

Her smile vanished when the parking lot came into sight. She could guess who Little D was, because standing next to him was Ford's No. 2 guy: Nate.

CHAPTER EIGHTEEN

"**Y**ou taking me up on my offer, Callie girl?" Nate chimed from across the lot.

His cheek bore pockmarks that were more obvious in the artificial glow of the nearby street light. Callie tried to focus on Nate's skin blemishes instead of her failure to tell Derek about this. He had enough to worry about, she'd told herself. Now, though, his fingers tightened on her shoulder, and the pool of fuck-my-life welling nearby was ready to crash over her head.

"Hardly." She edged back into Derek's arm as she said it. He only squeezed her tighter.

Derek side-eyed Nate in a way that suggested both that he wanted to crush the guy's skull and that he wanted to know what kind of proposition exactly Nate had made to Callie. He remained silent, though his arm stayed protectively wrapped around her. Callie took it as a modicum of trust she probably hadn't earned.

At least she wasn't going to have to talk through this one in public. Or maybe that kiss in the car was still scorching his brain. Either way, she was going to have to dance quickly to avoid getting pulled into the sinkhole of Ford's goons' nastiness.

"Ouch. You looking for me for another reason?" Nate waggled his eyebrows like a cartoon character who had never met a girl in real life.

"Stop talking." Iron met steel in Derek's voice, and the resulting clash was directed at Nate. Yep. They were definitely going to review that whole *proposition* thing later.

Nate puffed his chest and tilted his chin up. His attempt to hide his fear failed, but he shut up.

"We are here for him." Derek pointed at the short, stout kid standing next to Nate.

"Me?" The kid's voice squeaked. Fucking squeaked. Callie wasn't confident he'd actually gone through puberty.

Little D wore a coat three sizes too big for him, which was impressive given the width of his shoulders. He could probably give Derek a run for his money on shoulders, but where Callie's lover's shoulders were part of an overall tall, hulking, linebacker, gonna-fuck-you-up package of pure muscle, Little D's frame was more like he'd been squashed down. He wasn't much taller than Callie, but he was broad with wide hips and a wide stance. Little D was shaped like a box of pre-made oatmeal. Square, but probably squishy.

"You Little D?" Derek's question was a dare built

on a backbone of a threat.

The drug dealer and possible hit man didn't bother lying. "I'm Little D. What do you want with me?"

Nate smirked, and it didn't have anything to do with the disastrous nickname being bandied back and forth. "You need a hook up to get through bullshit with your boss?"

Callie shot him a dark look.

Nate continued like he hadn't seen her reaction, "I get it. Your friend Ford wants to help you out."

She was not playing these games. Not now, not here. Nate didn't have the upper hand anymore. He wasn't blocking her exit. He wasn't in charge. She could take a couple steps toward him and let her hands shift temperature to match his soul status. She could burn him with ice or fire. She could step out of the way and let Derek break his nose. She had options, and she wasn't going to squander them.

"I told you Ford isn't my friend. *You* aren't my friend, and I'm pretty sure he just told you that we weren't here for you at all."

Nate held his hands up in faux supplication. "Kitty's got claws."

Derek twisted his hips toward Callie and thrust the arm not holding her out, up, and into Nate's stomach. It wasn't Derek's real punch, but Nate doubled over and sucked in air with heaping gasps that echoed through the open lot.

"You leaving?" Derek asked.

Nate remained bent over. "I'll leave for now. Got to get to church, find some answers for my boss since you assholes won't help."

Callie mouthed, *Church?* Because of all the people she expected to seek their truth in the walls of a Cortean Catholic Church, Nate was less likely to plant his ass in those pews than she and the Soul Charmer combined. Derek held his stoic stance, but his lips tightened. Little D watched all this with wide eyes and parted lips. He may well have sunken into the concrete for how little he moved. If he hadn't been standing there, she could have asked about the church to be sure that Derek wasn't reading more into the comment. As it was, she needed to get her mind back on Cullen and ignore the mobster who cradled his stomach as he shuffled away down the block.

"Now. You." Callie tried to match Derek's badass tone as she addressed Little D, but it was the fact Derek had just punched Ford's No. 2 guy in public that kept Little D on his toes.

Their target swallowed hard. "Yeah?"

"Do you know who we work for?" she asked. Little D wasn't much younger than Callie, but somehow standing near him she aged.

"Not for that guy."

Callie almost smiled.

"The Soul Charmer," Derek said.

"Oh," Little D mumbled. Callie and Derek gave him a moment to process this. He looked to the edges of the parking lot. The others who used this lot as home base for slinging illegal goods had scattered. When he finally realized he was alone, he said, "Does the Soul Charmer need smack or meth or something? I could probably get some ganja if we needed."

What. The. Hell.

Callie said, "What?" the same time Derek said, "The Charmer doesn't need your drugs."

"Oh. So, um, how can I help you or whatever?" He grinned and plied a customer-service voice.

Seriously? He hadn't flinched at the Soul Charmer's name more than anyone else on the street would. Did they have the wrong guy? He'd thought they'd wanted to score. Maybe the tip had been wrong. Maybe there was more than one Little D? Callie's hesitation left the lot in a lull. The hum of the light bulb overhead, the whizzing of cars on the nearby street, distant laughter from an open door of one of the taquerias filled the air between the three of them.

Derek took the lead. "How do you know Nate?"

"Him? He's a supplier."

Drugs. Right. Of course Ford and his crew did more than threaten women like her and leave bloodstains to be shown on the 10 o'clock news. They had to make money on the backs of addicts citywide. Lovely.

"You ever do other work for him?"

Little D shrugged. "I do what they tell me, man."

The guy was a foot soldier and didn't have a single bit of shame over it. What would it be like to not feel everything? Callie shook off the thought. That's how addicts happened: the desire to not feel anything instead of solving problems. Her life might be shit, but she was clawing out of it on her own terms. Her brother was safe, she paid her bills the legal way, and having Derek at her side was an unexpected delight. Each day she'd regain a little more ground. What Little D sold wouldn't help her. Or anyone.

Callie's emotions were too frayed to let this run on any longer. She had to cut to the chase. "You know a kid named Cullen?"

Callie had thought Little D had locked up when they'd dealt with Nate. That wasn't true, though, because now the guy had turned into a living statue. His shoulders and chest barely moved with breath. His hands were buried in his pockets, but his jacket didn't shift. His eyes moved, though. His gaze darted from Derek's hard edges to Callie's widened stance.

Derek dropped his arm from around Callie, and took a step forward to put him within arm's reach of Little D. The kid wasn't about to run. Apparent fear had quite possibly turned the guy's legs to lead, but that didn't mean he was being helpful.

"Well?" a barrel-aged, smooth, deep nudge from Derek hit the dealer like a slap.

Little D flinched, but his body remained within striking distance. Brave or stupid, this guy. "Maybe."

"Maybe's not going to cut it."

Little D's nostrils flared and his mouth opened and closed damn near a dozen times. He knew.

He knew Cullen.

He knew Callie and Derek knew he knew Cullen.

And he knew he had one chance to get this right.

His answer was a torrent of truth and bullshit justification. "I didn't know he was protected or whatever. I just needed the cash. My mom, she's like sick, and I need to move up with the guys and I can't do that if I don't take on the other jobs. You can't get more work if you don't try new shit and I had to—"

"Did you just refer to what you did to Cullen as 'new shit' you were 'trying' to get a promotion?" Callie was out. No more need to play nice. No more thinking of Little D as a kid. This drug dealer could get fucked.

"It wasn't like that," he stammered.

"You did it then?" Derek asked. "Took out Cullen?"

It was the closest Callie had heard Derek get to saying Cullen was murdered. The closest he'd come to talking real crime outside the sanctity of her bedroom or the car. His voice was steady and his breathing even, but Derek was not okay. The miasma of ire coalescing around him pressed against both her heart and soul magic sense. The latter sensing the ache in his soul. Or maybe her heart was making that shit up. Either way, getting these answers hurt. Big time. Sharp. This needed to be a quick cut to their souls instead of a drawn out twist of a conversation.

"I had to, but I swear I didn't know it had anything to do with the Charmer. They didn't tell me that."

"What exactly did they tell you?" Callie spat.

"He needed to go. I was supposed to take him to

this alley and cut him with this little silver knife they gave me."

"Do you still have the knife?" Derek asked.

"No. The handle was like a weed cache, and they said it had something valuable in it and I had to give it back. So I did."

"Who paid you to do this?"

Confusion clouded Little D's expression. He jerked a thumb toward the street Nate had disappeared down. "Nate said it was for Ford."

"Fuck," Derek said mostly to himself. His chest rumbled deep and dissatisfied, but he reined it in. To Little D he said, "Nate tell you why you were going after a kid?"

At least Little D had the good sense to look ashamed. "He said he needed to send a message. Cullen used to buy molly from me pretty regularly. I learned he'd switched dealers and figured he'd moved on to new friends or something. That shit is cutthroat."

"And you thought killing a kid for buying molly from someone else was legit?" Callie's incredulity stretched to reach the tops of the nearby buildings.

"I…."

"Didn't think. Yeah. Got that." Callie couldn't look at him anymore. She stared instead at the meter box to pay for parking. The right side had a fresh 505 tag on it. The city would power wash it before the tourists got a taste of the shitty artwork.

Derek remained focused. "Ford ask you to do anything else?"

"No. Just slinging his new smack."

So he hadn't been a party to the knife they'd received. That was something.

"You want to make shit square with the Soul Charmer?" Derek asked.

"Hell yes."

"Good. Nate probably put it together that we know what you did. Your safest place is with us. You're done slinging for the night. Time for you to meet the Soul Charmer."

"What?"

Callie wanted to echo the objection. The Charmer wasn't a nice guy to anyone not flexing cash before him. Whatever it was going to take to make Little D square with him wasn't going to be pretty, and Callie certainly didn't want to be involved. Finding the fucker should be enough, she told herself, but she doubted the Charmer would see it that way.

"This is your only option, D." Derek sounded downright reasonable. If it weren't for the vein popping along the side of his neck, she might have believed that was truly the case.

Little D believed him, though, and within minutes the three of them were in Callie's car driving the narrow streets to the darkened lane near the Soul Charmer's storefront.

"Doll, why don't you keep the car running? I'll take him in and be back in a few." Whatever was going to happen inside the shop, Derek didn't want her to see it.

She remembered her interrogation of Tess. She couldn't handle burning anyone like that again. Not now. She wasn't steady enough to ask any useful questions at this point anyway. "What," "why," and "how could you?" probably didn't get the job done. She nodded in agreement.

Seventeen minutes later Derek returned.

Alone.

He didn't tell her what happened inside. She didn't ask.

He grabbed her hand. "Let's get out of here."

CHAPTER NINETEEN

erek's hands were heavy on Callie's hips as he urged her up the stairs to her apartment. They'd made the drive from the Soul Charmer's store in record time. Speed limits were for people whose lives were normal. Breaking a little traffic law wasn't a big deal when one had just interacted with a man who had so little heart that he hadn't been rocked with guilt in admitting he'd killed someone. Knowing people like that existed was wholly different than being faced with them. Having to talk with them and leverage what they know for a bigger, badder fish? Yeah, she and Derek needed out of the Charmer's view.

Callie's hand shook as she tried to insert her key in the front door. Derek took the key from her, unlocked the door, and then pushed it open. She stepped in first, and immediately missed the steady grip of his hands. She was afloat in a sea of guilt and fear with fucking frustrating rage simmering a foot below the surface. She glanced toward the couch. Empty. Thank God. She was full up on problems and having to deal with Josh now was not an option.

Derek closed the door. "We alone?"

"I think so." Callie checked to make sure the bathroom was empty, too. It was.

"Thank fuck."

"Right? I can't take one more conversation or interrogation or a second having to pretend this shit isn't fucking me up. It isn't just me, is it?" She hadn't meant to unload at all. Derek had been radiating tension for days, and it wasn't merely Callie's energy rubbing off on him.

He tossed his jacket on the near arm of the couch. Somehow his shoulders became broader outside of the leather confines. Derek stalked forward to meet Callie next to the kitchen counter. He stood only an inch, maybe two, away from her. He tilted his head to look straight down and meet her gaze. He was breathing fast; his chest almost grazed hers each time he inhaled. Was he touching her? She wasn't certain. Her heartbeat double-timed it, and her legs were threatening to go liquid. No, he wasn't touching her. He glowered at her, all clenched jaw and upper lip twitching like he was about to start a fight. The real kind. The emotionally driven, dozen blows when one will do kind. That kind of look should have scared her. His usual ominous scowl set others' teeth on edge. She had no intention of running. Sweat dappled her skin. Her shirt was too tight. Too warm. Too much. The air between them was electric, but Callie was ready to be shocked. She needed the zap of pain. Something to blind her from the shit storm swirling in her general region of late.

Another storm was forming. The thunder rumbling from Derek's chest was the precursor to the havoc about to hit. He licked his lips. It was a quick act, but Callie replayed it in slow motion in her mind.

"You ready to turn off your brain?" he asked.

Her body was electric, but her throat refused to work. She nodded once.

The bit of space between them was annihilated. He grabbed her hips and pulled her against him. He was on her. Hard muscles and seeking hands. Her palms found his chest. Her fingers curled around the neckline of his tee shirt. She tugged it down far enough that she could kiss below his collarbone. She shifted up on to the balls of her feet, stretching, reaching, and licked up to his neck until their height difference stopped her. The salt on his skin only made her thirsty for more.

He tugged his shirt off and threw it behind him. His lips found hers a split second later. He kissed her hard, and she matched the desperation behind it in kind. He slid his hands beneath the hem of her shirt to grab her sides. The power in his grip suggested he could lift her with a finger if he were so inclined. She parted her lips, and let her tongue seek his. Derek urged her backward with both his hands and his hips. The pressure against her stomach made it clear how much he needed this, too.

They fumbled their way through the short hallway. Callie's back collided with the bedroom door, and it pushed her more firmly into Derek. She nipped his lip. He hissed, and then pulled back for a second to turn the knob on the door. Callie took the moment to take off her shirt, and get a solid glimpse of Derek's abs. They were the kind of muscles people the world over would crave.

"Pink lace?" The question was wrenched from Derek like a final-word plea.

She'd actually forgotten about her bra. She rarely wore it because her wardrobe was black, black, and more black, but she'd had a feeling he'd like it. Sure enough. He grazed a thumb over the bra and right across her nipple.

Derek leaned back enough to make it apparent he wanted a better look. "Fuckin' see-through."

"Well, if I have my shirt off already, I probably am fine with anyone in the room seeing me naked." She cupped her hands around his upper arms and tugged.

He didn't resist. They practically fell into the bedroom. The soft breeze of the fan wasn't enough to cool Callie's skin. She and Derek were both gasping for breath already, and the sound covered the whirr of the fan. Pants, panties, and a pair of boxer briefs landed on the floor in rapid succession.

Callie edged toward the bed, but Derek stopped her at the edge. He slid one hand from the nape of her neck up into her hair. "Can I?" he whispered. The restraint in his voice hurt her. He needed something and was holding back. For her. He was good about putting her first, but right now, they both needed an explosion of sorts.

"Of course."

His left hand fisted her hair, and then his right gripped her hip and spun her to face the bed. He stepped close again so her back was against him. She arched at the pressure of his arousal against her rear, but his arms tightened. He leaned forward and kissed her shoulder and the side of her neck. His stubble scraped along the path, and the hint of pain, of friction was welcome. Her brain stalled out. All she could think of was Derek and the places where their bodies connected.

She tried to turn to kiss him again, but he only tightened his grip and pressed her more firmly against himself. A sharp sting of a yank on her hair centered her, held her in the moment. His teeth grazed the top of her shoulder, and she shivered. His right hand skated up from her hip to her breast. He wasn't gentle, but she didn't need him to be. He pulled and grabbed and tugged and shoved, and with each rough move her body became less real. She was *sensation*. She was *feeling*. She was no longer a woman with problems or drama or bullshit to handle. She was pure energy and decadent pleasure.

When he finally nudged her forward, she fell to her knees on the bed gratefully. Her skin was too tight, too much, again. She needed him. Needed freedom from everything except her body letting go.

The mind-numbing effects of sex lasted for more than the act. Thankfully. Callie and Derek lay side by side on the bed afterward and enjoyed the lack of conversation. It'd be a shitty thing to say aloud, but it was true. Not needing to talk. Not having anyone ask, order, or plead with you made it easier to relax, and this was the most relaxed Callie had been in weeks.

Callie turned onto her side to face Derek. The sheets clung to her legs, and she didn't bother trying to unwind them. She rested her cheek on his chest. It rose and fell at a slow, steady pace. Callie slipped an arm over his torso, and closed her eyes. She reveled in the quiet consistency. The room was still around her aside from the basic echoes of life between the two of them. Alone together. She inhaled against his skin. The clean, bright scent she associated with Derek now had a subtle layer of lavender woven through it. She'd intertwined with him in ways she hadn't with anyone in a long time. Though, he was certainly well versed in her subtle curves, this was more than their bodies. He knew her secrets. Not all of them, but some of the nasty ones. And he hadn't left. He was still next to her, breathing his giant breaths, and letting small, breathy rumbles escape his lips ever so often. A six-foot, brick-wall of a kitten she had beneath her. This time she did smile.

"Callie?" His voice rasped. Maybe they'd been more vocal than she'd realized. None of her neighbors had banged on the walls at least.

She didn't lift her head. "Hmm?"

"You good, doll?"

"Yeah. I'm actually pretty damn good right now."

His chuckle jostled her, but not enough for her to move off his chest.

"How about you?" she asked, because this wasn't only about her.

His chest paused beneath her, but a moment later he answered. "Better. I…"

The real world was about to crash into them. It wasn't fair to make him hold the dam against it by himself so she could nap naked on his chest for a few more minutes. Even if she really wanted to be that selfish. She told herself to relax. She ran her hand up and over Derek's chest. "What?" It was more a prompt than a question.

He shrugged beneath her. It reminded her how small she was, but also about how this was her chance to help him. Earning his trust wasn't easy, and she wasn't about to backslide.

She answered for him, because she understood. "You won't feel better until this is over. Until we know there won't be another body waiting for us the next time we go to drop off the flask."

His arms closed around her. "Pretty much. Ford's been a problem, but he isn't as easily handled as Tess was."

Callie flashed back to Tess bound to a metal chair in the basement beneath the Soul Charmer's shop, her skin melting as Callie's magic reacted to the woman's stockpile of souls. "I don't remember that as easy."

"She was one person. The people who worked for her weren't loyal. They didn't protect her."

"She wouldn't have let them."

"No, and Ford will use his minions like a wall

against the Charmer."

"What does he even want with poking at our creeper of a boss? What does he think he'll gain from that?"

Another big sigh from Derek. He held her close, and she had the distinct feeling he didn't want her to look at him right now. "Nate said he was going to church."

"And? Who doesn't go to Church around here?" She'd only been twice in the last six weeks, and only when Louisa dragged her along. Keeping face with the boss was worth the awkwardness for her.

"It's more than that. He mentioned wanting you to do work for him."

Callie's stomach bottomed out, and it had zero to do with being naked in bed with Derek. "He did."

"You want to elaborate, doll?"

Not really. "He wanted me to spy on the Soul Charmer."

Derek stilled.

"I obviously said no. I didn't think the two were related." She did now. "Fuck. I messed up, didn't I?"

Derek moved Callie off his chest and rolled to his side to face her. "No. Ford doesn't do soul magic. Why would you think it was anything more than him trying to get something on you again?"

"Last time he had Josh, not me."

"Having Josh is having you."

Callie's face flushed hot.

Derek quickly recovered. "He knows how to needle you. Makes sense, but he might actually be after something. I just don't know how much he knows or what he thinks he can do."

"Didn't that douchebag dealer say the knife was hollow?" The visual of the beer bottle exploding after she stuffed her mom's rented soul in it blasted her brain. The white band around her wrist was still there. She tucked her hand under the sheets behind her.

"Yeah. I don't know how that guy could be capable of taking a soul, though."

Shit shit shit. "We need to talk to the Charmer."

"He ain't going to be pleased with no action. We need to bring Nate in at least."

"No. I need to know why that knife worked and Little D didn't absorb the extra soul."

"What do you mean?"

"Every time I've run into a soul this week that wasn't in one of the Charmer's jars, a person, or my flask, it's been seeking the first open body—usually mine."

Derek's eyes widened like he was replaying the last few days over again with a new light. "Oh," was all he said, but those two little letters packed a whole lot of understanding.

She nodded. "I guess this means we have to get dressed, doesn't it?"

He kissed her forehead. "Yeah, but I won't bring up how we talked about the Charmer in bed again."

Callie squeezed her eyes shut in attempt to get that image out of her head. When she thought she'd succeeded, she opened her eyes to coat her corneas with the view of the hard planes of Derek's torso.

She spoke with the kind of hope she typically reserved for Josh's check-in day at rehab. "The sooner we do this, the sooner we can put this shit behind us."

She prayed she was right.

CHAPTER TWENTY

owntown Gem City was littered with pockets of darkness as the night waned. The low light, the men and women huddled in the alcoves in front of the closed shops for warmth, the sharp sting of wind cutting through narrow alleyways and up cobbled streets. All the splendor of the architecture and the vibrancy of the inlaid artwork on each building were scrubbed away.

Going to the Soul Charmer's storefront was never a pleasant experience, but added with the whirl of ominous energy of the 2 a.m. darkness it was legitimately creepy. They'd parked nearby, but Callie's stomach fell a little farther with each step they took toward the door. Icy gusts battered her face. She yanked the collar of her coat higher.

"Almost there," Derek said and stepped in front of her to act as a windbreak.

Almost done, she thought.

The chipped and peeling paint on the Charmer's door was barely noticeable. Derek pulled it open and held it wide for her to enter first. Touching the decrepit wood was the least of her worries right now, but she appreciated the gentlemanly act for what it was. Lamps offered small domes of light in two of the corners of the room. The incense tray on the counter was heaped with ashes, but the Charmer had burned the same Nag Champa for ages and so the stale scent clung to the walls. The same burgundy tapestries covered the windows as usual, but somehow everything looked older than before. Like the night had leeched the bits of life this room had held.

Derek rang the tarnished bell atop the counter. Callie quirked a brow at him. They never had called out like customers. Not together anyway. She'd only done it the once, and that was more than enough.

"He doesn't like late-night surprises." Derek's explanation did nothing for the heavy stone settling in Callie's stomach.

"Then he's going to love seeing us now without a flask full of his property," she said in a vehement whisper that told more of her fear than of the fake anger she was projecting.

Derek gave her a half smile. "I meant there's protection on the doors into his office."

Callie wasn't going to touch that one. She was here to talk about how souls could be contained outside of the body. That was far enough out on the fucking ridiculous scale.

"And what can I do for…oh, it's you." The Soul Charmer appeared through the heavy velvet drapes behind the counter with old-Hollywood gusto. He dropped the act as soon as he glimpsed Callie and Derek.

"You get a lot of late-night business that needs the full show?" Callie asked. The Charmer wore a purple smoking jacket like he thought he was playing host to pinups and not hawking souls to those slumming it.

"One doesn't command a market without always putting his best foot forward. Something to learn, Calliope." He flourished a hand toward her. He was probably pointing out that her jeans, Chucks, and a five-year-old winter coat were not peak style, but she was distracted by the way the glow from the banker's lamp on the counter refracted off the chunky gold rings on her reluctant mentor's fingers.

"You busy tonight?" Derek asked.

They needed privacy for the conversation they were about to have, but Callie appreciated the reprieve from banal talk with the Charmer. It was going to be hard enough to explain her concerns without mentioning that she'd worked for Ford and that he, you know, was trying to get her to spy on the Charmer. Callie didn't know the Soul Charmer that well. He was a guarded, volatile man. But in the short period she'd worked for him she'd learned one important thing: He considered theft—of property or secrets—a murderous offense.

"I have time for you." The Soul Charmer answered the real question, which was helpful and unnerving at the same time.

"We've got a lead," Derek said.

"Must be a good one for you to be here now." The Charmer barely moved his mouth as he spoke. An invisible brick smacked into Callie's chest. Whatever he was up to in the wee hours was eerie, and should probably remain a secret. From Callie. Forever.

"She's got questions," Derek said like it'd kick start the conversation.

"Do you have the flask?" The Charmer hissed.

Always. "Yes, but that's not why we're here."

The Soul Charmer nodded slowly. His beady eyes darkened as he stared at her. Something twitched beneath her sternum. She clapped a hand against it. Whatever was inside was hers, and he didn't need to be digging in there. His gaze narrowed on her wrist.

Her ribs vibrated against her hand when she spoke. "You've looked at my soul before. That's enough."

His responding smile did nothing to ease the twist beneath her rib cage. "You could feel that? Excellent."

If feeling sick to her stomach made him happy, he should prepare himself for a joy overload. "Can you stop? We… I… I need information to help us get the guy who is leaving you early, gross Christmas gifts outside."

Her fear was hardening to that delicious ire she could funnel into confidence. She could get through this if she could cling to her frustration and force it into action. Her problems were stacked blocks upon blocks reaching for the sky. She couldn't fix them as they continued to grow, but she could try to take this one tower out at the base.

The twitching quiver beneath her sternum stopped, but that rush of rage behind her eyes held steady.

"Derek already brought me the boy who left the first gift out there. What more information do you need from me that couldn't be extracted from him?"

Callie dropped her hand from her stomach and forced herself to keep her hands open at her side. Like she wasn't scared of what came next. Derek took a step closer to her, and the leather of his jacket covered the stale musk in the room. She wasn't alone. He wouldn't let this go awry.

She didn't take the Little D bait. "How does the flask work?"

The Soul Charmer keened his head to the right, and his gaze sharpened on her again. She almost expected to see a second set of eyelids nictate like a deep-sea creature. He wasn't peering at her soul this time. This was a completely different assessment. Probably not a good thing, but at least she didn't think she would puke anytime soon.

"You've been using it for some time now. You know how it works."

"I know how to use it to pull a soul out of another person. I don't know why it works, though."

"You know full well it's tempered with soul magic. You can connect with the energy." The Charmer couldn't have been less impressed if she'd told him the sky was blue. Asshole.

"We think the person who hired Little D gave him

a device to pull the soul from that kid outside." Derek played the mediator once again. She was going to have to make him breakfast one of these days as a thank you. Not pancakes.

"That drug dealer you brought here? You think he could pull souls? Interesting." The Charmer's eyes skittered right and left, like he was reading some invisible script on the wall behind them.

"Look, I know not every device can hold a soul."

There was that knowing, prurient smile she associated with a pleased Soul Charmer. "Do tell. How do you *know* this?"

Lying would be awesome now. Telling him that she picked it up because of the way the flask grew warm under her touch and the way it diffused the heat and cold her hands suffered when near soul renters. The problem was lying wouldn't get her answers. Plus, the fucker could see her soul and for all she knew that made him a human lie detector. That stuck her with honesty. The question was how much did he need to know?

For Cullen and for Derek, she pulled together her courage, tucked away her unease, and told him the truth. "My mom was renting again. Which I really hope you weren't giving her souls, but—" Callie shook her head as though to jostle the tangent out of her train of thought "—that's for another time. Anyway, some shit went down and I yanked the bonus soul out of her and shoved it in a beer bottle."

Callie stared at her feet. The dark carpet creeping up the sides of the white rubber on her sneakers. She swallowed a few times. Trying to pull herself together to tell him more.

Derek tried to help her. His hand was on her back. "The bottle broke, though."

The Charmer slammed a hand down on the counter. The clang of metal against glass snapped through the room until the tapestries swallowed it. "Of course it broke. It was made for beer, not celestial objects."

Why did he have to hoard knowledge like this? Wasn't part of being an apprentice that you got to know what was going on and how shit worked? Callie fixed her gaze on him, not backing down when the twin onyx blades within his pupils threatened to slash her.

"So what makes other objects capable of containing souls? Your jars are glass, and they don't shatter." She pointed toward the back room like he wouldn't know where the fucking souls were. She instantly regretted it, because she didn't want to go back there. She didn't want to be in a room full of souls that he could release at any time as part of his disturbed twist on the Socratic method.

"These are good questions." Surprise grazed his words and a smile softened his reptilian visage.

Callie and Derek shared a concerned look.

The Charmer laughed. It was a hiss and a roar—otherworldly. The twitch beneath Callie's breastbone now had nothing to do with the Soul Charmer testing her soul and everything to do with her heart reminding her she was alive and it wanted to stay that way.

"I made the jars strong enough to contain the

souls," he said finally.

"How?" The question bubbled to Callie's lips immediately. Just as quickly she regretted her eagerness, because there was no way the Charmer wouldn't use it against her.

"Not just yet." He parted his lips and his silver teeth flashed at her in a reminder of a threat. "First, dear Calliope, you're going to tell me what you did with this 'bonus' soul you took from your mother."

Callie tried not to roll her eyes, but failed. "It's in the flask," she muttered.

He held a hand out toward her, and motioned her to give it over. She sat the flask into his waiting palm, but made sure her skin didn't touch his. She didn't know why this fear still lingered, but her brain continued to warn her from making physical contact with the Soul Charmer. The white band of skin around her wrist was less stark in this lighting, and the Charmer didn't say anything when she tugged her sleeve down to cover it again.

He uncapped the flask, and held the opening beneath his nose. He took a loud, long breath, which might have been for show.

"Mine, but not mine," he said a moment later, and then capped the flask again.

"What does that mean?" Derek asked. He remained resolute at Callie's side.

"This soul was mine. One I harvested, that is. But someone else put it in Callie's mother."

"Probably the same person trying to send us a message." A hint of concern laced Derek's words.

"That's likely," the Charmer said. He turned his attention back to Callie. "Now, how did you get the soul into the flask if it was already outside of your mother?"

"I told it to go there." This was an oversimplification, but Callie couldn't think of another way to describe it.

The Charmer nodded, so it must have been the right answer. He turned and walked toward the curtains. Callie and Derek followed. They'd passed some test and now had to find out if their princess was in another castle.

As they moved through the hallway, Callie prepared herself for the thick layer of magic coating the entrance to the back office. Every time she'd moved through it, it had gotten heavier. For minutes afterward she'd swear the oily substance was still coating her. Sure enough it was there again, thick and viscous. This time, though, Callie picked up the energy. That's what it was. A layer of heat and power and unspoken command. She pressed outward with her mind, imagining widening her own energy to an inch outside her body. The sticky sensation still lingered when she moved into the room, but she hadn't fallen face-first on the floor and she wasn't gasping for air. Both major improvements.

The Charmer watched her out of the corner of his eye, but didn't say anything. For not the first time, she wished she could get a read on him. You don't grow up in a house with a con artist without learning how to read a room. Callie was good at picking up on emotional cues. She could spot the crier in every set of girls out at a bar. She could tell when a punch was going to get thrown. She could pinpoint the moment when a quick drink turned into five shots. She knew when to hide, when to run, and when to suggest that five-shot person buy her one, too, so they wouldn't have to celebrate alone. She'd learned all this to keep herself safe—and sometimes tipsy on a budget—but it did jack-all in this room. The Charmer was more reptile than human. Maybe his cold-blooded style made him unreadable. Maybe it was the magic. Maybe he was simply better at this shit than she was. She worked for the man and was trying to help him get answers and retribution, but she wasn't sure if he saw her on his side.

Fear sizzled in her veins. She did a cursory search of the room for any rogue souls or open containers. There were none. This discomfort was all her. She pulled off her coat, and laid it over one of the nearby stools. The room was heated, but the sudden warmth of her body had more to do with her emotions than anything inside this space.

The Charmer walked behind his oak desk. It appeared giant with his small frame behind it, but it was probably some boardroom standard shit. *Snick* and slide. He bent forward and reached into a drawer. Callie tensed. It wasn't until her back collided with Derek that she realized she'd actually moved backward. Derek steadied her with a hand lightly on her hip. She sucked in her bottom lip, and told herself to plant her goddamn feet.

The Charmer placed two jars on the desk. The slick

surfaces sent the sound to collision levels, though he had set them gently. "These don't have souls in them yet," he said like he could see the ghost of fear haunting Callie.

She lifted her chin in a tough-lady agreement and hoped the act would bolster her confidence.

"Well, come here and take one." He came around the desk and handed her a jar.

Sure enough it was regular, opaque glass. It was only three inches wide, but the base was heavy and it balanced well in the center of her palm.

He picked up the other jar and held it in the same fashion. "Now watch what I do."

Her gaze flicked from his eyes to the jar in his hands.

"Not with your eyes. Watch with that." He pointed at her chest.

He might have meant her soul or her heart or her breasts. She didn't ask. "Okay."

"Now feel what happens."

She did. The warm air rushing in from the vent in the ceiling stalled. The buzz of electricity powering the box fan set in the far corner disappeared. The energy rippling through the Soul Charmer's body pulled and stretched. She could sense it siphoning out of is chest and into his one palm. The glass vibrated. Or maybe it just hummed for her? A second later the ripple of energy in the Charmer's body dissipated. The warm air flowed again, the fan spinning, and the simple jar in the Soul Charmer's hand held power.

"Can I hold it?" Callie didn't disguise the awe in her voice. She could see Derek's confused look in her periphery, but this was an offer of understanding before her. She might actually be able to do something with this. Get out of the loop of scraping for answers and begging for freedom.

The Charmer held it out to her, and she took it with her empty hand. The glass thrummed against her skin. It bore the gentle warmth of her flask, but with a faster paced buzz. "Okay," was all she said, but it was enough for the Charmer.

"Now you understand. Not any device can contain a soul. My magic is what imbues it with the power. Much like how you can call a soul out, you can push that sense of soul awareness into the object. Then it tricks the soul into thinking it is in the safety of a body. For a time."

"For a time?" She snatched onto that caveat.

"Like anything else. If you don't tend to it, it can go wild." He hissed another laugh, and Callie remembered how different they were, even if they both bore this talent.

"Can anyone do what you just did?"

The corner of his mouth drew up. "You try it."

She wasn't really angling for an order. She was finally being taught something as part of this apprenticeship. She was actually learning how to use this magic he'd shoved inside her. She might finally get to own it. Own herself again. She should be focused on learning about the knife, but she had to know if she could do this.

She didn't say anything, but she sat his jar on the desk, and cradled hers in both her palms. The way the magic had moved through his body, it was as though he'd called it forward. Beckoned it. Like she had with the rogue souls. She sent a silent plea to the magic running beneath her skin. She begged it to come forward, to consolidate in her palms. At first nothing happened. The prickle of sharp energy of the magic snapping against her nerves was there, but it wasn't moving. *Please*, she thought. It ebbed and flowed, but eventually the magic pooled in her palms. She asked it to jump to the glass, and it did. When she looked up the Charmer flashed his shiny teeth at her again. Derek's hands went to her shoulders. She didn't need to read his soul to know he was panicked. She was breathing hard and her head spun, but the thrum of magic in the little jar buzzed delightfully against her. Warm and gentle and hers.

The process took her several minutes, which the Charmer was quick to point out meant she'd need practice. "Once you both stop whomever is threatening me and mine, you'll be prepping jars for me. You should be able to do it in ten seconds or less."

Nice. At least he was teaching her. "Does it work with any container?" She could almost feel the snap and fizz of the broken beer bottle in her hand.

"Depending on skill, perhaps. Opaque glass and organic containers will hold the magic the longest. The darker the container, the better."

Callie focused on the flickering energy she'd

forced into the jar, because it was best not to let the Charmer know how excited she was to get actual, tangible answers from him. Her breath stuttered. Cullen. They were supposed to be getting answers for him. She diverted her dizzying deluge of questions to one that might help solve the big problem. The dead kid problem. "Can anyone do what I just did?"

His brows knit together. "No. You'd have to be adept in the magical arts to craft a vessel for souls."

"Could someone buy something already made for catching souls?" Derek offered.

The Charmer's nod was slow, but gained certainty with momentum. "That's a possibility. There are several artifacts from my predecessors that one could get their hands on."

Callie tried not to imagine what the other soul magicians might be like. For her it was hard to imagine anyone but the Soul Charmer hawking souls, but then he had to learn somewhere, right? "Would any of those be a hollow knife?"

Derek and Callie explained the knife they'd heard about again, and how Little D returned it to his handler after the job was done.

"A knife like that, if it is from one of the original soul magicians, would be very valuable. Someone would have to be quite desperate to let someone as irresponsible as that cretin use it." The Charmer sounded incredibly pleased by the fact his nemesis was desperate.

Whatever got him through the night, Callie supposed.

The bell chimed from the front of the store. The wall clock put it close to three. Callie guessed that's when all the good souls got rented. The Charmer tugged down the sleeves of his smoking jacket, and started toward the front room.

"We've got a solid next step for taking care of this," Derek said to the Charmer. He sounded like he had a plan.

Callie didn't know what it was, but from the grimace on her lover's face, it wasn't going to be fun.

CHAPTER TWENTY-ONE

Callie's mind was already buzzing with dozens of fresh questions for the Soul Charmer, but as the below-freezing night air snapped against her skin she realized she was fucking tired. Her brain wasn't up for next steps right now. It was up for a pillow and a well-worn comforter. She had been awake almost a complete twenty-four hours. She couldn't remember if the last time she'd done that was while on rotation at the hospital or the previous time she nursed Josh through withdrawals. Either way, it'd been a minute.

"What's next?" she asked both because she was curious of his plan and because she wanted to hear the answer was nothing because this bullshit was over.

"We need to talk to my brother."

That shot a second wind into her. Her gaze sharpened and homed in on Derek. His brows were furrowed and he was studiously tracking the path to her POS car like he thought someone would jack it at any second. Derek had never mentioned a brother. He'd commiserated in the natural baggage people come with and he acknowledged family was one of those. But never mentioned a fucking brother. Holy shit. She mentally shifted gears from sleep-deprived delirium and soul magic wonder to straight-up dying-to-know levels. While her mind whirred at 150 miles per hour, her mouth managed to cultivate the very articulate question of, "What?"

At least it was better than "Who?" she supposed.

"My brother. He knows something." Derek's teeth were gritted. Where Callie wanted to yell at her brother and shake sense into him, she got the distinct impression Derek would like to land a heavy fist on the bridge of his brother's nose.

Um. Okay. Since when was his family involved in their shit? What had happened to make him think his brother was part of this? "I thought it was Ford. I mean, I know we didn't name names to the Charmer, because if we do so without a why then we're stuck being the ones extrapolating it later, which is gross and makes you want to bust out the brain bleach."

"It is Ford," he said, like he wasn't even listening to her.

"Is Ford your brother?"

That stopped him. "What? Fuck no."

Callie stepped in front of him. The car was a few feet away, which put a soft yellow glow above their heads and stretching black shadows at their sides.

"Then what does your brother have to do with this? Like, I'm curious as hell, but my brain is running on fumes, and I don't get what's up. Does he deal in ancient magical artifacts? Do we think he sold someone that knife? How is he involved, and how have I not heard of him before now?"

Derek's shoulders sagged. He took a half-step to close the gap between them, wrapped his arms around Callie, and sighed heavily enough it moved her bones, too.

"Nate said he was going to church." His words hit her hard enough to shake her spine.

Her hands were on his shoulder blades, and she tried to pull him closer by pressing on them. As though it would spare them both any more battering ram phrases. "Him and almost everyone else in Gem City," she said as softly as she could. Which at 3 a.m. with a two-degree wind chill blasting her every few moments was, perhaps, not the most delicate.

"No." Derek slipped his hands to her upper arms, and held her a few inches away. Like he was both scared of his strength and like he needed to see her reaction. Callie shivered. He sucked in his lower lip, but when he released it, he continued, "Nate didn't bother to hide his connection to Little D. He knew that we knew that corner dealer was the one who killed the kid. He knew we were looking. Instead of threatening us—"

"He wouldn't threaten you," Callie said. They'd encountered Nate together before, and he didn't have the balls to try anything against Derek.

"He didn't make a crack toward the Charmer. He

wasn't scared enough of me to keep his fucking mouth shut about you. He couldn't resist telling us he was going to church."

"But what's the big deal with him going to church? Is he on a goddamn mission from God?"

He looked left and right, as though he expected to find a crew of crazy people ready to jump them. The street was empty. "We need to get in the car," he said with the urgency of the aforementioned fictitious crazy people.

"Seriously? Who's here to hear us?"

"Just get in the car."

Her car had been a safe space for secrets between them. As silly as it sounded, she hoped the roomy, if deteriorated, interior would comfort him. Or at least make this less of a head-spinning conversation.

Once inside, he turned the key and revved the engine. He left the car in park, though.

"Okay, we're in the car. Now will you tell me?"

"The Charmer ever tell you where souls come from? Like during your training or whatever?" His words fell over one another, which only made the question itself more ominous.

"Until today he hasn't been big on revealing his secrets. You'd think he was fucking Houdini."

Her joke fell flat.

Derek's brows knitted together, and he flexed his fingers like he was holding back from gripping her far too tightly. "So, he's never mentioned where the souls come from?"

"I've seen the rockers come in to pawn theirs," she said with confidence. It failed to carry her, though, and when she continued that hesitation coated her words like mud. "I've never seen him take a pawn on a pure soul. Nothing that would rate top dollar, by his standards."

The knowing look Derek gave her made her stomach hollow out.

"Where does he get them?" her whispered voice cut the air between them. As though even the junker car decided this moment required silence and it quelled its rattling muffler and the rumble beneath their feet. Her words lingered between them, the question caught on a non-existent heat flow from the less-than-fully-functional vents.

"I've never seen the actual place. I feel like I have to say that."

He was stalling, but instead of calling him on that, she offered a non-judgmental, "Okay."

"I know you've heard him say shit about filling the well. Or going to the well. Or whatever. The well is real."

"There's a soul well?" Even now, knowing magic was real, that souls could be parted from their bodies without making some kind of celestial progression to light perfection or fiery abyss, it was hard for her to keep the skepticism out of her voice. Because, let's be real, it sounded made up.

"Yeah. And the Cortean Catholic Church owns it."

Callie's head was mushy with the impossibility. She sputtered a few objections, but none were coherent or valuable. Derek had no reason to lie to her, but how could this be real? Was the Church making a buck off circumventing actual redemptions? Had they become so jaded as to quit seeking salvation the old fashioned way? Or was this the old fashioned way? "How long have they had it?"

"Supposedly it's the reason the Conquistadors came here. The reason the Corteans set up shop and founded Gem City."

"But the Charmer is new. It's been a decade of soul magic. Not centuries."

"It's been a decade since the Charmer went public. Doesn't mean this stuff hasn't been happening for a long time. Charmer never says."

The Charmer didn't say a lot of things. He didn't point out that he had a regular gig with the church. He didn't mention the vast network that had to exist for this to be a thing. No wonder he had competition. Soul magic wasn't new. He wasn't the originator…unless he was doubling up on lifespans.

Callie shook her head, but the images wouldn't dispel. She tried closing her eyes, and when that didn't help, she pressed her hands over them until flickers of stars burned before her. When she pulled her palms away from her face and opened her eyes again, Derek was watching her. The pained expression cutting across the harsh planes of his face cut her. Maybe one had to be bleeding to accept this kind of truth. You had to be raw, and broken, and too beat-down to fight the facts. Callie wished she could reject the knowledge. She wished she didn't know what it felt like to be so *done* as to no longer fight the unbelievable.

She licked her lips. Once, and then again. Derek didn't say more, but then, what should he say? It wasn't a joke. It wasn't something he'd made peace with. It was fact without context. He'd given partial truths because that's all he had.

"Okay," she said, more to confirm she was still alive than to agree to anything. "What do the Charmer and the Cortean's soul well have to do with your brother?"

"He's a priest."

Callie didn't say anything for a long time. She'd worn out her ability to react to batshit comments. If she'd still had energy, she would have been aghast. She would have thrown her hands wide, she would have shook him, she would have asked a million questions. Instead, she simply confirmed the fact. "Your brother is a priest."

Disbelief shrouded the words, but without the fire of her previous indignation. She watched Derek for a sign of fear or regret or any emotion at this point. He simply looked tired. An echo of herself. Dark bags beneath his eyes. Shirt rumpled. Shoulders rolled forward, chin almost to his chest. They were two broken beings holed up in the sanctity of a very old car, parked on an abandoned street, on a winter night. The wind whistled around the cars, as though it was attempting to nudge them into action. The car remained in park, but Callie's hand found Derek's.

"You never mentioned him."

"I don't like talking about him. Or to him."

Why? she thought, but bit the urge to ask. It wasn't something he could explain. When people wondered why she couldn't stop coming to Josh's aid, they'd ask why she let him pull her down. There wasn't a simple answer. It was what family did. It was what he'd earned by being there for her when she was younger. Maybe she was earning Josh's care in the future? She wasn't keeping tally of who did what for whom. Helping him felt right. That wasn't an answer that sated anyone. Not even Callie. Derek had to be in the same boat. Whatever kept him from his brother wasn't simple. There was something dark and delicate in his past. She wedged those secrets between her ribs, and occasionally coated them with various shades of booze. It hid them, but didn't actually make them disappear.

"Do you think he would help us?" It was the safer question to ask.

"He gets off on helping people." Derek's tone suggested it would not be the first time his brother held assistance over his head. At least the Delgados didn't rub each other's faces in their good deeds. Zara didn't count because she'd never done anything good for Callie, if you didn't count the whole birth thing. Some days—when she was running double shifts, fielding Zara's texts about how Josh was so much better than her, and she was trying to remember the last time she'd done something that wasn't for her mother or brother—she didn't.

"Got it." She scrambled for more to say. She was simply worn too thin to excel at comforting him. How had Derek done this for her when they'd first met? Shit. "Does he know about the Charmer or the well or…" she trailed off because she figured listing all their problems and the various human components wouldn't help the situation.

"He knows." Derek pursed his lips for a moment like he was holding back more. It must have worked, because instead of elaborating, he shifted the car into drive, and took them east and toward the Plaza again.

A couple minutes passed with neither of them speaking. The window on Callie's side rattled as they hit potholes. She would have to have that looked at eventually. Going anywhere with a busted window in winter was a bad idea. She'd have to start putting some cash away to cover it. Somehow.

"Will he be there now?" she asked to distract herself. She avoided mentioning "brother" for Derek's benefit.

"He lives on site." He was shutting down. Going into that gruff, Spartan mode. He'd be grunting his replies soon. She wouldn't admit it aloud, but she was too raw for him to do that with her right now.

"Stay with me," she muttered.

He peered at her. The green of a traffic light lit one side of his face. As though the universe was telling her to stick with him, and hoping she didn't notice the darkness bathing the rest of his body.

"Not going anywhere, doll."

"Never thought you'd take me to church," she offered with the kind of delirious laugh that came from fear or lack of sleep. Both, in her case.

"I'll make sure to tell your mom I took you to see a priest next time I see her. I'm sure she'll invite me over again." His laugh was as ridiculous as hers, but it was better than the booming silence that had held them captive in the minutes before.

"We need one of those clear plastic dividers. Like they use in ICU. We need to quarantine her from us before we try to sit down to a meal again." Callie didn't realize what she'd said. She'd be the one quarantined if this got out. She was the aberrant one. The one who lit on fire and snatched souls. The more she became like the Charmer, was able to use the magic he had forced into her, the more *other* she became. At least she could defend herself now. Mostly.

Derek parked the car right in front of the cathedral. There were no tourists littering the street or strolling among the statues or gardens. Saint Catalina, Callie's favorite, was lit with three ground lamps. Beautiful and glowing. Callie almost crossed herself at the sight, but then remembered why she was here. There was probably some rule about not acting pious as you went in to question a priest about soul magic and possible murder. She wasn't an expert, though.

CHAPTER TWENTY-TWO

It had been twelve years since Callie had been inside the cathedral in Gem City's plaza. It had always been the cornerstone of the faith, and as such had limited seating. Plus, Zara had never wanted to drive downtown and fight for parking for "the same service we'd get at home with our people." Callie had never been completely certain if her mother had meant their neighbors, non-tourists, or criminals and their kids. The cathedral boasted ornate spires and lush gardens and the most intricate depictions of the apostles in stained glass anyone had seen. All those things didn't keep out the criminals. There had been a shot on the news the other night of Ford walking down the very steps Callie now climbed. The headline was about the investigation into Ford's father and some failing machinery in one of his factories.

Maybe Ford already had looked into the soul well.

He'd been in this behemoth of faith before. She sucked in a breath and held it as she crossed into the church.

"You know He doesn't actually smite people, right?" Derek said with forced humor.

"I was thinking about who has been through these doors before us." Her church whisper was on point.

He nodded, and she chose not to explain further.

"Shouldn't we be going around the side of the building or something?" She had to admit she flinched at every creak of the floorboards beneath her. There was church quiet, and then there was this. Eerie, unreal silence that carved a space near her heart for *more*. Moments like this, when both fear and awe struck her hard and fast and real, she could see the appeal of coming to church. She'd never experienced it when in the pews before. Squished between the judgmental or drunken men and women. Those who would rather pay penance than do the right thing out of the gate. Callie carried a cargo-trailer of guilt. It didn't make her a better person that she lamented her numerous fuck ups. If she could get past it, she'd probably be one of the grinning, perfectly coifed people in the poster on the far wall. Some church propaganda professing the power of prayer to lead to wealth. God didn't shower people with money. Good or bad. If he showered them with anything it was challenges and awkward "I'm not mad at you, but I'm disappointed in you" love. Callie bypassed the holy water, and tried not to make eye contact with Jesus on the cross ahead of her. She wasn't sure where she stood with his father, other than she disagreed about the church's function, but she was pretty sure doing anything wrong in this place was a red-hot ticket to the kind of fire she couldn't overcome.

"He's in the confessional."

"I didn't see anyone assigned to the 4 a.m. shift." Though she probably wouldn't have recognized it anyway. Was there even an overnight shift for the confessional? Most of the churches in her neighborhood locked the doors at night. Vagrancy was more an issue in the plaza, but the cathedral doors had opened to them and nary a person greeted them.

"He's there. Trust me." She could tell Derek didn't doubt her faith in him, but his bad mood doubled inside these walls. As if the burnished wood and the waxy remnants of candles were convening to attack him at any second.

She didn't bother asking more. She followed him toward the back of the room and the series of seven wood doors laid into the far wall close to the rectory. Only one of the doors was ajar. She'd been to St. Stephen's down the street from the retirement home with Louisa dozens of times, and to St. Luke's near Zara's place hundreds more. She'd never see the confessional doors closed unless a parishioner was seeking absolution inside. The streets outside the cathedral were barren aside from Callie's car. The sanctuary was equally empty. Why would the premiere house of worship in their city close its doors to confession, but keep the building entrance unlocked? A sharp shiver shot down her spine. She was certain if she moved close enough to the doors she'd feel energy simmering and snapping behind them. Souls in motion. Perhaps this explained why she stopped edging forward.

Derek got four strides ahead before he paused to realize she had stalled out in the middle of the aisle. "You feel something?"

She was certain he meant magic, and he wasn't necessarily wrong, but it didn't fully cover what was happening here. This was more than soul magic at work. It was this place at this time, and it was fucking with her head. She couldn't explain that, though. She couldn't speak freely here in this cavernous room. Her secrets would rise to the rafters. Others might find peace in that, resolution, absolution; she didn't. "I…" she fumbled for the right way to say it. "Can I wait here while you find you brother?"

He furrowed his brows so tightly she wondered if they'd permanently knit together. His lips thinned into a hard line, but Callie wouldn't let herself think she'd taken a misstep with him. He was quiet for several moments, and she stilled the urge to explain. Finally, he said, "I'll bring him out. Grab a pew."

Her sigh of relief made it to the Madonna sculpture in the far corner. The Mother didn't flinch, so Callie held her shit together and found a seat in the closest pew.

Derek pulled open the one confessional door that wasn't shut. He didn't step into the booth, but leaned forward until all she could see over the pews was his hand on the door, knuckles turning white around the outer edge of the dark wood. Callie had often wondered how private the confessional booths were. The hard surfaces inside didn't offer much in the way of sound barriers, and though the kneeling bench was padded, that didn't count. Surprisingly, though, she couldn't hear the conversation within. A hard *thump* echoed in the vast room, jostling her secrets from the rafters and allowing their escape. A rumble of male voices emanated from Derek's general direction, but Callie couldn't make out any of the words.

A small panel popped open to Derek's left. Derek straightened. The deepening red on the back of his neck was visible from where Callie sat four rows back. "You can't make demands in the confessional. Please. I can help," said the man who stepped out from the hidden panel. He was more than six feet tall, and the collar he wore was so white it could blind a room. His dark hair matched Derek's, though it was slicked back. His nose had never been broken, and his hands didn't bear the telltale signs of hard labor. He'd planted his back foot slightly behind his front, as though basing for a fight, in a mirror of Derek. They were almost a before and after. The priest was what Derek could have been if fate hadn't dealt him hard choices. Maybe what he'd have been if he weren't the older brother, the caretaker, the one who fell into league with the Charmer. Callie shook the thought off. It wasn't her place to cast stones about dealings with the Charmer. She'd signed up for round two all on her own. Like the idiot she was.

The priest, though, was younger than she'd expected, but undeniably related to Derek. He still bore roundness in his cheeks that Derek must have lost ages ago or simply never inherited. But the shrewd gaze the priest locked on Derek was nothing short of pointed. That was the look Derek deployed to get souls returned in record time. A look like that should probably be off limits for a man of the cloth, but Callie expected rules were bent for family. It didn't matter how hard you tried, family had a way of pulling the worst out of you. Not that Callie was thinking about the shattered bottle from earlier or the thwarted attempt at a meet-the-parent event. Though, by the red blotches creeping up the side of the priest's neck, Callie wondered if Derek might out-do her on the fucked up family re-union for the day. At least hers hadn't gone down in the wee hours of the night in a location that—should the situation escalate—would slip right on into sacrilegious. She stood and moved toward the men, because the thought of letting Derek break a priest's nose inside a cathedral would signify a serious issue.

Her stomach fluttered with every step she took toward the confessional. The tense lines of Derek's shoulders reeled her forward, though. Callie stepped up behind him, tapped his shoulder, and he angled enough to see her. She edged around his side to stand close. Her butt was pressed against the edge of the nearest pew, but at least she wasn't against the confessional. She was sorry for so much shit that the thought of all she'd have to unload in that tiny box made her think of another box…the six-feet-below one. Hard pass.

"This is Callie," Derek said. The "and you better be nice to her or I will break your perfect nose" was silent, but clearly understood.

"Callie, it's nice to meet you. Even at this hour." Maybe Zara was getting her guilt grinds from the church after all.

She nodded, because she didn't have the energy to absorb passive aggressive behavior.

Derek pointed at his brother. "This is Henry."

"Father Henry," his brother corrected, in a lighter tone. The hint of a smile suggested it was an old joke. The guy wasn't much older than Callie. When had he taken the cloth? His freshman year?

Derek ignored his brother's comment. "Look. I need to know if Ford's man Nate was here."

"Or Ford himself," Callie interjected.

"Right. C'mon, Henry."

Derek slipped an arm around her, and she was solid again.

Henry sighed in the way good parents do when their children make poor choices. Callie hadn't been on the receiving end, but she'd watched the other kids' parents at after-school meetings. "You know I can't share who has come here. Those who seek solace deserve what we grant them."

"Henry, I swear—" Derek started.

Callie cut him off. "Isn't that whole priest/penitent thing only for confession? We didn't ask if they came to seek forgiveness. I don't want you tell me their sins, Father Henry. We need to know if they were here for other reasons." Callie wasn't sure how much to say. She wasn't even supposed to know about the soul well, which suggested mentioning it in conversation within moments of meeting a person, even a priest, was in poor taste.

Father Henry's gaze sharpened and focused on Callie. He slowly, deliberately tilted his head to the right. So much Derek's brother that she forgot for a moment where they were. "At least he found someone who has faith."

Neither Callie nor Derek laughed, but her gut kicked with the urge to do so.

"Henry," Derek used a pleading tone Callie hadn't heard before. "Lives are on the line. Are you going to help me or not?"

"I pray for you twice a day."

Derek's fist shot out from his hip into the door on his right. It slammed shut, and the resulting rumble resounded for seconds upon seconds. Blood marred the wood, but it was solid enough to have held under the duress. Better than the lot of them could do.

Once the sound softened, Callie said, "It isn't our lives we are here for. Innocent people will be hurt if we don't take action. We need you to help. Please."

Maybe it was the tacked on supplication. Maybe it was seeing pain ravaging his brother's face that had nothing to do with the freshly split skin on his pinky. Father Henry dropped his gaze. The sight of a priest with blatant shame dropped heavy stones into Callie's stomach forcing it to both sink and ache with the acidic knowledge of what she was doing. Henry swallowed twice, audible in the stillness. When he finally spoke it was in a whisper. It couldn't hide his secrets in this space.

"Both have been here. You know why." He looked

at Derek, open and pleading.

"I have a guess," Derek muttered.

The night was edging toward four in the morning like a frat kid, staggering and bordering on incoherent, and Callie needed more than implied answers. Confirming Ford's interest in the church and this location was important, but if they didn't say more it could be a coincidence. She was not interested in acting on assumptions. Not anymore.

"Did you or someone else let them see the well?" she asked.

Henry reared back as though she'd struck out at him. She held steady. Josh was as stubborn as she was, even if he made shittier decisions. She had to hope that the DNA Henry shared with Derek meant even if he didn't like hard questions he would be able to handle them.

It was almost as if Henry siphoned the panic and stress from his brother. The more red-faced Henry grew, the more Derek's shoulders relaxed and his breathing evened out. His hand reached out to rest above Callie's hip. It was a steadying move, not a possessive one. That one touch told her she hadn't shoved her soles in her mouth. At least not any more than was appropriate in the situation.

"I would never allow anyone without divine access in there." Father Henry was trying for the stoic, serene gaze the Cortean priests epitomized—hands folded loosely in front of him, gaze open and interested—but Callie caught the flickered gaze toward the confessionals a little farther back. There was a dark imprint in the upper corner of the frame. A wing. A beak. The same dark bird she'd spotted on the Soul Charmer's wrist the other night.

"That's a dodge of the question, Padre. Did you allow Nate or Ford inside? Does either of them bear that mark?" She pointed at what she was starting to think might be one of the little hawks she'd spotted near Juniper bushes on early mornings.

Both men followed her gesture. Derek offered a, "huh," as though he'd never noticed the mark. Father Henry offered a variety of negative noises, but none with any confidence. Finally he let out the kind of sigh that Callie would use when she finally got home and didn't have to continue solving shit for the day. "Neither have the mark. Neither were let in, but they don't know that's the reason they aren't gaining access."

Giving up the fight wasn't something Callie did often, and when it happened it was usually against another Delgado. The memory of broken determination and the halo of failure that had wrapped her for weeks later stole the front of Callie's mind, and she recognized the same marks forming in Father Henry's face. She'd broken a priest. If the Charmer said her soul was still pure, he was a fucking liar.

Derek picked up the questioning as Callie's brain sputtered. "Did they know what they were asking to see? Did they call it by name?"

"They brought an old book with them. It merely referred to the well as 'the source,' and that is what they were seeking." Father Henry's resignation rippled through a sigh. He continued, quieter, but also somehow more sternly. "I don't believe they understood they wouldn't have been able to access it or pull souls from it. They aren't built for it. Using an ancient gateway our Lord provided isn't a task any person off the street can do. Speaking to Him isn't a simple task."

The urge to ask about prayer and its validity burst in the back of Callie's brain. She stomped it out. That was her exhaustion speaking. The clergy spoke to God. That was the deal. Which made one dark concern rot at her gut until she expelled it. "Are you suggesting the Soul Charmer speaks to God?" Because that man was the least pious, righteous, man of God she'd ever seen in her life. If he was a conduit to the Lord, then she might as well forget any standards for getting into Heaven.

"No, no. But he does understand the right way to ease the overflow of the source of souls. It's a symbiotic relationship," Father Henry explained.

"You're calling him a parasite," Derek deadpanned. His eyes held that glimmer of joy Callie recognized as the delight in watching a stiff and prim person squirm. She stood inside a church, so she wasn't about to lie and say it wasn't a *little* amusing.

"Your words, not mine, brother."

"Wait he's helping control the well?" Callie latched on to the important part.

"I can't say more." Henry shot a furtive glance behind him, as though they weren't the only people in the cathedral at this late hour. In a whisper Callie had to lean forward to catch, Henry added, "It isn't my place to speak of the well. I keep people out of it, but the men you ask about, they are determined. It's why I'm here now. Bishop Bianco is concerned they will attempt to break into the well. If they were to try to reach in, only death would follow. All criminals deserve the chance to repent."

Callie wasn't so certain that was true. She could certainly think of plenty of people—including Ford and Nate—who maybe deserved damnation. Still. If they got in, there was a problem. The Charmer knew more about what was happening here, but did he actually know that it was part of why people were being killed to get his attention? Could Ford learn how to conduct soul magic from a book? The energy that allowed her to sense the magic in others swirled bright and beckoning at her core. It wasn't something she'd had until the day the Charmer turned her into this. This power wasn't a natural one. Could Ford conjure the same skill?

If Callie had learned anything in her apprenticeship it was that the Soul Charmer of Gem City always had a leg up on others, and anyone who tried to knock out that leg would pay in fire and blood.

The stones in Callie's stomach settled heavy in her center. Could she avoid getting burned from the sidelines?

Fuck, she hoped so.

CHAPTER TWENTY-THREE

The night was charged outside the cathedral. It wasn't the statutes of saints and their watchful gazes setting energy snapping along Callie's skin. It wasn't even soul magic. It was that sharp sense before a storm slams into the city. The air was thickening, preparing. Stars sparked in sync across the endless black sky. Callie watched them, as though their electric energy would ignite something fantastic. As though the answers could be laid out in specks of hot white above her instead of the pools of black tar congealing within her stomach.

Taking the truth to the Soul Charmer—that a mobster known for cherubic looks and a hankering for hacking body parts was after access to an infinite source of additional souls, was after *the Charmer's* prime source of business—was not going to end well. She didn't need the cosmos to tell her so. She scrubbed her left hand across her face. Whether it was the pressure or the frigid air, her cheek stung afterward and sobered her thoughts. Her other hand was clamped around the flask in her pocket. She had been stroking her thumb over the onyx inlay absently. She stilled it. The external container for magic, for souls, shouldn't be the source of comfort. Unfortunately, fighting her feelings hadn't ever changed them. So she didn't bother releasing her metaphysical blankie.

"You okay?" Derek's rumbling voice was behind Callie's ear. No wonder the wind wasn't slicing into her neck.

"I honestly don't even know anymore."

"That sounds like a no."

Callie shrugged. "I'm happy you didn't deck your brother."

"Punching a priest is off limits." The humor in his voice was strained, but at this late hour everything had been pulled past its limits. Humor shouldn't get to be an exception.

"Isn't there a family clause or something? Does he ever get to be something other than a priest?" It was a silly question. A man of God was always a man of God. There were times life would have been easier if Josh had been a junkie who had come into the emergency room on her rotation and not someone she'd dive into a well to save over and over and over. It was hard to not be able to give up on people. It was a shitty thought, and Callie was shitty for acknowledging it. It wasn't the first time Callie had contemplated how her life would be different if she could cut ties. And like every other time, she had to bite back the bile of imagined betrayal and subsequent shame. What the fuck was wrong with her for considering skipping out on those who mattered most?

Derek dropped his heavy arm over her shoulders, and the weight grounded her in a way she couldn't fully describe. It was good though. He'd chosen to be part of this complete mess. Maybe she had, too. She wasn't going to cut and run. On him or on the job. She'd picked both. It was rare she had the chance to choose, and she wasn't about to let that go.

"Next time he drops his collar outside of a church, I'll knock him once for you," Derek said.

"Now, I didn't say I wanted you to punch him." She almost smiled.

"He's earned at least one solid pop. He did hold back about people trying to get to the well."

Callie's mother and brother weren't in her good graces at the moment. Broken beer bottles and thwarted magic and all. But they wouldn't have kept secrets about her from her. Zara would have told the truth to see Callie squirm, she admitted to herself, but Josh would have had her back. Henry should have had Derek's. "He knows what you do with the Charmer, yeah?"

"He's part of the reason I ended up with the Soul Charmer." He offered this morsel of his past, but it came with a finite cut. The hard edge of finality suggested Derek understood Callie wanted to know more of him, to understand him, but he wasn't ready to divulge. She couldn't blame him. They were still new, and already broken. Shattered people don't build a foundation for a relationship in weeks. She had secrets she couldn't imagine ever sharing. Begrudging his privacy would only make her an asshole.

The interior of Callie's car wasn't any warmer than the street outside had been, but at least they were blocked from the frigid gusts. Callie tugged on her seatbelt, and then slouched in the seat until her chin was forced to her chest. "Can I just sleep like this?" she mumbled.

Derek turned the car on, and cranked the heater. It pumped cold air at peak volume, but would eventually warm up.

"You care if we crash at my place?" Derek asked.

She'd never been to his place. They were always on the move or he was coming to check on her, pick her up, keep an eye on Josh. It had made sense to stay at her apartment. Curiosity had twitched in the back of her brain about what his place would look like, but she hadn't ever questioned why they hadn't stayed there. Her heart squeezed at the opening to see more of his life, but the rest of her body was too burned out to react appropriately. "Is it close?"

He nodded. "Just a few blocks."

"Works for me."

The car didn't have time to warm up before Derek was pulling into a covered space outside a squat row of adobe homes. He turned off the car, but Callie didn't move. She wasn't asleep per se, but her body was ready to give up. Between being awake for more than twenty-four hours, the emotional explosion with her family, the discovery of the soul well, and meeting Derek's brother, she was tapped.

She got out of the car and followed Derek around the front of the houses. The third one in had an aquamarine front door and a slightly overgrown bougainvillea out front. Derek's. Callie got the sense he hadn't changed a thing since he'd taken over someone else's lease. The interior was all grey furniture and black tables. Derek helped her take off her coat and hung it in a front closet. His home was a reprieve from the whistling wind and wicked cold outside. Burning wood simmered in the air. His tiny fireplace was empty, but one of his neighbors must have been utilizing theirs. The scent lodged itself in Callie's nose, and the comfort of its subtle warmth only added to her drowsiness.

"Bedroom is straight back. Bathroom's on the right just inside. I'll get you some water."

Even after all they'd been through today, even after having an awkward conversation with his brother less than ten minutes ago that had to be battering his mind, Derek was looking out for her first. Like this was any other night. She should have been sweet or gone to hug him, but she was simply too drained to do anything more than stumble down the hallway to his bedroom. She hit the bathroom, and then stripped down to get in bed. His mattress was far firmer than hers. She was so used to sinking in that the lack of give when she sat on the bed startled her. Derek walked in with a glass of water. He brought it to her. She gulped down half the glass, and then set the cup on the nightstand. Derek met her beneath the sheets, and pulled her to him. She curled against his side. His pulse tapped a steady beat beneath her ear, and she fell soundlessly to sleep.

Fingers of light stretched toward Callie when she woke. She squinted against the bright sun from the window on her right. She rolled to face the other wall, and remembered where she was. The hard bed, the dark grey sheets, the poster of Springsteen on the wall? Right. Derek's house.

The whining groan that escaped her was three parts "oh, God, what did I do?" half a cup of "Do I still have to fix everything?" and a pinch of FML. She chased it with a confused, "Where are my pants?" for good measure.

The door to the bathroom opened. Derek exited in a wall of steam with nothing but an orange towel around his waist. His hips were angled forward and his shoulders back, every bit the peak of causal masculinity. He was relaxed, which Callie delighted in seeing almost as much as she liked the sharp groove his muscles cut just inside his hips. She pulled in a long breath, and flounced back on the bed. Languid and contemplating pulling herself together enough to take advantage of a fresh-from-the-shower Derek. Citrus and soap filled the room, and Callie held the clean relief of both in her lungs as long as she could.

"Doll, you leave your phone on vibrate?" Derek asked, already bending down to nudge through Callie's discarded jeans.

"Almost always do." She sat up, and held out her hands like she was expecting a communion wafer and not a phone to be placed within them. Spend one night outside a confessional and all the habits come pouring back.

He tossed it her way, and then moved to grab her clothes from the floor and placed them at the foot of the bed. He didn't hover as Callie unlocked the phone. Derek grabbed a pair of black jeans, yanked them on, and headed out of the room. "I'm going to see if I have anything edible in the pantry," he called as he left the room.

"Okay," she mumbled.

She stared at the screen. Four missed calls. Two voicemails. All from Cedar Retirement Home.

Fuck.

Fuck. Fuck. Fuck. Fuck. Fuck.

There were not enough fucks in the world for this.

"What time is it?" she snapped her gaze from one nightstand to the dresser and then to the other searching for a clock. Completely forgetting her phone displayed the time at the top of the screen. The digital read-out from the alarm clock on Derek's side read 11:52 a.m.

She wasn't just late for work. She'd missed almost the entire thing. She hadn't called. She hadn't texted. Callie stared down at the notifications of the missed calls, and began to shake. Tears weren't falling. Maybe her body already knew it needed to conserve water, because she sure as shit wasn't going to make enough to cover both rent and the water bill now.

4:42 am Missed Call

4:44 am Missed Call

4:45 am Voicemail

5:22 am Missed Call

8:02 am Missed Call

8:03 am Voicemail

Callie's thumb hovered over the button to access her voicemail. Imagining the disappointment in Louisa's voice would be worse than the real thing. It had to be. Right? Callie tapped the button, and brought the phone to her ear.

"Callie, are you okay? Is Josh okay? Worried about you, honey. Please call." Louisa's genuine concern poured over the line like agave nectar. The sweetness stuck to Callie, choking her pores and reminding her how she'd let someone down. Someone that *chose* to care about her.

Callie sucked in a ragged breath. Derek peeked in the door. "Callie, are you…" he trailed off. Her face was hot, and her vision beginning to blur. She probably looked as much of a mess on the outside as she was on the inside. He stalked toward her, and sat next to her on the edge of the bed. Callie's feet didn't reach the carpet. Derek's bare foot slid beneath hers and his arm curled around her waist. He would keep her grounded. She would not completely lose it. She bit her lower lip, and tapped the second voicemail.

Derek stayed quiet, because he was a smart man and her rock and better at handling crazy crying girls than anyone she knew.

Louisa's second voicemail opened with a long sigh. More than three hours of waiting, worrying had changed Callie's boss's attitude. "I don't know what's happening with you. Know that I'm worried. That I care. I want to hear from you, to know you're okay, but also you left me short staffed this morning. I've given you more freedom than we give other employees, but we have a firm policy about not calling in. I'm sorry Callie. A no call-no show, means no job. We will mail anything in your cubby along with your last paycheck to your apartment." Another long sigh. Then Louisa added in a rushed whisper, "Please let me know you are all right. If you're in the hospital with Josh, I can make them give you your job back. I think. Just call me, Callie."

Callie slowly lowered the phone from her ear, and then tapped the button to lock the device. She didn't want to see the screen and its accusing list of missed calls again. She stared at the chipped purple polish on her toenails. She focused on Derek's hand now on her thigh and the raised, patchwork of scars on his knuckles. She wanted to punch something. To scream. To earn scars to match how badly she'd ruined things. Instead she let tears track down her cheeks and topple onto her lap. Derek wiped them away with a touch so light she almost couldn't tell he'd done so. He rested his forehead against the side of hers.

"How bad?"

"It's good you have room for me in your bed, because I'm not going to have a place to live within four weeks."

"You got evicted? For what?"

Callie shook her head, but couldn't appreciate his

indignation now. "No. I was supposed to be at work at four thirty this morning. I was here. Sleeping. After spending a day trying to solve the Soul Charmer's bullshit problems."

Derek made nonsense calming noises and rubbed her back. The effort was appreciated, although it didn't change anything.

"Can you call and explain?"

"No. Explaining that my unpaid apprenticeship took priority over the job that pays my bills would not go over well."

"It wasn't just your apprenticeship. We're trying to find a killer." He was so earnest. The plea on his face almost stung with how much Callie wanted to simply acquiesce.

"That's not something we can tell other people, and you know it. It doesn't change anything. It's not something other people would understand. Hell, Louisa thinks the Church has signed off on soul magic. She isn't going to take the idea that people are killing one another over souls well at all."

Derek frowned, and Callie could almost see his mind spinning and seeking an answer for her. A way to fix it. She let out a long breath and leaned into him.

"I don't have a job now. I…I…I don't know what to do with that." It was the understatement of the century. She'd spent her entire adult life trying to make her way with honest work. Legit, hard work. No cons, no crime, steady hard work for steady meager pay. And she'd blown it because she was off hunting a person who killed a kid and stole from the Soul Charmer? She didn't carry a badge. It's not like she was a cop and would get to do the right thing and put the bad guys in jail. There were too many grey areas at this point to even be sure that she wasn't classified as one of the bad guys. Ford was definitely worse, so on the scale that made him the relative bad guy, but fuck. The lady who made breakfast and lunch for senior citizens was definitely a whole lot farther away on the evil bastard scale. She'd liked being that person, and now she wasn't her anymore.

She could try to get a job somewhere else. It wasn't like Cedar was the only retirement home in Gem City. Who would want to hire someone with erratic schedules and who came in with dark circles under her eyes because she'd spent the evening extracting souls from delinquent soul renters or tracking the kind of nasty person who would kill a kid to get one over on a business rival? Hell, at this point she wouldn't hire herself.

"We need to talk to the Charmer," Derek said with the finality of someone who had a plan. Only he hadn't shared it and whatever plan involved going to see that sketchy fuck right now was not something Callie was emotionally prepared for.

"I can't. I need to call Lou. Apologize. Whatever."

"Is she going to give you your job back?" Pointed question. He definitely had a plan.

"Not unless we want to doctor some medical records to say I was in the hospital."

Derek scowled at her.

She was having a crisis and he was scowling? "What?"

"You're doing complicated, dangerous work for the Charmer, yeah?"

"Yeah," she said weakly.

"You lost your day job because his shit spilled all over your life, yeah?"

"Yeah."

"Fucker needs to pay you, and I know for a fact he pays well."

"I need him, though. Until he takes this magic out of me, I can't do shit about it."

"He's a shit teacher. You learned about pulling souls out and putting them in bottles without his help. You'd manage if he didn't offer more lessons."

He had a point, but the idea of being on her own doubly in one day was not appealing.

"He needs you. He doesn't have anyone else who can do what you do with the souls. He needs an apprentice, even if he won't admit it. We tell him he needs to start paying you, or you're done."

"That kind of ultimatum sounds like it would end in me getting blackened with flames again."

"Maybe, but afterward he'd agree to pay you. I've worked for him for years. You're going to have to trust me on this."

"Okay," she agreed, though it lacked any enthusiasm.

"Put on some clothes. I'll make coffee—it's all I've got—and then we'll go talk to him. We'll get you a paycheck, and then I'll buy lunch."

He made it sound so simple. Like he solved crises of potential homelessness everyday.

"Okay," she said again, but this time with actual agreement.

Callie had only ever wanted to live a straight life. No crime, no cons, nothing she would be embarrassed to tell a priest she did for a living. She'd already been doing underhanded shit for the Charmer for weeks. She'd struggled with what it said about her. Her days were dealing with the very people she'd been trying to escape her whole life. She was hiding crimes from the cops. Yet the Cortean Church was a part of it. A priest had told her as much last night. The job was borderline legal, if not ethical.

Rationalizing was a skill one learned over many years. Callie was rationalizing at a professional level at this point. She told herself if she could get the Soul Charmer to put her on a real payroll—W-4 and all—then she could spin this in her head as okay for a limited time. She'd do what needed to be done, get paid, keep her apartment and fill her 'fridge. She'd survive, and continue to convince herself it didn't mean she was a criminal.

If she was lucky, it might actually work out.

CHAPTER TWENTY-FOUR

Entering the dilapidated storefront of Gem City's premiere soul renter never got easier. Callie had pushed open the chipped black door dozens of times. She'd soft-shoed her way across the sagging carpet just as frequently. She'd ignored the aging tapestry on the far wall, and the way the embroidered conquistadors watched her through their bits of black and gold thread. The first time she'd entered these walls she'd been desperate to save Josh, to get a soul to keep Ford from killing him. The Charmer had seen right through her, used her, bribed her, and it had led her to this. To being his apprentice. To coming into this den of moral dereliction of her own volition.

Now she was going to ask for more of it.

To make it official. Real. On the books. Whatever words she conjured couldn't capture the idea that she was taking another step toward becoming fully part of this world. It was easy to convince herself she was going to escape this gig. She'd been doing it for Josh, and then to keep herself safe as the soul magic within collided with every other magical element outside of her. She'd needed the Soul Charmer to learn to keep from freezing to the cart in the middle of the grocery store. She still needed him for that, but she'd deluded herself into thinking there was an end. Now she was going to up the game and ask for a paid apprenticeship. She wanted to believe she was better than this. Better than the kind of woman who would dabble in the barely legal.

The truth was, at her core, she wasn't. She was a survivor, and if that meant doing the wrong thing to keep herself or those she loved afloat, she'd do it. At least this could be honest work, if not noble work. That was all true if Derek was right. If the Charmer really would pay her enough to cover her rent, food, the heating bill, and the other essentials.

A portly man in a business suit blustered in the door behind Callie and Derek. He shoulder-checked Callie as he hurried his way to the counter. Did he think there was a run on souls at the Charmer's shop? It wasn't like there weren't enough to go around. Even without knowing that apparently the Charmer could swing by the well for a cup of souls, there'd never been an issue with people having access to souls for rent. As long as they had a handful of cash or a valid credit card. Callie bit back the urge to call the man on his rudeness. She shot Derek a "that fucking guy" look, and his pursed lips mirrored her internal irritation.

The guy tapped the bell on the counter three times in rapid succession. At least he thought he was the most important to the Charmer, too. Derek inclined his head toward the back curtain. Callie nodded, and the two walked passed the business suit asshole and toward the back. The Charmer exited the curtained doorway as the portly man was beginning to huff. Their boss gave Callie a wink, which made her stomach spark like she'd eaten twelve habaneros in as many seconds, but he let them pass. For the best. The Charmer could help the customer while Callie attempted to corral her baser thoughts.

She forgot to buffer her energy as she moved through the doorway, though, and spent the first fifteen seconds in the backroom trying to scrub the invisible, oppressive tar from her skin. She sucked in quick breaths, which echoed throughout the room until the walls were hyperventilating and she was more shaken than before. Fucking great.

"Callie, grab one of the 454/2000 jars and bring it up here," The Soul Charmer practically crooned from the front of the store. He must be putting on a hell of a song and dance for the business guy.

Callie moved to grab the appropriate jar from the nearest shelf. She slid a hand into her pocket to wrap around the flask. It was a steady buzz beneath her palm. She took the jar in her other hand, and was pleased when fire didn't rake her bones. Another day she'd think about how her life had gotten to the point where it was a surprise not to be burned, but today her brain was too mired in staying alive to think about the finer points of her situation. Getting on the Charmer's good side was paramount. She needed cash. At least for a little while. Until the apprenticeship was done, he took his magic back, and she was able to find a normal job that didn't involve any mafia lords, underhanded businessmen, or junkies looking to escape.

She mentally pressed against the air around her as she moved through the doorway. The trickle of tar teased the side of her neck, but she managed to escape without being coated in the thick protective magic. She stepped back into the storefront, and the businessman straightened upon seeing her. She hoped he remembered whacking his shoulder into her earlier as she cradled the soul he was paying for in her palms.

She tried to hand the jar to the Soul Charmer, but he pretended not to see the move, and stepped into the main area of the room. She followed, because the counter wasn't protecting her from anything in this musky, moldy room.

"Mr. Gillem here would like to rent that soul," the Charmer said.

"Don't use my name," the customer squawked.

The Soul Charmer smiled and shushed the other man with the gentle kindness of everyone's favorite TV grandpa. Seeing him soothe only set Callie's teeth on edge, but she didn't move. She heard snakes could detect fear. "She's my apprentice. My secrets are her secrets. Fear not," he told the customer.

Callie bit into her tongue hard enough the iron tang of blood welled. She wished she knew half of the Charmer's secrets. Now wasn't the time.

"She's going to place the soul in next to yours now. Are you ready?"

Callie wasn't completely certain if the Charmer had been talking to her or the client. The businessman took two calming breaths that his wife probably taught him and then closed his eyes. He held his arms out wide, palms open, as if he expected to be raised to Heaven any second from the freedom of a bonus soul. Since he couldn't see her, she rolled her eyes. The Soul Charmer shrugged in response, like this kind of show wasn't anything new to him. Preying on idiots and the desperate were his bread and butter, she supposed.

"I don't know…" she whispered to the Charmer like the business dude couldn't hear her.

"Go ahead," was all the Soul Charmer said.

"Do I have to do the…" she waved her free hand around. Most of the time when the Soul Charmer placed a soul into one of his clients—mostly those dropping more than a dime on the deal—he put on a showy production with anointing them and the soul and making the sign of the cross like he was a priest and not a shady, vindictive man who would take more than he gave.

He shook his head no. The client was twitching a little, probably from his attempt to hold his crucifixion pose longer than his weak muscles could maintain.

If she was going to ask the Soul Charmer to make her an employee, she had to do this. You couldn't decline tasks when asking for more money. That was like pay raise negotiation 101. Fine. She took a tentative step toward the businessman. He didn't move. She pulled the lid off the jar, and peered in at the gossamer tendrils of the untethered soul inside. She focused on what was inside the jar, on each thread, and told them, "I have a home for you." She hoped they'd heard, because if she went flame-on next to this dude there was no way she wasn't going to scorch him.

Callie pressed the lip of the jar against the man's squishy chest, and tilted the jar up until the opening was sealed above his sternum. The soul remained coiled within the jar, though.

The Soul Charmer hissed in her ear, "Give it a nudge."

Her reflex was to shove the jar firmer into the guy's chest. He groaned, but didn't stop his posing. That wasn't what the Charmer had meant, though. Callie grabbed onto the magic tendrils tingling below her skin. The ones that would ignite if the soul escaped. The ones that locked up and hid when there was minimal soul magic to feed on. She pushed them toward her hands. She was a mama bird nudging her chick out of the nest. She tapped her magic against the bottom of the jar, and urged the soul to, "go on now." It worked. The subtle warmth of the second soul seated beside the host's emanated from the man. Callie didn't mind her body's reaction this time. The dappling of sweat on her forearms from the not-quite-hot sensation was fine, because she had experienced the alternative. She'd just put a soul in another person's body. She was part of this in a way she couldn't revoke. Paystubs wouldn't change how finite her involvement was. She'd helped someone evade sin. She'd put someone else's soul in them. There wasn't a way to return from something like that.

Perhaps that had been the Charmer's goal all along. He beamed with paternal pride, which only made Callie want to upchuck the cup of coffee she'd downed before arriving at the shop.

"Be sure to be back in 72 hours, Mr. Gillem," the Soul Charmer said with that cutting undertone she'd never heard from another human. "And do enjoy your class reunion weekend."

Oh, ick. That dude was going to try to relive misspent youth. Probably all over the backseat of a Camaro.

The customer left, and the Soul Charmer transferred a wad of cash from the pocket of his PJs to the cash register.

The act was so odd she had to ask, "Why didn't you put the money in there from the beginning?"

"If they want to feel like they are cheating the system, making it a standard business transaction doesn't achieve the desired effect. Showmanship is more important than customer service in our business." His toothy, silver smile did not put Callie at ease.

Callie set the now-empty jar on the counter, and squared her shoulders before the gnarled old man. He was deceptively small and frail, but Callie wasn't new to his moves. He could be across the room in seconds. He could rip a soul from a body in less than that. She had to focus, because this was important. "Speaking of business transactions, I have a request."

"A request? Now? What could you possibly need? Did I not just teach you how to place a soul into a host?" The Charmer hadn't moved, but he had pushed Callie on to heels nonetheless.

"Yeah, um, thanks for that. I didn't know I could do that."

"Of course you could. Commanding souls takes focus. You finally have some."

Right then. "Here's the deal. I need to be paid for said focus."

"Excuse me?"

"This needs to be a paid gig." The words tumbled from her mouth like pebbles in a deluge of melted snow down the mountain. Sedentary stones forced to flee or be buried in the wake of change.

"You demanded this apprenticeship. You wanted to learn. Your payment for services has been in knowledge."

"Do you know what I've lost in *learning* here?"

"Certainly not any skin. You've gained a valuable weapon, too." His arm snapped out like a whip, his knobby fingers around her wrist in less than a blink. "Did you think I didn't notice?"

His fingers were clammy, but the white band circling her wrist cooled beneath his slick touch.

"I didn't know…" Callie trailed off. The list of what she didn't know was lengthy, but she also wanted to believe this puckering white of her skin was not related to the Charmer.

He squeezed a little harder, and when he finally released her the back of her wrist had returned to the light brown, but the inside a halo of white the size of a silver dollar. "This means I was right about you. It means your body can handle the magic."

Fucking seriously? He was so proud that she was still his damn tool. "Were you not sure I'd survive when you shoved it into me before?"

The click from the back of his throat was more derisive than outright rolling his eyes at her. "Get over it. Honestly, tell me how awful your life is, child."

"Thought you could see my soul," she shot back.

"Your soul doesn't share your memories with me. You should have learned that by now."

He could touch her and change the world. One squeeze of his hand, and the mark of stealing a soul from her mother shifted. And he didn't get it. He didn't think her life had changed? Fine.

"I have lost my freedom. I've lost my sense of right and wrong. I've lost the ability to sleep at night because I'm stuck staring at a dead teenager I found outside your building every night when I close my eyes. I've lost plenty, Charmer. So don't fucking act like this is pure charity you're giving me. You're getting answers. You're getting to find out who is after you and your business. You're getting a backup for grunt work with souls. You're getting a second set of hands. And you've been getting it for free, which I managed until solving your shit lost me the job that pays my fucking bills. So quit being a bitch and pay to keep me around. I can tell you're going to need me, because shit is not about to get any easier around here."

Tirades were not typical for Callie. Letting loose on the Charmer should have left her elated. She'd told him off. Yet she was left merely exhausted, and a little scared of what her antagonistic throes had done to her prospects for food and shelter for the next few months.

The Soul Charmer ratcheted his neck to the right until his ear almost grazed his shoulder. Then he did the same on the other side. Callie could almost hear a *click-click-cli-click* in between each of her breaths. His serpentine motions served to shove those scattered pebbles from her diatribe right on back into her mouth and down into her stomach. The weight made her knees shaky, but she refused to move. She couldn't afford to.

"You want to be employed."

It wasn't a question, but Callie still managed force herself to reply. "Officially. Yes."

The Soul Charmer made a series of noises in the back of his throat that were probably designed to unnerve her, but mostly suggested he was thinking. Perhaps she'd spent too much time around Derek to be tossed off kilter by a rasp or a rumble. "I will make you an on-the-books employee…"

"Great. Thank you." Callie tugged her sleeve down again, and let some of her unease fall away.

"With a caveat. You expected to have information for me. Who is after me?"

Derek approached from the back room, but Callie wasn't about to consult before answering. "Ford is at the core of it. He's after your business, though one of his henchmen did much of the legwork."

"Ah. His business with me has dwindled since I added a frequent-use tax."

"Wait, you made them pay more because they bought often?"

"Souls don't grow on trees. Supply and demand. I had what they needed."

"They know about the well," Derek said from safety behind the counter.

A flare of pure black flashed over the Soul Charmer's eyes. "How?"

"We don't know enough yet," Derek said.

Callie added, "We heard they had a book."

"They haven't been to the well. The church won't let them in," Derek said.

"Of course they can't access the well. Even if they were to find a way in, the soul well wouldn't grant them entry. They couldn't tend the magic required to quell the offload. They'd die trying." The Charmer said this last part as though he was considering letting Ford and his cohorts do just that.

"At least we know who is behind it now and why," Derek said with the confidence of a man who was used to solving finite problems.

"But he hasn't been stopped, has he?" The Charmer's icy tone cut through the room until even the incense in the far corner quit smoking.

"He will be," Derek said with the menace that probably got him this job.

Callie did not have much in the way of menace, but she had a hunger to keep the lights on in her apartment. "What do you need?"

"Find Ford. Resolve this."

Oh, was that all? "Already working on it," she said through gritted teeth.

The Charmer simply smiled. "Good. You take care of this, and you're employed." He threw out a salary figure that was triple what she was making now.

Derek coughed loud enough to act as an elbow to the side. Callie was about to graciously accept, when the Charmer upped the figure to quadruple her wages from the retirement home. Almost crime definitely paid.

"Done," she said before the Soul Charmer could take it back.

His tongue darted to wet his lips, and Callie swore she heard a hiss. Derek hadn't flinched, though, so maybe her mind was playing tricks. "Take care of this Ford business today. Now."

"On it," Derek said. He rushed out from behind the counter, slung an arm around Callie, and ushered them both out the front door. He hadn't run, but even outside the building the two moved with purpose to Callie's car.

He opened the passenger-side door for her. "You want food first, or are you ready to convince Ford he needs to stay out of the soul business?"

Derek was so matter-of-fact about it. No matter his nonchalance, she *knew* this wasn't something he did every day. He hit up petty people and dads stepping out on moms and junkies hiding their addictions, and made them return what didn't belong to them. He did not have to go toe-to-toe with the mob on the daily.

"I'm going to need sustenance so I don't topple over in the middle of pretending I'm scary. So, food."

"I'll handle the scary side," he said as he slid in to the driver's seat. "Though, if you could do a little fireworks show that probably wouldn't hurt our case."

She wiggled her fingers at him. "Fireworks?" That was a nicer word than suggesting she threaten to immolate the man.

"It'll be fine," he said, softly.

Two kinds of scary had to be better than one. "Get me a sandwich, and we'll get this over with."

That was, if she managed to keep the lunch down and not get knifed the second she stepped foot onto Ford's property. Easy enough, right?

CHAPTER TWENTY-FIVE

Derek held his gaze steady when Callie told him the best way to approach Ford's house. He didn't even question why she'd know where the private entry was located. Her lover was smart and would have pieced it together, but she had to bite back the urge to explain she'd been here for Josh. She didn't need to justify herself. He didn't require that of her. Unfortunately that left her to peer at the expansive home. Though it was only a single story, like most houses in Gem City, Ford's home *sprawled like it was claiming desert territory the way its owner claimed city blocks.*

They'd bumped along a gravel road to reach the winding driveway. It would be difficult to sneak up on the man out here, unless you had serious survival skills and not a single fear of snakes. She heard one rustle in the nearby bush when she exited the car. Callie did a cursory inspection of the path to the doorway. Suddenly more concerned with her rubber-soled Chucks' ability to withstand snakebites than the sharper stabbing that could greet her within the building.

One thing at a time, she reminded herself. Derek's hand was a steadying presence on her lower back, and the two moved up the walkway with little fanfare and zero snapping snakes. Her nerves had pushed her body into red-alert. Her jacket was too tight. Her lungs too small. Her stomach toyed with rejecting the BLT she'd eaten, but she swallowed hard and willed her body to *hold it together.*

They stood before the oversized door. It was probably crafted from a single plank out of some historic tree only found on a mountain or some shit. Whatever it was, it was expensive. A camera above the door panned toward them. "Do we knock?" she mouthed the question, as though the camera had ears.

"I do." He didn't modulate his voice. He didn't care who heard him. His balled fist slammed hard against the stained wood. It thudded hard. Again. It was a pure demand. The camera in the corner to the right of the door whirred, but didn't move. Callie assumed it was zooming in on them, and flipped the bird. Her insides were mush and weak and scared to the point her stomach was trying to shuffle behind her spleen for cover, but Ford liked a game. He enjoyed using his power to put people in their place, as he saw it. He wasn't the first man she'd met who liked to treat others like doormats. He was arguably the most lethal, though. None of that mattered. She needed inside. She hoped the taunt, which he might read as playful if she were lucky, would get them through the door.

The deadbolt clicked, and the knob twisted. Callie's gut did the same thing. An anesthesiologist she'd once worked with told her he was paid to wake people up, not put them to sleep. She was starting to understand him. Getting in was the easy part, and getting out was the part that would require finesse.

The door's hinges whined, and Callie straightened her spine. As though good posture could improve this situation. The last time she'd been here was a haze outside of her terrifying interactions with Ford. She couldn't recall who had escorted her into the house before. Today, though, she'd remember.

Nate held the door open, but stood in the frame. Every bit the bouncer he'd likely been before Ford gave him his criminal wings. He was gnawing on the end of a strip of beef jerky. He yanked off a piece and chewed and chewed and chewed. As each millisecond passed his eyes ripped over them. Callie could feel when he lingered on her. She'd have bruises from that gaze in the morning.

He finally swallowed, and then sniffed hard. She had to remind herself that if she walked out of here with bruises and a fucking cold, she would be lucky. Walking out alive was a win. Staring at Ford's henchman's craggy face slathered with derision, Callie began to wonder if this was, you know, a really bad idea. Unfortunately, her life had become a series of poor choices, and that wasn't going to change today. Getting in that house, convincing Ford to leave her boss alone, and possibly dragging him back to the Soul Charmer's shop were required. She needed to succeed if she wanted a chance at her own life not devolving into homelessness, dead kids, and iced or torched skin battling it out for dominance in a soul-magic-heavy world.

"What do you want?" Nate asked like she and Derek were selling magazines door-to-door.

"We need to talk to Ford," Derek said. His arm tensed around Callie's back. She pulled in one of those heady breaths of leather and soap, and kept herself steady.

Nate edged forward enough to close some distance between them without actually exiting Ford's house. He bobbed and weaved like he was listening to music only he could hear. His eyes met Callie's. "You change your mind? Ready to level up and work for my man?"

The obvious ridges of a pistol printed through the workout shirt Nate wore. If she stumbled forward, she might even be able to snatch it from his hip. Only she'd never held a gun. Shit would get worse if they started to bring weapons into it at this point.

"No, but we do have business with him," Callie said, injecting as much calm professionalism into her words as possible.

Hopefully he would use his words, too, and not the weapon at his waist.

Nate shrugged, and stepped aside. Derek stepped forward, but urged Callie through the door first. His hand remained pressed to her hip.

"Your funeral," Nate whispered as Callie walked

past him. She bit the inside of her lip, and reminded herself that the douche couldn't resist needling her. He had no power here or over her, and it was making him extra asshole-y. She strove to focus on her surroundings. The last time she'd been here, it'd been overwhelming and fear for Josh had redlined her nervous system. This time she was here on the Soul Charmer's behalf. She was employed by one of the other bad guys. Less bad, if that was a thing, but still a bad guy. No matter how hard she scrubbed in the shower or how much booze she doused herself with, she was still a part of this. She was entering enemy territory, wearing the specter of the Soul Charmer's protection, and doing it by choice.

Callie's shoes were silent on the plush rug running the length of the hallway. She moved forward enough for Nate to close the door and come to meet them. This house was a maze. A large sitting room opened on her left. The walls were ocher and a painting of a big-city skyline filled the far wall. Grey skyscrapers cut through the golden glow. Bulky beams ran just below the ceiling. They extended from the cheery yellow room to over Callie's head. The last time she'd gazed up at them, she'd been rendered unconscious. She righted her head and focused on what was immediately in front of her: the back of Nate's head, the extending hallway, and the silver sculpture of a siren singing to those off shore.

Nate finally paused in front of a door painted a rich plum color. He rapped his knuckles against it with the syncopation of someone who did it often. Callie had wondered why Ford would keep a guy like Nate around. He didn't come off as particularly smart, but she supposed since he ran around doing errands for Ford that Nate must be good at following directions. She'd still rather have to dance with Nate than Ford, but the time for dealing with middlemen was over.

A muffled "yeah" reached through the door and granted them entry.

The inside of the room was yet another bold color. How had Callie forgotten how ridiculously bright this place was? For a den of inquietude meant to shudder spines and rattle brains, the décor was downright cheery. The Saltillo tile and a broad window in the far wall only brought more warmth into the room. Ford waited for them behind a behemoth of a desk. He had those cherubic cheeks and soft, light eyes. When he smiled, she shuddered despite his dimples because she knew the checkered button-down and the well-worn jeans were all a front. He was not the boy next door. He was not a child at his daddy's desk. He was the butcher down the block. The one you took the extra fifteen-minute route home so you wouldn't have to see.

Callie and Derek waited in the center of the room. Sitting in either of the wingback chairs wasn't going to work. You couldn't threaten someone while sinking into expensive leather. She hadn't ever tried, but she was pretty sure her knees would be trying to bump her chin or something equally as awkward. This meeting was rattling her enough without having to worry about seating swallowing her.

"Didn't expect to see you back here, Callie," Ford said. He nodded to Derek as way of greeting, but kept his eyes locked on Callie.

"I hadn't planned to be back, either. Things change, I guess," she said.

Ford rose behind his dark desk. A small stack of papers sat within a bin at the corner, but otherwise the wood was unblemished by work. Last time she'd been here three severed fingers had lain on top. Zero fingers this time, which Callie counted as a good start. He walked around to the front of his desk, and then sat on the edge of it. He was only a couple feet from them now. He folded his arms across his chest, and kicked out a booted foot. He looked like he should be the high school football hero leaning against his fancy car. Callie wasn't fooled anymore. She saw the sharp glint in his eyes, the dirt darkening his nails, the causal lean that was too slick to be anything but a tool. She couldn't see knives, but he was close enough to cut her before she even realized a blade was out. He'd wanted her to know these things about him. The last time she'd been in this room, the threats had fallen thick and heavy and real. He didn't have her brother hidden away any longer, but the hint of a smirk smeared on his lips said he had something on her. Something he could do. Someone he could hurt. Some way to break her.

What he didn't know was she was already broken. She'd already lost her above-the-board job. She'd already committed to being a part of the Soul Charmer's business. She'd already accepted this was her life. She wouldn't have been in his study if she didn't have to be. That was as true as last time, but what had changed was the reason for her resolve. Last time she was here for Josh. This time she was here to save herself. To stop people being murdered and dropped where she had to see them, deal with them, mourn them, because no one else would.

"Change can be good. Are you here to accept a job offer?" Ford asked.

"I've already done that elsewhere."

"Derek, you're welcome into the fold, too. I can always use more clever muscle." Ford's words were genuine, or well rehearsed, but that didn't change the tone of dismissal they were built on.

Callie had made the mistake of thinking Derek would beat his way to answers and action when she'd first met him. She now understood, he avoided violence when he was able. It was easier, he pointed out, to get results when you didn't make the person spit blood. Ford had known him longer than Callie had. She should have picked up on it by now, but maybe Ford wasn't as smart as Callie had thought.

"Not interested." Derek's response reverberated against the barren, blue walls.

"If you aren't here to accept a generous offer, can you tell me why you felt it was appropriate to barge into my home?"

"We knocked. Not exactly barging." Callie sighed, and then straightened at the realization she'd just sassed a man who fileted human beings for fun. "We are here on business, though."

"Business?" He arched a brow like he was a cartoon super villain. It was not funny, though. Not even a little.

"Word is you're interested in the Charmer's work." Derek wasn't meeting Ford's gaze, but at least his voice carried a bombastic punch.

"Did she tell you that?" Ford's accusation stung. It shouldn't have. There would have been nothing wrong with her telling Derek anything. Why did she care if a mobster thought she was untrustworthy? She hadn't imparted his secrets. They'd been hers to share. This shouldn't be a "snitches get stitches" scenario.

Derek's shoulders rolled forward, and he inclined his head toward Ford. A full-body act of contempt. "We heard you'd hired an idiot to kill a kid. Want to explain that one?"

Ford laughed with all of the air in his lungs. It was loud, harsh, and meant to underscore their mediocrity. Callie wasn't new to games meant to dismiss and hurt. She'd been raised on that shit. Ford couldn't cut her too deeply with emotional barbs. It was the knives she worried about. This? This she could handle.

Ford's shrug was for show. "The Soul Charmer could lighten up."

How could he be so goddamn casual? "Are you saying you had a teenager murdered to rib someone?"

"Well, not anyone. The Soul Charmer." Ford pulled a pen from his pocket and twirled it between his fingers. His attention was tuned to the shiny exterior. "He has a monopoly and refuses to make smart business deals. There's value in reminding him that he is not the preeminent power in Gem City."

Callie almost asked if they should just solve this with a couple of rulers. Was this really about whose dick was biggest? Because she could handle a lot of wicked things, but the concept that a kid had been killed because Ford had his ego bruised was going to send her in a rocket ship to rage town.

Derek spared her from shoving her shoe in her mouth. "Let's not pretend that's what it's about. I hear your boy Nate is trying to rile the Cortean priests at the downtown cathedral."

Derek didn't have to say anything about the well or about soul magic. He was good at this careful dance. Callie hid her delight when Ford's face stretched tight. He didn't pale or flinch, he sharpened. Those chubby cheeks melted away to reveal nothing but defiance and menace. That was the face of a man who had killed people. It was the sharp stare of a man who would kill *them* if they didn't play this right.

"I don't know what you're talking about. I attend mass at the cathedral twice a week." The lie was so blatant it should have burned his tongue.

"Are you trying to say that priests lied to us?" Callie asked. Ford's gall was cranking her own.

"I...I...I..." Ford sputtered. Seeing a kingpin of violence unsure only unnerved Callie further.

"You what? What is it that you want, Ford?" Derek asked.

Ford pushed off the desk, and took the three steps to close the gap between he and Derek. "What I want is for you to tell me where your boss gets all those souls.

No one does business like him. He wants to screw me over on costs, but everyone else has ten souls at a time. Max. He has a hundred."

Callie didn't correct Ford. The Soul Charmer had hundreds—plural—in the back storeroom. "So you had a child murdered because you wanted a better rate on a soul loan? Are you kidding me?"

"That was no child. I had a drug-addicted soul user leveraged to get my point across. If you two are here, then it worked. Now, the question is are you going to help me get access to those souls or do I have to make you the next example?"

Ford's right hand flashed to his hip pocket. Silver glinted in it as he rotated his palm and shoved it straight toward Derek's stomach. Callie's hands were over her mouth. She might have been screaming. Her ears rang and the sound pinched her mind. Derek's hand darted forward, too, though, and his fingers wrapped around Ford's wrist, flipping and twisting and using the momentum of their joined motions to force the knife out to the right. Derek rushed forward to Ford's side, and shoved the blade and Ford's arm the opposite direction. The knife was tipped in blood and pointed toward Callie.

What the fuck was she supposed to do? She didn't know anything about knives other than that a sharp one stung like a motherfucker when you slipped while chopping chiles. Her butt collided with a bookcase. She hadn't realized she'd taken a step backward, but the knife wavered in Ford's hand mere inches from her. He and Derek were twisting and elbowing one another, but the knife was still pointed at her. She slammed her palms down on either side of her body, and was greeted by a thick, heavy book. Probably one that Ford put on the shelf to impress people, but have never read. She grabbed the book, pulled it from the shelf, and then swung it down hard on top of Ford's hand holding the knife. The blade clattered against the floor, and Ford let out an anguished battle cry.

Nate darted into the room. He shoulder checked Callie hard enough to send her wheeling back into the bookcase. The shelves slammed against her spine and beat her breath from her lungs. She gasped and gasped, but couldn't get air down. Her vision blurred and a heavy hum droned in her ears. She took another hard hit to the outside of her thigh and went down hard onto the tile. The familiar smell of warm leather met her before she'd fully registered that she was pulling in full breaths or that Derek was next to her.

The scent disappeared, and Callie fought to focus. She needed to get up. She steadied a hand on the tile. It slid in liquid. Her gaze sharpened to see she'd smeared blood across the beige block. She scrabbled backward, and shoved with her legs until she managed to walk herself upright. Derek had the knife. It was bloody. So was his shirt. Nate was a couple feet away. Blood smudged his right sleeve.

Nate blocked the exit.

"Let me go after him," Derek hissed with enough grit-laden force that Nate should have staggered.

Nate held steady. "Not an option, man. I told you both to work with us. Why would you want to side with that creepy old man?"

Derek edged to the right, and then the left. Nate mirrored his movement. "Honest living," was all Derek said.

Nate's laugh was cut off when Derek took a step forward. Nate reached for his hip.

Callie yelled, "Gun!"

Derek already knew though. Nate pulled the weapon from its hiding place with smooth proficiency, but the old adage about bringing a knife to a gunfight was wrong. Derek charged forward with the sliver of steel in his hand. He slashed down across Nate's torso from shoulder to hip. Nate began to double before he had the gun raised. Derek's forearm collided with Nate's hand and the gun flew across the room. Callie didn't track it. She was too focused on her boyfriend and how he rammed his body into Nate's. The two landed on the ground. Derek's forearm pinned against Nate's neck.

Callie scanned the floor for the firearm. She found it lying sedate and unthreatening on the floor against the wall. She picked it up. The black plastic was weighty in her palm. She yanked back the slide, and it made a satisfying *ca-click* that drew both men's attentions. Despite the powerful protection in her palms, her hands shook. She had never held a gun before, and she was scared she'd accidently shoot someone. She kept her finger away from the trigger, and hoped Nate would be more focused on the barrel than anything else.

"Where's Ford?" she asked between shaky breaths.

Nate smiled, and his gums were coated with blood.

"Gone, baby girl."

Derek hefted his weight forward, and Nate coughed. "Then I guess we have you to get answers from."

Callie tried to convince herself she could stay calm even with her heart racing and her palms sweating and her knees wobbling. Totally calm and collected. "Derek, we need to get him out of here. Somewhere to talk."

Derek looked at her for a long moment, before rising up. "Keep the gun trained on him."

Nate stayed on the floor, his grey shirt now a deep red. Derek's shirt was matted to his chest, too, but Callie couldn't tell whose blood was the source. She'd seen Nate slashed, but she wished she could run a hand over Derek to confirm he was uninjured. Instead she let him take the gun from her. The barrel stayed trained on Nate the entire time.

Derek leaned down toward Nate, and punched him hard in the head with the barrel of the gun. It was enough to make Nate go limp. Derek passed the gun back to Callie, and then squatted to heft Nate over his shoulder. "We need to get to the car fast. Grab his bag and the blanket on the back of the chair, too."

Callie hadn't even noticed the chair near the door. It had a dark blue woven blanket draped over the back. It was scratchy beneath her fingers, but she folded it over her arm and was pleased that it hid the gun in her hand. She grabbed the black knapsack from the chair, too, and then she and Derek were rushing back through the hallway to the front door.

She'd expected to be stopped by other members

of Ford's group. No one was in the house. Either this was a good sign, or they'd rallied around their boss and something ten times worse was waiting for them elsewhere.

She couldn't worry about that now. She had an unconscious man to finish kidnapping. Maybe she was more like Ford than she wanted to admit.

CHAPTER TWENTY-SIX

Heavy, grey clouds loomed overhead. They were low, and scratched with impending snow. Though the heat was cranked inside Callie's car, the air pushing out the vents remained cold. Callie didn't mind. Her skin was prickling with heat beneath her coat. Derek had tucked Nate in behind them and tossed the rough blue throw blanket over him. His unconscious body was wedged behind her seat, and the secondary soul seated behind Nate's sternum was igniting the energy around her. Callie popped open the glove box, and retrieved the flask.

"What are you doing?" Derek asked as she unbuckled and began to pivot in her seat.

"I can't take this." He held her hand up, but flames didn't lick her skin. Nate only had one extra soul inside. She'd gotten used to the hot flashes, but stacked on to her peak anxiety level she couldn't stand the nonstop pressure of the heat. She shook her head at him. "He's got a rented soul in him."

"Oh. Okay." After a moment, Derek added, "Give me a second to pull off the road."

He eased the car to the shoulder. Traffic was minimal this far outside of town, but it was better to have both eyes on Nate. Knocking someone out wasn't a precise thing. He could wake at any moment, and the shoelaces they'd used to bind his hands weren't exactly police grade.

Derek tossed the blanket back. Callie flipped open the lid of the flask. She bent around to wedge herself in the channel between the front seats. She pressed the opening against Nate's chest with less precision than she typically leveraged, but with more mental focus on what was happening. The onyx beneath her fingers came to life and offered that soothing, sweet, steady warmth that said the magical object was pleased. Her own skin released the excess heat as quickly as it had manifested it. She snapped the lid back on, and tucked the flask into her front coat pocket.

"That's so much better," she said, relaxing into the cushion.

Derek covered Nate back up, and then buckled back up, too. "Can you tell anything about that soul?"

"It didn't belong to him, but you knew that part."

"I wondered if it might feel different than the Charmer's. Could give us an idea where they're sourcing."

Callie sighed, but the exhaustion wasn't directed at

Derek. "I wish I could tell you it had a different energy. Maybe if I wasn't zapped, but it just felt like a soul. But Ford did say he was worried about a business deal, and he said everyone else only had around ten souls to rent. If the other, street-level soul magicians are offering up less than a dozen, they're probably pulling them from real people."

Derek made a sound of thoughtful agreement deep in the back of his throat. He pulled them back onto the road.

"The Charmer will get it out of him." He jerked his head toward the heavy mass under the blanket.

A heavy scarf of fear and anxiety wrapped around Callie's neck. She scratched at her throat, but the sensation wouldn't dissipate. "We can't go there."

"Why not?"

"I know what happens if we go there."

"Charmer sees we got one of the guys, and he gets answers. What's wrong?"

Callie's heart tried to leap out her mouth. She gritted her teeth and swallowed. She shoved her arms out of her coat. The cold in the car was a welcome slap. "He doesn't get the answers. He makes us do it. Me do it. I know what happens when I show up with someone with secrets. The Charmer pushes me to do things I can't forget or live down or whatever. I'm not letting him do that to me again."

"I can take him there on my own," Derek said quickly. His protective streak was usually pretty hot, but in this moment it only further riled her.

"No. I don't want him forcing you to do anything else that haunts you. He's already done that to us enough."

"Then why do we have that asshole in the back of the car?"

Callie wasn't the only one nearing her emotional limits. Derek's wounds were superficial, but the cuts were real nonetheless.

"We need answers," she said. "The Charmer demands them. Cullen deserves them. Even your brother would be safer if we knew them. It's important. We just…" Callie paused, not believing she was digging herself in deeper of her own volition. Better than being shoved into the hole, she supposed. "We just need to get the answers on our own. If I'm going to do some fucked up shit, I want it to at least be fucked up shit I choose to do."

"That doesn't mean it won't still haunt you." She hated when he used that voice that suggested deep scars and dark memories.

She softened. "No, it doesn't. It won't be the first thing I regret, but at least I can blame myself."

His hands tightened on the wheel, and the speedometer jumped five notches. "I don't want you to have regrets."

"I don't want you to have them either. We'll have less if we don't take him to the Charmer." Her tone was shockingly steady. The pressure around her neck eased. It wasn't that she was doing the right thing so much. Kidnapping anyone—even a murderous asshole like Nate—was firmly on the "not okay" list, but the fear of where the Soul Charmer would push her now, what he'd make her do, made this the better option. When it came to shades of grey, Callie would take pigeon tones over slate every day of the week.

The Soul Charmer's shop was wedged in a dank alcove downtown. A place where a brave tourist might venture or a drunk one might stumble. Callie didn't need prying eyes. She didn't need the Soul Charmer's gaze either.

So they drove away from town.

Toward new troubles. The kind she'd have to own alone.

The air above them rippled and shook. A small airplane streaked through the sky. Little black wheels visible beneath it. Callie hadn't had much reason to visit the Gem City Airport. It was small, remote, and required a fuckton of cash to get on a plane to go somewhere. She didn't have anywhere to go and zero money to get there regardless.

Derek had driven them to this squat warehouse in the shadow of the regional airport. The road leading them here had been riddled with potholes and pebbles that had plinked against her car like vicious rain. Their guest of honor had awoken, and bitched about the bumpy ride. Losing consciousness was not healthy. Doing it multiple times was worse. Callie knew they weren't doing Nate's brain any favors, but let Derek knock the guy out again. Typically she was anti-brain damage for anyone, but she wasn't about to let herself forget Nate's role in Cullen's death. There was a reason Derek was dragging the man out of the backseat now, and hefting him over his shoulder. Nate wasn't the abject bad like her mom or even the dealers who peddled meth to Josh. Nate was the kind of bad that took joy in pain, in sorrow, and in death. She needed to hold on to that truth if she was going to get answers. If she was going to be able to stop Ford.

And, damn it, she was going to stop him.

The metal building was long enough to house an airplane. Derek punched in a code on the keypad near the door, and then Callie was able to pull the metal gate back. It rattled and squeezed on rusted wheels. She flattened herself against the cool, pocked metal.

"It's okay. We don't have to be quiet here," Derek said. She could hear the smile on his voice, but didn't deign to look his way. She didn't need to feel anything other than fury going forward. Not if she was going to actually scare a mob guy and convince him to flip on his boss. Fuck. Even in her head it sounded idiotic. Luckily, the absurd was becoming more and more finite in her life with each passing day.

She stepped close enough to Derek and the unconscious sack that was Nate to let the shiver of his less-than-whole soul slither across her shoulders. The chill lit her anxiety, but also snapped something sharp and eager beneath her heart.

The warehouse's interior was barren and dark. Zero airplanes in this hangar. She found a light switch and flipped it. The overhead bulb gave them a single halo ten feet above. Each wall was cut with fogged windows that merely showcased the dim glow outside and didn't allow any warmth to peek into the building. The vast black creeping in from the walls ate the edges of illumination. Derek dropped Nate on the concrete floor with a soft smack, and then moved to close the door. The wallowing wind was somehow louder with the room sealed. Was that the bay of a coyote or another gust? Derek wrapped an arm around her, and pulled Callie in close.

His chin rested atop her head, and she felt both tiny and safe. "You sure you want to do this, doll?" he asked.

No, she didn't want to do this. That didn't change the fact she needed to do this. "Let's get it over with."

He kissed her forehead, and then went to pull zip ties from a nearby drawer. He bound Nate's hands and feet, and left him in the center of the bright circle. Who had ready-made restraints on hand? If she wasn't enamored with Derek, she might have considered this hangar a murder den. She whispered to him, "What is this place? How do you have all the…gear?"

He stared at his shoes for a long moment. Long enough to make it clear this *was* his place and she wasn't going to like his answer. Finally, he said, "I've been getting answers for the Charmer for a couple weeks. This is how we make sure the upstart soul magicians stay little league."

He worried at his thumbnail. Nate groaned incoherently behind them.

At least now she knew what wound the Soul

Charmer had been rubbing salt in the last few days. This wasn't a murder room, but it might have been a torture chamber. Derek, who abhorred overkill, had been stuck in this place because of their asshole boss. "The Charmer makes us all do nasty shit, doesn't he?" Callie sighed. "It's on him. Not you."

She took his hand, and then he met her gaze. His dark eyes were shimmering, the pain and relief bare for her. She kissed him.

"I hate that you have to see this," Derek said softly at her ear.

"I hate that he made you do this. At least we're together. We'll get it done, and get it done fast."

Derek gave her a stiff nod, but his fingers lingered between hers for another half second. He then nabbed the grey backpack they'd brought along and passed it to Callie.

Nate began to rouse in earnest on the floor, but Callie tried to ignore his low grumbling. She unzipped the main compartment on the bag and poured the contents onto the slim workbench where Derek had found the zip ties. There was a small work lamp clamped to its edge, and she flipped it on.

She wasn't sure what she'd expected, but a couple Marvel comics wasn't it. He didn't even read Deadpool or Ms. Marvel. She shoved the graphic novels aside. The bag had held a full pack of smokes, a tiny silver flask that did not ping Callie's soul radar, an Allen wrench, and a notebook. Why would a mob guy take notes? Hell, she and Derek didn't even talk in specifics when outside of one of their designated safe spaces.

She picked up the tattered, black book. At first she'd thought it was one of the hipster Moleskine ones. A couple of the doctors at the hospital had loved them. Pretended they were Hemingway or some shit in between rounds. This notebook was thicker, though. The edges of the pages were gilded like a holy text. The cover was pebbled leather, and the corners were bent and fraying. Everything about the petite book in the palm of her hand made her want to clutch it tight. To keep it safe. To keep it with her. She loved a good paperback—as the overdue library books on her nightstand attested—but this was a clawing need to protect.

Groans rumbled louder behind her. The scratch of denim against concrete. Derek moved toward the sounds, but Callie remained transfixed on the unmarked volume she held. This was a book of secrets. The thought delighted her enough to make her wonder if that joy should be shoved beneath her stomach like the other inappropriate feelings she'd buried. She needed honesty, though. Callie carefully peeled back the cover.

"This was a bad choice, Callie girl," Nate's voice strained behind her. A soft *thwack* and a raspy groan followed. Nate was mostly quiet again, and she focused on the title page.

STUDY OF ST. PETRO

PRAYER FOR

ORIGIN BALANCE

Callie could draw the Cortean Catholic crest in her sleep. It was on the page next to a delicately drawn bird. The outline was a thick black, but the sharp eyes and even sharper beak were clear. She'd seen this hawk so many places now she wasn't about to pretend it was a coincidence. The Charmer bore this mark. The Cortean cathedral downtown had etched this symbol into its confessional. Now this aged tome between her fingers had a more refined version of it. Whatever origin balance was, it clearly had to do with soul magic and the Church's well.

She began leafing through the pages. Prayers and diagrams rippled together. Talk of rejuvenation, redemption, and rebirth. Talk of the importance of praying for balance, and the strategies for doing so. The language was complex and steeped in the kind of overwritten double-speak the Cortean priests loved. It was like they thought they sounded smarter by saying something in twelve words instead of two.

Why did Nate have this book? How had he gotten an ancient text written by a saint? Did he think this would act as a ticket to get him access to all the souls Ford could handle? There was an obvious way to find out, and it was squirming its way into a sitting position on the floor not ten feet from her.

"That ain't yours." Nate's caustic accusation lost its power from his current, grounded location.

"Not yours either, though, is it?" Derek asked. His shoulder grazed Callie's.

He peered down at the book she held. From Nate's position, Derek didn't react. He didn't blink or smile or raise an eyebrow. The man was a master of the stoic visage. Callie, though, knew his body. Recognized and read the ripple of tension running down his forearm, the one now pressed against her back. He understood what this book meant, too.

"Is Ford trying to turn you into his own version of the Soul Charmer?" Callie tried to capture some of Derek's faux casual energy for herself.

"Ford doesn't make me do shit." Nate all but spat the words.

"Do you really believe that?" she asked before she thought better of it.

"Not all of us have to be blackmailed into a better life." Nate shrugged. He grazed Callie and Derek with blatant physical assessments. "Or bribed with a good lay, I guess."

Derek took a long step forward, and then planted the toe of his boot into Nate's ribs. The crunch was quick but replicated within the vast space. Nate coughed and sputtered. Derek merely said, "Guess you missed the part where you're tied up on a floor, but this isn't like on a street corner. We don't care how big you think you are. You're going to answer our questions or you're going to hurt. It's that simple."

"And does the Soul Charmer make you do that?" Nate taunted between gasping breaths.

"The Charmer didn't tell us to bring you here. He doesn't know you're here. No one does." Callie's cool tone was enough to send chills coursing across her shoulders. She managed not to tremble. This was the man who had picked Cullen to die. Who had used a teenager's death to poke at his boss's rival. For what?

"Ooo, kitty's got claws."

That earned Nate another jab from Derek.

Nate slumped on the floor, but his words remained sharp. "He's touchy about you. Interesting."

"Focus, Nate. Where did you get this?" She held up St. Petro's book.

"Library?"

Derek started to move toward Nate, and their captive quickly amended, "From a priest. I got it from a priest."

"Why would a priest give you that book?" Derek asked, not bothering to school his features. His brows were drawn tight enough *they* were ready to punch someone, too.

"Because not everyone loves your boss."

"It can't be that simple," Callie said, mostly to herself. "Nothing is that easy."

"Look, Ford already told you he was sick of your Charmer's fucking games. He changed the prices on us, wanted more and more cash, and didn't want to give us pure souls ever. Not that I fucking care. I get a high and escape the cops either way." As the words left his mouth, he seemed to realize he was not high in any shape. "You do something to me?"

"Other than the whole bound in a warehouse thing?" Callie was incredulous. How was this her life now, and how did it involve people as awful and idiotic as Nate?

"The buzz is gone," he said mostly to himself. Was he talking about the thrum of energy of soul magic or simply the way an extra soul affected him?

When Callie had accepted a second soul from the Soul Charmer she hadn't noticed a difference. If no one had told her she was toting a second soul around, she would have been none the wiser. She was alone there, though. The Charmer's clients spoke of euphoria, of instant easement of their minds, and the more one used rented souls the more physical signs appeared. The milky eyes, the scratching, the shaking, the full-blown addiction. Nate wasn't rocking, and his eyes were their standard dirt brown.

Callie shrugged. "Maybe playing with souls just isn't for you."

"Give it back," Nate snapped. He was working to get his legs under his body. Derek knocked him back down, and held him to the floor.

"No one gets to leave yet. Not without answers." Derek may have used his ripped-from-tar voice for Nate, but his face held a silent plea for Callie. They had to step this up soon or shit was going to go sideways. She nodded, though she wasn't sure if she was truly agreeing with him or making a promise to herself to keep moving forward.

"Ford wants souls. Why does he think he can do that without the Soul Charmer?"

"He is already," Nate said through gritted teeth. "He's got souls. Little D pulled that one out of the kid no problem. I have it now."

No, Callie had it now. In her flask. "How'd a dolt like Little D get that soul out? He doesn't have any magic to him."

"He slings souls just like your man."

"No, he doesn't," Callie said.

Derek punctuated the message by pressing his forearm harder against Nate's throat.

"The knife did all the work. I just had to tell him where to cut." The squeaking voice ripped from within the tight grip no longer sounded like Nate, and maybe that made it easier to continue.

Container magic didn't entirely work like that. Derek couldn't pull a soul into the flask, but Callie could. She didn't need a special skill to do it, though. The Charmer had "seen" she could do it. Little D was a murderer for hire. He was an idiot. Apparently, he also had enough latent ability to suck a rented soul out of a person.

Callie's mind was pulling more questions and deeper problems like taffy off the line, but Derek remained focused. "How did you know where to cut?"

"The book," Callie answered for him. "This told you how, didn't it?"

Nate's eyes were a bold white against the red of his puffed cheeks. He gurgled and squeaked, but didn't answer.

"Why'd you have to kill a kid? Why put him at the Charmer's doorstep? How does that help you get access to souls? There's no way that shit is in this book." She shook the bound pages at him, as though they'd compel the truth out of him. Leather and paper weren't magic, though.

"Derek, ease up on him," she said, wishing the words would reach only her lover's ears.

Nate slurped in air. "That kid was a junkie. Same as the rest of us." He paused to pull in a rattling deep breath. "Really? Do you have to ask why? I did it because the Charmer's a bastard and getting him worked up is fucking funny."

Callie sputtered now, too, but not due to a forearm pressing against her trachea. A junkie? The rest of us? Cullen had been damn near a child. He had liked to roll on molly. That wasn't the same as a junkie. She was well acquainted with the difference. She'd helped a real one get sober several times over and even then he wouldn't have deserved to be sliced and dropped at some enemy's door like an appetizer to war.

"Ford wants nothing from the Soul Charmer then?" Derek asked.

"We aren't going to need him soon enough. We just wanted him to suffer. Looks like it's working if he's got you two running around like this." Nate arced his stomach back toward Derek as much as he could, then whipped it forward bowing his back and rocketing the crown of his head into the bridge of Derek's nose.

Blood began pouring from Derek's nostrils. It spattered Nate's head, but he was already trying to move away. Derek's arm had loosened enough for Nate to gulp down air and inch away. He was still bound, though, and Callie hadn't learned anything useful. Finding the book was a start to understanding things, but how could Ford really make it work without the Soul Charmer? Ford had as much as told them there weren't enough souls to rent outside of the official business. Did he plan to murder people for their souls? They'd have to have rented ones inside their bodies while doing so, and it would only lead to a nonstop cycle of killing and more killing. As much as these men had no compunction about murdering anyone, including teenagers, she didn't think they would want to have to do it out of necessity. That'd ruin Nate and Ford's fun.

Callie planted the sole of her shoe against Nate's chest and kicked him backward. She followed him to the ground. She gripped his hair, Derek's blood slipping between her fingers, and yanked hard.

"You can't do soul magic. If you could, you wouldn't need the Charmer. How do you think you're going to get souls for everyone? How is Ford going to win?" With each question she pulled a little harder until her knuckles were wedged against his skull.

"I've read that book cover to cover. I know how it works. Give me time. If you can do it, I'm sure it isn't hard to figure out." He squirmed beneath her and bucked. Once again trying to turn everything into sex. Trying to use it against her. Trying to pull her down into whatever depraved version of her he pictured. He was a slug who had kids murdered to get a rise out of people. Fuck. Him.

Callie reached into her pocket and pulled the flask out. Her hand was slicked with blood to the point she couldn't see the icy webs covering her fingertips. Her anger kept her from stiffening, though. She hadn't known that was possible, but she hadn't ever been this outraged either. She flipped the cap open. The black stone set into the container sparked against her palm. She imagined it slurping the energy from Derek's blood. Her partner's life could be fueling her ability to stop this cruel person. The soul inside the flask chirped in the back of her mind. A tiny voice begging for safe harbor. She wasn't about to shove it back into Nate. The soul in this flask carried an echo of Cullen. She doubted Nate had read *that* in his books. A piece of the renter always left with the borrowed soul. She wasn't going to give Cullen back to the man who had paid for his murder.

Callie slammed the mouth of the flask against Nate's sternum.

He laughed. "We have a network now. I can get another soul."

Callie laughed, too, but it was the kind of cruel cackle that offered no humor or reprieve. It was the rumble of rapture on the hill ready to rain rocky retribution. "You can't replace your own soul. You'll be alive, but never whole."

"Wait! What? No. I have that kid's…"

Callie waited for the truth to wash over him. His ruddy cheeks tempered to a ghastly shade of realization. Derek had shoved some cloth under his nose. He held it there with one hand, the other pinning Nate to the ground again. He wasn't going to make her do this alone. Callie was too far gone into her fury to appreciate the act in the moment, but later she'd be glad that they'd both taken part. Even if it meant he'd have to share her remorse.

Maybe Nate saw it, too. Or maybe he'd resigned to how totally fucked he was. Either way, words gushed from him. Vulgar facts flowing hot and fast over the potential kindness they all used to have, but no longer remembered how to use. "Just. Just don't do that. I can't get into the well. The priests won't let us in. We—we—we have a group. I mean, Ford is building a cooperative of potential soul magicians. He's finding people who can take souls. He needs to get the Charmer to work with him or get out of the way. That's the only reason we were needling him. It'd be faster to use him to get access to the soul well, but Ford will get it either way. So hurting me doesn't change anything."

"It doesn't change anything about Ford's plan," Callie said, nodding. "It does get some justice for Cullen, though. I'm not about to let that kid go unremembered."

She didn't give Nate more time to talk, to tell her how he was actually a good person, or how this proved she wasn't one. She'd accepted that she wasn't going to get to lead the pure life she'd always dreamed of. She could, though, exact revenge for a teenage boy who was leveraged as a pawn. He'd deserved more. Nate didn't.

She cooed and called to Nate's soul. It was sticky and heavy behind his breastbone. Its weight pressed on her mind. Her fingers locked around the flask. Chills wracked her body until her stomach was convulsing. Bile burned bright at the back of her throat, but she focused. She couldn't beckon his soul. Whether this was because it was permanently affixed to Nate's body or because it was squishy and rotted, it wasn't clear. So instead she insisted.

She demanded.

She ordered.

She tried once more. This time pushing her energy into Nate's chest and wrapping her own flickering sense around his soul. "It's time to leave this place. Come with me," she commanded.

It did.

Nate's soul slipped soundlessly into the opened flask. Callie's energy snapped to her center, and she rocked back. Her fingers loosened on the flask. They'd blanched to a fresh shade of white, and cold sat deep in the bones. She could move them enough to cap the flask, and tuck it back into her pocket.

"Tell Ford to back off. Or this soul disappears forever."

Derek helped her stand.

Nate remained in a pile on the ground. A tiny flap of mottled black soul remained within his body. Enough to keep him alive. She hadn't killed him, but he'd never be whole again. The darkness of what she'd done worried her, but she couldn't find a way to feel bad about punishing him in that very moment.

Later, she would have to wonder who she had become.

CHAPTER TWENTY-SEVEN

The Soul Charmer drove a slick, classic sports car. It was not made for icy roads or frigid temperatures, but fortunately only tiny snowflakes were falling and the ground was still warm enough to keep from icing over. This did not make Callie feel any safer inside the metal box with her boss at the wheel.

She'd never pictured him outside the shop. It was a juvenile way to view a person, only thinking of them in the way they engaged with you directly. He was so smarmy and at home surrounded by his jars and his tapestries that she had pictured him a pure recluse. When she'd told him of Ford's plan to craft his own network of soul distributors, he hadn't taken it well. To say the least. The Soul Charmer bowed to no one, especially, he had said, "to bottom-feeding thugs like that." The fact they hadn't caught Ford did not count in her and Derek's favor with the Charmer, but he'd been pleased to see St. Petro's book.

"This is a treat. I can see how they thought they'd be able to learn from this, but even if they had potentials—like you—they couldn't have done much without access to the well," he'd said more to himself than to Callie.

It was then the Soul Charmer told Callie they were going for a drive. It sounded like he was going to take her someone to kill her, because being alone in a vehicle with a man who could steal your soul was inherently dangerous. Only Callie was now someone who could steal a soul, too. She hadn't told that part to the Charmer, and Derek hadn't as so much as nudged her to do so. Some shames need to stay secret. But the Charmer didn't let Derek come with them. As much as he'd become her shield in the shop, this was comforting. He had enough problems as it was. Instead the Charmer sent him to find Ford's whereabouts. An innocuous enough task, but one that mattered and suggested this chess game had already cleared the pawns.

Callie ran a thumb underneath the nylon seatbelt strapped over her chest. It was smooth, but with little effort could burn her. Like the Charmer. He was humming a children's song as he turned the car toward the plaza.

The sound, the song, the space, all of it was unnerving.

Callie sucked in her bottom lip, and released it slowly. "What is it we're looking for?"

"Looking for?" He jumped like he'd forgotten she was in the car. Great. "We aren't looking for anything. We're going to make it impossible for Ford to take what's mine."

Nothing about that sounded good. Especially not the *we* part. "He's locked out as it is, though, right?"

"He can't get to the soul well right now, but if he's already started using containers through his potentials, then he'll find a way. Kill the right person or torture the wrong one, and one can achieve horrible goals. Not my method, mind you, but effective."

Okay. The Charmer had never been kind, but he sounded a whole lot closer to the type of person she wouldn't feel guilty about ditching. Unfortunately, tucking-and-rolling out of the car was not a skill she had nor in her best interest. "So what are we doing then?"

"You're going to visit the well. With two of us we should ward off more usurpers. As long as your power actually grows." While the words were clearly a jab, there was this bubbling pride beneath them. He *did* believe she'd become stronger. He shot her a cutting glare, and while his coal eyes carried no emotion, the corner of his mouth suggested he wanted to smile at her potential talent.

The desire to be special was the most cliché of dreams. Every kid wants it. They want to be better than their siblings, the brightest star, the best at *something*. Callie hadn't been the valedictorian—not by a mile. She couldn't sing worth a damn. She wasn't a clever chef. She could only run fast if the cops were behind her. She didn't have any traditionally noteworthy skills. She was kind when she could be, and tried pretty hard to keep people she loved safe. That's what she had to offer the world. Only now maybe she had something else. Was soul magic a way to make the world a better place? Un-fucking-likely. But at least she could have something to hold on to for the moment. Something to keep her head above the rapidly rising remorse for losing the little bit of honest work she'd had.

Questions about this, about everything really, were setting stage in the back of her throat to bum rush the Soul Charmer. She hadn't opened her mouth yet, but he shook his head. "Not now."

She bit back her irritation, and tugged the seatbelt taut against her. She was locked in to whatever batshit thing was about to happen. Might as well hold on.

The Charmer parked his bright blue car across the street from the cathedral. She wanted to be surprised, but she'd known the soul well was here. The Charmer hadn't even bothered to act like she wouldn't know its location. She'd learned quite a bit during this apprenticeship, but very little directly from him. Perhaps he'd wanted it that way.

She unbuckled, and reached for the door handle.

"One moment. You're not ready yet."

Understatement of the century there, bud. "What do I need to know?"

"Plenty," he deadpanned, and Callie's stomach hollowed in response. "Give me your hand."

She did. "You going to teach me the secret handshake?"

"Something like that," he grumbled. The Charmer reached for the cigarette lighter. He yanked it out of the holder unheated. The one in Callie's car was charred on the end from Josh's use. The Charmer's was pristine silver. She didn't know if that was from proper cleaning or disuse. She was simply happy the tip wasn't red. The Charmer palmed the lighter. She could almost see the white of his knotted bones in his hand.

His grip on her right hand tightened. For a gnarled old man, he was strong. Her tendons grinded against one another. Her fingers began to tingle.

"One must earn passage into the origin well. You haven't learned as much as you should. You will, though."

"I will," she promised, unsure where this supplication was coming from, but unable to deny it.

"You make a promise by entering."

"What promise?"

"You can never take more than you need, and you must always give back."

"The soul well lives by the kindergarten principle of sharing to make friends?"

He yanked her hand hard enough to tug her one inch closer. "You will not ruin the balance. Once you visit the well, you can't *not* visit again."

The Soul Charmer was the one holding a lighter, but Callie was the one filling with heat. Her shoulders shook slightly at first, but a moment later she doubled over. Her ribs were caving in and her lungs attempting to punch their way out of the calcified cage.

The Charmer moved his closed hand over her wrist,

right atop the ghosted white halo that refused to fade, and brilliant blue flames rose from her skin. "To take souls and to bring them back, you must be willing to ferry them. You can carry souls, yes?"

Callie began to hyperventilate. Pain shot down into her hand and up through her forearm. The slashing flames cut as sharply as she'd imagined Ford's blades did. She was certain her wrist was being butterflied beneath the azure flickers.

"Callie, I asked you a question! Now! Can you carry souls?"

He wanted her to answer questions when her arm was being devoured? He yanked her hard again, and she eked out a "yes" in the hopes it would make everything stop.

It didn't.

"Calliope. Focus. You're almost done. Vow to be loyal."

"To whom?" she spat so hard through her clenched jaw she should have shot an incisor at the Charmer or at least specked his green robe with blood.

"The balance, child. You will be the nighthawk. Will you ferry souls to keep the balance?"

Had he just called her a bird? He might be able to do some pretty insane magic, but he could not turn her into a fucking bird. The flames arced around her wrist, snapping and burning until she was caught entirely by the flame gauntlet. She couldn't see any blood seeping from the inevitable wounds. As much as this hurt, it was magic. Like before. Like always. She would recover if she could simply make it end.

"Yes." It was a sigh and a plea and an agreement all in one.

That one word was more magic than she'd mustered all week. More magic than corralling rogue souls. More magic than taking Nate's. Her arm cooled quickly, but the prickling sensation of energy she associated with both the dangerous magic moves she'd made this week coiled around her wrist and coalesced on the inside slightly below the heel of her hand. The Charmer still held his hand over the spot, but all the skin she could see was healthy and unmarred.

"Good," was all the Charmer offered her. He released her hand, and placed the lighter back in the dash.

Callie gawked at her wrist. Unmarred had been the wrong assumption. Her skin was not the same. She hadn't been charred and her skin was certainly not falling off. The white circle from the debacle with Zara was gone. This should have been a large comfort, but instead she was transfixed by what she found instead.

"We have matching tattoos." There was no inflection in her voice. She wanted to scream, because they weren't sorority sisters. She hadn't signed on to get inked. But there it was. On her wrist. The same mark the Soul Charmer bore on his.

"That isn't a tattoo, but the mark of the holy nighthawk. That ungrateful tone is why I didn't want to show you this."

"You burned my wrist and marked me with a fucking bird and a *holy* one at that, and I'm the emotional problem here? Think not."

"That mark can only appear on those with the ability to move souls from body to body. Are you unable to pull a soul from a body or to put one in a container for safekeeping? No. So quit your whining and get out of the car. We need to see the well. You need to pull from it or none of this will stick and that weasel of a mobster will try to steal our power."

She'd been the one marked against her will, and yet the Charmer made her into the asshole. She kind of believed him. Overstepping is what the man did. Curiosity had her eager to see the soul well, but fear was what got her out of the car. It wasn't fear of the Soul Charmer. It was fear of what would happen if she didn't stay on his good side. Ford had already proven himself a realistic threat. If going with the Charmer into this church offered her another layer of protection from the gangster—protection she'd be able to leverage for her family and Derek—then she was going to suck it up and get her ass to church.

Callie examined her fresh mark. The petite hawk on her wrist had a dainty-but-vicious beak and wicked black eyes. White slashes at its neck and near the ends of its wings were both a relief from the dark, arcing feathers and a threat. This was a bird that would fuck you up. She'd seen them flying in the early mornings outside the retirement home. Hunting. They were beautiful and small. A sweet, soft shape from afar, but fast and savage when the time to strike arose. Callie wasn't certain she could epitomize this bird, but the part of her that craved the ability to protect others sure liked the idea of being able to bring the beak, as it were.

Sets of spotlights set the statues of saints aglow throughout the plaza. Even the lights looked up to the Cortean saints. Tourists milled between the opulent artwork. Callie couldn't recall seeing a portrait or sculpture of St. Petro, but the way the Charmer reacted to his book suggested he was of great importance. How had she never heard of him? Yes, she only attended services now to appease Lou or her mom and to generally keep face in the community, but there was a time when she spent hours and hours with the Cortean texts. Now wasn't the time to ponder her patronage of the faith.

A teenage boy held the door open for them. The Charmer didn't bother thanking the kid, but she did. She hoped no one recognized the curmudgeonly man with her. Or wondered why they were together. She had lost plenty this week, but apparently her pride was still intact.

A few people sat scattered in the pews near the front. Another knelt near prayer candles. One petite, older woman sat in the pew closest to the confessionals. The curls of her white hair sent a sharp stab of panic through Callie. No, she sighed, it wasn't Louisa. Seeing her former boss for the first time would be hard, but doing so at the Soul Charmer's side was something she couldn't bear. A tall man in work boots and a white tee splattered with paint exited the nearest booth, and the woman moved to fill the vacancy.

The Charmer waited until the woman was in the confessional to scuttle forward. He reached blindly behind for Callie and took hold of her wrist again. From afar it probably looked like she was helping him find his way. Her wrist heated beneath his, but no pain erupted. Thank God. A priest appeared from a rear door and rushed toward them. It was not Father Henry. This priest was middle-aged with a robust moustache and wary eyes. This man of God had seen too much.

"I'm so glad you've arrived. Things are… volatile." The priest had amended his language upon seeing Callie.

"Show him your wrist," the Charmer hissed at her, before realizing he was already holding on to said wrist. He tugged her forward, and let go.

The priest stared at her fresh hawk mark. His brows pulled together tighter and tighter with each second he examined the bird. Finally, he nodded. "It'll be good to have help," he said to the Charmer.

To Callie he added, "I am Father Giles. Please come with me."

The priest opened the door to the confessional at the end of the row without any fanfare. After the way Derek's brother had behaved, she thought there would be a special lock or code or password to get in. Nope. Just a pocket door. However, when she stepped through she understood. The heavy, oily barrier ricocheted around her, reverberated against every bone. The energy was stickier and thicker than at the Charmer's doorways, but she could sense the magic ordering her to prove herself. Unlike at the Charmer's she couldn't simply step through. Her wrist heated again, but emitted no flames. The invisible goo smashed into her face and squished up into her nostrils. A magical lard choking her pores and cutting off her airways. The panic rose with explosive intent, but Callie fought it back. She focused on the energy whirling around her center. The same energy she'd suffused into Nate to pull his soul out, she now used to part the energy acting as gatekeeper. Musty air rushed into her lungs, and she didn't mind the peaty notes. It was oxygenated and welcome.

The priest led them down a spiral staircase. It was black and metal and shook beneath the weight of three adults. Neither man showed signs of worry. Callie figured if they went down, at least she'd land on them. When she was close to getting dizzy from the tight corners and continual descent, they reached the floor. The painted concrete absorbed the light from the series of industrial bulbs overhead. Each was caged in a thick steel bracket. It was as if they were coal miners and not magicians in the basement of a church. Someone had secured wood paneling on each side of the corridor, but age had left the corners of the veneer to peel. This space had been tended once, but other than the lack of debris littering the hallway Callie didn't think it got much attention these days.

The Soul Charmer was shitty about maintaining much other than money and souls. Carpets, walls, cleaning, plumbing, signage, and every other essential a businessperson worries over were all at the very end of his to-do list. This had to be his doing.

The hallway ended in a bauble of a chamber. More of the industrial lighting circled the outer edges of the space. The whole look reminded her more of the middle-class cul-de-sacs where she had soul pick-ups than a majestic source of souls. It was the center of the room, though, that carried all the power. The well wasn't merely a descriptor. Black lava rocks were stacked as high as Callie's hip. They were smooth and the grout between them was so fine she could barely tell where one rock began and another ended. Radiant gold filigree adorned the top of the stack with shiny swoops stroking down the edges until every piece of the soul well looked otherworldly. It didn't sparkle, but the shine somehow stretched into Callie's chest. She closed her eyes and pulled in a long breath. She held it as warmth suffused her bones. The good kind of warmth. Not the same as the delightful touch of Derek, but close. Safety, certainty, and a steadfast focus seated in the base of her mind. She exhaled and opened her eyes.

The men were watching her. The Soul Charmer was clad in his loose pajamas, and the priest was in a well-starched suit. Both wore the intense gaze of a man peering beneath the surface. She'd seen that look before. The Soul Charmer wasn't the only one who could see her soul. Whatever they saw, neither commented on it.

Father Giles turned his attention to the well. "You can see the problem."

The grey smoke within the well churned and roiled. While Callie couldn't see anything wrong, she could feel it. Everything in this space was too much. The energy pouring from the well was packed against the walls, it was digging into her shins, it was dimming the lights, and it was exhausting her.

"You had quite a lot of souls decide they wanted back into our world." The Charmer's chuckle rattled against the walls. The lights tinkered in response.

Father Giles grumbled, but didn't argue. Whether this was an understanding or dismay, Callie couldn't tell. She, however, was full up on fear.

"What do you mean? Where did the souls come from?" she asked.

"The Lord!" he said. The priest's face puffed and reddened, and this only sent the Soul Charmer into a true fit of laughter. Callie thought she might hurl.

Father Giles pulled himself to his full height, and evenly reminded the Charmer, "Do not misunderstand our agreement as an opening to disparage the church or commit acts of blasphemy within its walls."

"He's no fun," the Charmer said to Callie. "This well connects our world and the other side. Sometimes there are too many souls in the in between, and it is our job to make sure the balance remains."

"So these are souls of people who aren't living any-more?" Callie's nose curled and her mouth pinched. She couldn't taste sickness in her mouth yet, but if this continued she wouldn't escape it this time.

"Or who haven't lived yet. Just think of them as unattached souls."

No one was saying limbo or purgatory, but the words banged the sides of Callie's skull loud enough to drown out her thunderous heartbeat.

"No. No, it can't be that," Callie took two quick steps away from the well. "The souls you sell aren't that pure. If these souls haven't even lived yet, they can't be carrying sin."

"It is very rare for us to get a pure soul from the well. That isn't the way the balance works." It was Father Giles trying to calm her. How was he okay with this?

"Oh, well, then explain how it works." Her combative words couldn't conceal her crumbling confidence. Her desire to tuck and run was apparent, and she couldn't do a damn thing about that either.

"Some souls need more to work through in order to progress celestially. I can't explain more to you than that. You're simply not ready. But allowing the Charmer to take from the well allows those souls a chance to come back and mature. Some souls are ready to move forward and get tangled elsewhere. He also can bring these travelers' souls back here. I can see the bitterness on your face, child, but if we do not maintain a balance of which souls need to be in the in between and which need to continue processing on earth, the well will no longer balance between the worlds."

Had he just suggested hell or purgatory or some shit was going to eat their world if the Charmer didn't poach souls to rent? Callie opened her mouth to ask what the fuck that meant, but he held up a hand.

"You can't understand it from simple conversation. The more you interact with the well, the more you will understand and know. Until you begin to work with it, and earn its knowledge, I can't give you more."

Callie was fairly certain that was the priest version of 'you'll understand when you're older,' but her brain was stretched to its maximum limits. She hadn't trusted the church before, and she'd been right. She'd have to relish in that one for a moment, because she might explode if she had to try to reconcile the truth of where the Soul Charmer acquired his wares.

"Enough jibber jabber. I need to get back to my shop, and we need to stop his magic from overflowing. I could feel it upstairs. You should have called me."

"You don't always take my calls."

Callie's phone buzzed, and it was so out of place all she could think was how it was a miracle to get reception here. She peeked at the screen and it was a message notification from fifteen minutes ago. From Josh.

"Calliope. Focus. You need to earn that hawk. Get over here."

She wanted to argue, but the man had branded her one of his. She wasn't prepared for what that argument would lead to. She tucked the phone back in her pocket and stepped closer to the Charmer. The lava rocks brushed her knees, and they were heated and slicked like the stones her cousin used in massage. The Charmer pulled three jars from one of his deep pockets, and handed them to her.

"Pull five souls from the well."

Callie stared at the trio of jars in her hands, and then back at her boss.

He flicked his fingers at her like she was a pet he was urging indoors. "Double up. They don't mind, and I'll put them in their own jars when we get back."

He pulled out another set of jars, and twisted one

under and over his palm. He then reached out over the well. A wisp of grey smoke rose slowly from the mist. It corkscrewed upward, and then dove directly into the jar the Charmer held.

His black gaze had once left her certain she'd be shredded. Now, though, with those beady eyes targeted on her she simply sensed the shove. The inherent 'do this or else' in his stare didn't scare her the way it should, but perhaps that was because the six-foot well of souls in front of her had claimed all her terror. That fear was all she had and she let it guide her. She set two of the jars on the edge of the well, and uncapped the third. She didn't have the flourish the Charmer did, but she still reached out over the opening and called to the souls.

There were so many. Her body didn't alight despite the fevered energy. The layer of magic over the top of the well bent and bowed. Though it didn't have any tangible qualities, Callie could feel it straining beneath her hand. Her mind darted from one wisp of a soul to another.

"How do I know which one to take?" Her voice echoed as though the chamber had expanded a dozen feet.

"Ask who is ready to return. They'll run to you." The Charmer's plain words were actual help. He could be a decent teacher if properly motivated, she guessed.

Callie called to the souls, beckoning those who were ready to come back to this world. She didn't promise them a life or anything good. The mule-kick to her gut made her add on a reminder that their journey would be inside another host, alongside another person. It didn't slow the souls straining to reach her. Whether they knew or they couldn't understand her, she needed to pull these free. The Charmer had filled his jars, and his stare burned bright on her back. Finally, a grey swirl broke through the barrier and buried itself into Callie's offered jar.

They repeated this process until the souls were secured in the jars, and the well had quelled. Callie hadn't believed the men that taking souls from this "in between" would stop the roiling energy in the room, but it had. The room had brightened, and the air had cooled. The vibrating hum that had pressed into her lower legs was gone, and even the grey mist in the well hovered in a pastoral cloud.

"We will tend the well. No one else." The Soul Charmer's firmness made Father Giles pull back.

"There are no other nighthawks here. You know this."

"It stays that way. She is my apprentice. Let her in without me."

"She bears the mark, Soul Charmer. You know the wards will always let her pass." Father Giles bit his lower lip and watched the Charmer. The gaze was much like that he'd given Callie earlier, as though he was examining something others couldn't see. Whatever he found in the Charmer, he didn't share. The priest clapped a hand on the Charmer's back, and then led them out of the basement and back up the winding staircase.

Altar boys were preparing for mass when they returned to the sanctuary. Callie thanked Father Giles because she probably was supposed to, and she and the Charmer exited the building without another word about the nighthawk, the well, or the souls in their pockets.

CHAPTER TWENTY-EIGHT

Callie's phone buzzed again as they exited the cathedral. She checked the screen, curious what Josh needed now, but the incoming messaging was from Derek.

Who never messaged if he could avoid it.

"Need pickup. At that house off Paseo de Real," the text read.

"Fuck," Callie said. She still stood on the church steps. Several parishioners shushed her. She didn't care. Derek was at Ford's house.

She typed back quickly, "Bring backup?" It was her best guess at how to code the question of if he was being held captive.

His reply pinged almost immediately, "No. Just a fast car. Hurry."

Callie turned to the Soul Charmer. "Your car is

fast, right?"

He grinned in that unctuous way that sent ants marching across her skin. "Of course. What do you need?"

It sounded like another bartering request from him, but minutes ago she'd pulled souls from some godly place on his behalf with minimal questions. She was not about to quid pro quo any of this shit right now. "Derek needs us now."

The Charmer's full-tooth grin made Callie suck in a breath to steady herself, but he was in. "He was taking care of a job for me. Of course, we'll help him."

The Charmer's lithe movements across the plaza and over the car didn't align with the visual of the hunched elderly man in bright pajamas. Callie didn't have time to care about the stares they received, because they were a solid twenty minutes from Ford's house.

For once, Callie appreciated the Soul Charmer's ego. He revved the engine, and she believed he could cut the drive time.

The Charmer didn't slow as he whipped onto the private drive leading to Ford's house. Callie hadn't needed to point out the obscured drive. Whether because he'd been here before or because of some supernatural skills, Callie didn't care. Black smoke stretched above them, thick and billowing. The cloud above them grew darker, denser as they zipped up the driveway. The Charmer stomped hard on the brake pedal with both feet. The car slammed to a stop. Callie caught herself on the dash before her head could collide, but her wrists sang from the impact. She was about to chide the Charmer, but then she looked out her window.

The front door of Ford's home flew open. It banged against the frame, and starbursts lit its glass inlay. Callie instinctively ducked low in her seat. She peered over the window ledge. The man followed the door in blasting from the house. Shoulders wide enough to graze each side of the frame.

Derek.

Running.

He was waving, and yelling, but Callie couldn't process any of it.

His cheek was a deep purple, and red streaked his chin and most of his shirt. Were those from earlier? His wounds hadn't been deep. His hands were blurs of black smudges.

He was almost to them.

Still yelling.

Shouldn't they be calling 9-1-1?

Derek coughed, and bent over. Callie shoved open her door and scooted over.

His words finally hit her. "Go, go, go!"

The earth shook, the car rocked, and Callie was thrown hard against the Charmer. His bony frame caught her with surprising strength. Steely fingers gripped her shoulders. "Move your legs. Let him in."

Derek was mere feet away now. A pillar of flame rioted behind him. Ford's house was unrecognizable wrapped in gold and tangerine swaths of fire. It was nothing but fuel for combustion now. No more pretentious bookshelves. No more expensive art. No more safe haven for a murderous mobster who had it out for their boss.

Derek jumped in the car, landing halfway on top of Callie, and slammed the door shut. He reiterated his earlier plea, "Go. Now."

The Charmer had no problem taking direction from Derek. His foot pressed on the accelerator with the same vigor he'd employed to the brake earlier. Callie was thrown back against the seats, but she couldn't feel the center console grinding into her back. The car fishtailed out onto the main road kicking gravel back at the darkening sky and the blaze obscured by a row of trees.

"Scanner." The Soul Charmer's word allowed for no argument, but Callie didn't understand the demand.

Derek eased Callie up onto his lap. His arms were shaking and rocks rattled between his bones with each breath he took. She rested a hand on his chest. It might have been in her head, but his stuttered breaths smoothed slightly. She needed it to be real. He reached behind her and flipped on the radio.

Her car picked up a classic rock station, two pop stations, and about eighty percent of the time an oldies station. The Charmer's car radio picked up police chatter. It was all numbers and call signs at first, and Callie couldn't follow. She was distracted by the way the cut below Derek's eye was puffing and oozing. He needed to get ice on it quick or he wasn't going to see out of his left eye for a couple days.

"Are you okay?" she whispered low enough for only his ears.

"Yeah, doll." He hugged her like there was more to say, like he needed it. After the things she'd learned about the Soul Charmer today, she didn't blame him for avoiding giving the man yet another secret.

"…correct. Three sites. All plastic explosives. Over." The radio had Callie's attention now.

"Bombs?" She was unsure which of the men she was asking.

"Necessary," the Charmer said.

Derek said nothing.

"What the fuck is going on here? Is that what happened back there? Did we blow up Ford's house?" She almost asked Derek if he'd blown up the house, but based on the way the Charmer and she were also in the car bolting back to downtown Gem City, it sure looked like it was a group effort. She had missed the planning phase, apparently.

"We sent a message," the Charmer said.

"We ended it," Derek added with a blend of gravity and gravel in his voice.

Seriously? "By bombing his home? How is that going to improve anything?"

"We took out his home, his office, and his father's slaughterhouse. It's over. Quit fussing." The Charmer *shushed* her. Callie's back was mostly to him, but she could *feel* that sneering grin against her back.

She turned her head to see him. The casual fucker

eased back in his fancy car. No tension, no fear. She would have punched him if she thought it'd do any good.

"How does that help exactly? Do you know how he'll retaliate?" She didn't, but she could sure as shit guess it would be bloody and painful. Everything related to this battle between Ford and the Soul Charmer had been foul and violent and ended with innocent people caught without their souls. She was not a part of that kind of shit. Only now there was a tattoo of a nocturnal carrion bird on her forearm saying she had vowed to be a part of the Soul Charmer's what-the-fuckery, and she carried a flask in her pocket containing a soul she'd stolen from a mob henchman.

"It's done," the Charmer snapped.

"He can't come at us again." Derek's rough rasp against her cheek could have melted her any other time. He settled the weight of his hand on her upper thigh. Calm, steady comfort. He wasn't shaking anymore, but Callie didn't know if that was a good sign.

"How do you know?"

"He's dead." The words grew in the subsequent silence until they pressed hard against the roof and the windows, until Callie's ears ached from the potential.

Her brows pulled together so tight her nose pinched, too. This couldn't be the way they solved problems. This couldn't be true.

"He gave me this." Derek gestured to the rapidly swelling gash on his cheekbone. "I'd tried the two other places first. He was knocked out, and now he's gone.”

“Why burn it down?” Her voice was tiny and meek and she didn’t recognize it.

“Fire is permanent,” the Charmer chimed in, either delighting in interrupting Callie’s moral indignation or unaware of it.

Derek’s gaze dipped to Callie’s chin. Her one safe place was Derek now, and even he couldn’t look her in the eyes.

“Why would you do this?” Her quiet question was for him alone.

Derek met her eyes. His were wide and filled with a churning grey sea.

“No more kids killed. No more threats to you. No more nightmares. Permanent fix.” The words were measured, balanced, and with zero inflection. His eyes though? They glistened with the tears he wouldn’t shed. His fingertips dug into the denim of her jeans with a blatant clawing need to hold on to something real. He didn’t like his solution any more than she had, but the relief was palpable.

It was *done*.

CHAPTER TWENTY-NINE

allie and Derek went straight from the Soul Charmer's car to Callie's apartment. Their boss didn't comment or complain, which meant he could read a room. Callie drove them to her apartment. Derek's was closer, but she had medical supplies and hospitals were off limits after a firebombing.

Though Derek was the one with visible injuries, Callie's soul ached. She wasn't certain she could sense souls the way the Charmer did, but hers hurt. She unlocked the apartment, and for once was happy to not see Josh surfing her sofa. She'd have to message him back in the morning.

Derek wrapped himself around Callie once the deadbolt was in place. His hands were in her hair, around her back. His chest was pressed against hers. The scruff on his chin scraped her temple. All of it was welcome. His closeness ebbed some of the resounding pain in her heart. It couldn't make her forget what had happened today.

She slid from his embrace and tugged him to the couch. She sat first. Derek took the corner cushion, but pulled Callie closer until she was wedged in the crook of his arm. "Are you going to tell me what really happened?"

His sigh echoed throughout Callie's bones. "I wasn't lying. I did it to protect us. Ford wasn't going to stop. He'd keep coming, and he's had eyes on you for some purpose since before the Charmer shit. So, now it's done."

"That's not all, though. I don't want your half-truths. This—" she gestured between them "—doesn't work if you can't tell me the truth." If she was going to treat him like family, he needed to be honest like they were.

He licked his lips as though wetting them would ease what he had to say, and then wiped a hand across them. "The Charmer wanted the bombs. Killing Ford solves our immediate problems. Burning down his house and all the other places he does business was all about the Charmer's retribution."

Callie had heard their boss go on tirades. She understood. "Fire and brimstone."

He nodded.

"How many other people…" She couldn't bring herself to say the words.

"Did I kill? There were a couple other guards at the house, but I made sure the other buildings were empty."

"So three?"

He nodded. "Yeah. Can you accept me still?"

It was such an odd question. He was holding her, in her home. She'd asked for truth and he had given it to her. He had no idea the things she'd done this week or in the past. She had luggage-store level baggage. "The Charmer took me to the well," she blurted.

"Oh."

Is that all he had? "Do you know how it works?"

He shook his head. "It's the source, like I said before, but anything more than that isn't something he's shared."

She didn't want to share it either. Here she was preaching about truth and the thought of throwing another log onto the bonfire of a bad day rattled her core. "It's the most fucked-up thing I've ever seen. If I drank twelve bottles of vodka, I couldn't forget it. Bottom-barrel, break your mind kind of shit."

Derek wrapped both arms around her so tightly it hurt to breathe. She didn't tell him to stop. "I think that it's part of me now. The soul well," she whispered.

"We'll figure it out." He didn't have answers, but she didn't need them now.

Callie silently siphoned Derek's warmth for a few moments longer, but finally turned her face toward him. She needed to see his eyes when she asked this. "Would you still want me even if something horrific was part of me?"

His answer was immediate. "Of course."

"Good, because I don't know if I can do this without you, and I'm pretty sure I love you." There. If she was going to go down with this soul magic thing and Derek was going to kill mob bosses to help keep her safe, she might as well make a fucking commitment.

A slow smile slid over his lips. He tucked loose strands of Callie's hair behind her ear.

"I love you, too, doll." He kissed her softly.

His touch was gentle, but Callie hadn't let go of her fire yet. It wasn't that simple. "As soon as I can find an out, we need to be done with him."

"You mean quit?" Derek asked like he'd discovered it was an option for the first time.

"Yes. We'll look for the moment when there isn't an imminent threat, and then we're done with him."

"Done." Derek tasted the concept like it was aged whiskey, and he liked it.

"Yes, and soon. We'll be done with him. With the souls and the danger. With the death. With the regret. You and me. That's real."

This time when he kissed her it was hard and devoted. Her heart sang and a tingle of anticipation skated along her nerves. She curled her fingers into his shirt and pulled him closer. She let her fingertips graze his cheek. He winced.

She pulled back and reexamined his wounded cheek.

"Kissing later. Ice first."

CHAPTER THIRTY

Callie had cooked eggs a dozen ways in her tenure at Cedar Retirement Home. It'd never been special. It'd been solid, clean work. She'd expected to miss it more than she did. Sure, Louisa was on her mind. She'd texted her to make sure the other woman didn't worry about her. It probably didn't help.

A week had passed since the night of the bombings. Josh had pinged her almost every day asking her to check in on Zara. Callie wasn't ready to face her mom yet. Josh was the favorite child. He could look in on the woman.

The Soul Charmer held up a bargain for once, and she got paid for the first time. She'd slipped on some cotton gloves, and hit the grocery store for the best produce her money would let her buy. She'd promised Derek breakfast, and she was going to deliver.

The pipes in the wall behind her hummed. Derek

was still in the shower, and she was mixing ham, bell peppers, onions, and a healthy handful of cheddar into the eggs. Omelets were special. All timing and delicious ingredients. Using her newfound cash flow to nourish him made her feel like she could actually keep up her end of the dating deal.

In this apartment they were safe from the Charmer's drama. They escaped the pressures of soul magic, and pretended the soul well didn't tug at Callie's heart every other day.

The pipes quieted. Callie checked the temperature of the skillet, and then poured the mixture in. Her spatula was on the spoon rest, but she knew better than to touch it too soon.

"Smells good, doll," Derek said by way of greeting. "You didn't have to go to all that trouble."

His mouth widened into a grin. Yep. That's why she was doing this.

It also smelled amazing. "You're going to have to share."

"Fine. Fine. Let me go put on some clothes, and then we'll see how this omelet stacks up to the Plaza Café."

Pssh. "Homemade is always best."

His laugh carried from her tiny hallway, and then he disappeared into the bedroom.

A light knock tapped at her front door. Probably the local pizza place flyering the doors again, she thought. The handle jiggled. The pizza guy did not try the doorknob. She was being paranoid. Her soul magic radar wasn't buzzing.

She shook away the thought, and headed to the door. If she left the door hanger on too long her neighbors complained. She peeked out the peephole. Empty hallway. She unlatched the deadbolt and pulled the door open.

The handle was empty of advertisements, but there was a bold message by her feet. Two fingers and a folded sheet of notebook paper rested on an ornate silver platter. The soft arc of the metal was memorable. The plate was the same one from the failed dinner at Zara's house. The nails were painted lavender and a thin silver band rested again one of the knuckles. The ends were ragged and oozing blood. The edges of the paper absorbed it.

She didn't remember screaming. Her body locked, and she stared blankly at the long, delicate fingers of her mother served up like afternoon fucking tea. Derek hauled her back into the apartment, and deposited her on the couch.

The door latched, and only then did she look up. The platter was out of sight, but Derek held the blood-soaked page. She held out a hand for it.

"No," his voice was barely audible.

"Yes," she said a little stronger. Anger began to bubble in her belly. The ire ready to cover the terror. "I need to know who did this."

He didn't move. She stood, and then took the note from him.

Callie girl—

Splitting a soul stings. Did you know? She does. Now.

I'll keep cutting until I get what's mine. Your mom is the tip of the fucking iceberg, bitch.

Pay up.

N.

Callie's brain stuttered. Nate? Idiot, side-muscle Nate was sending her threats? He'd taken her Mom?

"I thought the Charmer had him?" This didn't make sense.

"He did. He was in the basement yesterday." Derek had yet to escape checking on the Charmer's version of lockup.

"He's not anymore, and he has Zara."

"It says we owe him?" Derek said slowly.

"His soul. He wants his fucking soul back."

"That's doable. We can fix this together," Derek said like this was a perfect plan. An easy plan. Like they'd fucking succeed.

"Now I understand the Charmer. He needs in on this. He mutilated my mother. We need to save her, and then burn it all down."

"I thought fire and brimstone wasn't your thing. We can do this easy." Even he didn't believe that. His eyes couldn't lie to her.

"When it comes to family, Delgados demand retribution."

Derek leaned his forehead against hers. They'd already been through so much together, and she could see those memories tugging his brows together. "I told you I'd ended it with Ford. I didn't know Nate would…"

Callie cradled his jaw. He'd shaved and the skin was still cool. "You couldn't have known. Help me find him?"

"I'll protect you, if you'll let me."

"We'll protect each other." Callie said. Now she needed to hold up her end of that promise.

ACKNOWLEDGEMENTS

I have to start with a shout-out to my husband, who is convinced I can do anything, and doesn't flinch when I tell him my most twisted plot ideas for this series.

Huge thanks to my literary agent Cheryl Pientka, my critique partners Amanda Bonilla and Megan Frampton, publicity powerhouse Kristin Dwyer, and my beta reading queens Joanna Hoskinson and Laura Helseth.

Thanks to Amanda Bouchet, Stacia Kane, Chloe Neill, Melissa Marr, Jeaniene Frost, Bree Bridges, Donna Herren, Lauren Dane, and Darynda Jones for being such stellar support for this writer friend in Texas.

Thank you, readers, for being so enthusiastic about the Soul Charmer series. This book is for you, and there's more magic and mayhem planned for Callie.

ABOUT THE AUTHOR

Chelsea Mueller writes gritty contemporary fantasy. She founded the speculative fiction website **Vampire Book Club**, blogs about TV and romance novels for numerous websites, and is co-chair of **SF/F charity Geeky Giving**. She loves bad cover songs, dramatic movies, and TV vampires. Chelsea lives in Texas, and has been known to say y'all.

For the latest updates, join her email list at ChelseaMueller.net or follow **@ChelseaVBC** on Twitter and Instagram.

www.ingramcontent.com/pod-product-compliance
Lightning Source LLC
Chambersburg PA
CBHW051605100726

47898CB00001B/241